THE WAYWARD PRINCE

ALSO BY LEONARD GOLDBERG

THE
WAYWARD PRINCE

A Daughter of Sherlock Holmes Mystery

Leonard Goldberg

MINOTAUR
BOOKS
NEW YORK

First published in the United States by Minotaur Books, an imprint of St. Martin's Publishing Group

THE WAYWARD PRINCE. Copyright © 2023 by Leonard Goldberg. All rights reserved. Printed in the United States of America. For information, address St. Martin's Publishing Group, 120 Broadway, New York, NY 10271.

www.minotaurbooks.com

Designed by Omar Chapa

Library of Congress Cataloging-in-Publication Data

Names: Goldberg, Leonard S., author.
Title: The wayward prince / Leonard Goldberg.
Description: First edition. | New York : Minotaur Books, 2023. |
    Series: The daughter of Sherlock Holmes mysteries ; 7
Identifiers: LCCN 2023004461 | ISBN 9781250789617 (hardcover) |
    ISBN 9781250789624 (ebook)
Subjects: LCGFT: Detective and mystery fiction. | Novels.
Classification: LCC PS3557.O35775 W39 2023 | DDC 813/.54—
    dc23/eng/20230208
LC record available at https://lccn.loc.gov/2023004461

Our books may be purchased in bulk for promotional, educational, or business use. Please contact your local bookseller or the Macmillan Corporate and Premium Sales Department at 1-800-221-7945, extension 5442, or by email at MacmillanSpecialMarkets@macmillan.com.

First Edition: 2023

10 9 8 7 6 5 4 3 2 1

For Mia and Jackson and their wonderful moms

CONTENTS

Contents

The prince who relies upon their words, without having other-
wise provided for his security, is ruined.

NICCOLÒ MACHIAVELLI, *THE PRINCE*

THE

WAYWARD PRINCE

CHAPTER ONE

An Unforgettable Date

It was as if the Great War, now raging on the Continent, had driven London's criminal element even deeper into the underworld. Only the most trivial of crimes were being reported, and those were usually buried in the midsection of the daily newspapers. A prime example was the recent attempted robbery of a jewelry shop on Bond Street in which a clumsy thief tripped over a leashed poodle as he made a hasty exit with a diamond brooch in hand.

"A failed snatch-and-grab," my father described, placing the morning edition of the *Daily Telegraph* onto his lap. "Hardly worth the attention of the daughter of Sherlock Holmes."

"His daughter would find a tidbit or two of interest in this case," said Joanna, who was stationed at the window overlooking Baker Street.

"Pray tell what catches your eye but escapes mine."

"The omissions, my dear Watson, the omissions."

I, John Watson, Jr., M.D., the husband of the famous daughter, leaned forward in my overstuffed chair and pricked my ears for the interchange which was about to occur. How many times,

I wondered, had my father carried on a similar conversation with his long-dead colleague and friend, Sherlock Holmes? For the senior John Watson, who had been the sounding board over the years for the Great Detective, now served a similar role for the daughter whose adventures I had the privilege of chronicling.

My father carefully reread the article before pronouncing, "I see no omissions."

"Describe the gentleman holding the leash on the poodle," Joanna prompted.

"None was given."

"Yet he unintentionally or intentionally thwarted the robbery. Surely, this hero-by-chance merits some description which would be of interest to the reader."

"Perhaps he chose to remain anonymous."

"He would have been seen by others or in the company of a constable who no doubt would have questioned him."

My father gave the matter further thought. "Are you implying he simply disappeared?"

"Which brings us to the second omission," Joanna went on. "What of the diamond brooch?"

"It was not recovered."

"And I would wager a guinea it disappeared in the hands of the man who vanished along with his leashed poodle."

"I cannot believe this apparent gentleman was involved in the robbery itself."

"I am of that opinion as well, but there is the distinct possibility he took advantage of the situation."

"So the gentleman walking his poodle, who was the unlikeliest of suspects, appears to be the thief."

Joanna nodded slowly. "These are desperate times, Watson, which tend to bring out the best and worst in people."

"But should not desperate times bring out more crimes rather than the lull we are currently experiencing?"

"Oh, the crimes are being committed, but these are of little consequence, and thus do not warrant publication," Joanna replied. "No one wishes to read of arson in Whitechapel or an assault in Limehouse, but an attempted robbery on Bond Street is of interest because it is upscale and involves an item of considerable value."

"But what of murder?" my father queried. "I very much doubt those have diminished in number."

"I suspect you are correct, but murder is of small matter unless it is attached to wealth, sex, or the aristocracy. Moreover, a single death or two is unlikely to draw the reader's attention, whilst there are thousands being killed daily on the Western Front."

"One would think that stolen masterpieces would still be in demand," I interjected. "Surely, there remains a market for a stolen Rembrandt or Caravaggio even during wartime."

"Not with the outcome of the war undecided," Joanna reasoned. "Buyers here and on the Continent would be skittish when it comes to parting with large sums of money for famous works of art. They would take into account that the Huns might triumph over the Allies and, with that being the case, who knows what the victors would choose to confiscate for their museums and private collections."

"So the lull persists whilst we sit and wait."

"I am afraid so."

A sudden, deafening explosion rang in our ears and violently shook the walls and ceiling at 221b Baker Street. In an instant, Joanna grasped and closed the thick, dark curtains as the windowpanes behind them cracked and shattered, causing large slivers of glass to fall at her feet. We waited in stunned silence for the vibrations to cease, whilst the chandelier above our dining table continued to sway in a wide arc.

"To Miss Hudson's kitchen!" I shouted, then helped my father to his feet for the journey down the stairs to the kitchen where our landlady had recently installed large timbers to brace against exploding German bombs.

"Hold!" Joanna commanded as we reached the door which led to the hallway.

An eerie quiet hung in the air, with no further explosions or vibrations. The chandelier became stationary in the dim light.

"There may be more bombs on the way," I cautioned. "We should hurry to the safe space."

My wife hesitated at length before shaking her head and guiding us back into the parlor. "It is near noon and the Germans never bomb in open daylight when their chances of being shot down are greatest. Furthermore, we did not hear the drone of overhead bombers nor the shrill whistle of a constable warning of an oncoming raid, which occurs without fail. And finally, there was only a single explosion. The Huns always drop their bombs in clusters."

"What caused the blast, then?"

"Most likely a delayed detonation of a bomb from last evening's raid," she surmised, and led the way back to the tightly closed curtains that allow no light out from the inside, which at night could provide a target for German bombers. "Whether the delay was done intentionally by the Huns is open to question."

"I saw a similar device during my service in the Second Afghan War," my father recalled. "Such bombs were left behind by the treacherous Afghans, which inflicted devastating misery on the advancing British troops."

Joanna parted the curtains to reveal multiple cracked windows which were badly shattered in places. Glancing over her shoulder, we could see a billow of black smoke arising into the air from a westward location no more than a block away. No flames were visible, although they were surely present. Below, ambulances and other emergency vehicles began racing by with their bells clanging loudly. Across the way red bricks from the façade of a dress shop were falling onto the footpath and causing passersby to scamper away from the danger.

"The war draws nearer and nearer, and is now at our very doorstep," said I as the dense, black cloud of smoke drifted toward us.

"But at least our Johnny is safely tucked away at Eton," my father noted.

"Yet I worry for my son," Joanna said, the concern obvious in her voice. "Keep in mind that Eton is just across the Thames from Windsor Castle which would make a very tempting target for German bombers. Can you begin to imagine the depressing effect a Windsor in flames would have on the British people?"

"There is a rumor that the Kaiser has given orders not to bomb Windsor Castle, for that is where he plans to reside once a German victory is secured."

"And you believe that rumor?"

"He is pompous enough to have said it."

"And dangerous enough to ignore it," Joanna retorted. "Take the word of a Teuton at your own risk."

Quiet once again returned to our nicely warmed parlor, but it was soon broken by the loud ring of our telephone. Our collective eyes and minds went to the phone, all hoping that London's lull in criminal activity was about to come to an end. But the call was to be that and much, much more. It was of such great importance that the precise time and date it reached us will forever be fixed in our minds. Big Ben was tolling the noon hour on May 21, 1918 when my father lifted the receiver and heard the voice of none other than Sir Charles Bradberry, the commissioner of Scotland Yard, who requested our immediate presence at 10 Downing Street. A motor vehicle would shortly be at our doorstep to transport us to one of the most famous addresses in all England. No further information was given.

After hurriedly changing into attire more appropriate for a

visit to the seat of the British government, we dashed down the stairs, passing a startled Miss Hudson who was carrying a tray laden with tea settings.

"Will you be returning for lunch?" she called out.

"Unlikely," Joanna replied.

"And dinner?"

"Perhaps."

A black, chauffeured limousine awaited us as we exited the front entrance. The driver opened the rear door of the motor vehicle, giving us the slightest of bows. His dark suit was well fitted, but there was a noticeable bulge on the left side of his jacket. He gave no greeting.

We traveled through the Marylebone district of West London at a reduced speed, slowed by the ice-covered roads and intermittent swirls of falling snow. In addition, the wider avenues had been badly damaged by the recent attacks of German bombers. There was one bowl-shaped crater after another which interfered with our drive, and off to the side were adjacent homes reduced to smoldering rubble. The last air raid two days earlier had been so massive it resulted in forty-nine killed and a hundred and seventeen injured, with damages amounting to well over 100,000 pounds. And adding to the misery of many, there were shortages and rationing of bread, meat, and sugar, which were becoming more severe. Surely, our urgent summons to the prime minister's office had to involve some aspect of the dreadful war. But what?

My dear wife, Joanna, studied my face at length before commenting, "It is hopeless."

"What is?" I asked, coming out of my reverie.

"Attempting to decipher the reason for our call to 10 Downing Street," said she. "We have neither the information nor clues to guide us. As my father would have told you, we cannot make bricks without straw, and we have no straw."

"May I inquire how you were aware of my inner thoughts?"

"Your actions revealed all," Joanna deduced. "First, you stared at the ruins caused by the German bombers, prompting your jaw to tighten and your expression to turn grim. Next, you removed a piece of lint from your lapel and straightened your tie, indicating your thoughts had shifted to your appearance on entering 10 Downing Street. Connecting the two observations, you assumed the prime minister wished to see us regarding some aspect of the Great War, but could not fathom what services we might render."

"Entirely reasonable logic, I would think," my father interjected. "I would suggest there might be more espionage afoot, or, Heaven forbid, yet another traitor in our midst."

"Possibilities, but unlikely."

"Why so, pray tell?"

Joanna smiled briefly at my father, keen to present her reasoning for his consideration. "There is a history to be considered here, Watson. Think back to the other cases of spying we have been called upon to solve."

"Are you referring to *A Study in Treason* and *The Disappearance of Alistair Ainsworth*?"

Joanna nodded, then reached for one of her Turkish cigarettes and lighted it carefully before continuing. "And what was the common denominator in these cases?"

"Acts of treason," my father replied at once.

"The highest and most treacherous of offenses, you would agree."

"Beyond question."

"And in both cases we were called upon at 221b Baker Street," she went on. "Yet, now we are asked to appear at the prime minister of England's office. What do you make of that, my dear Watson?"

"It must go beyond treason or espionage," he responded.

"It must, for there can be no other answer."

"Beyond what, then?"

"A serious threat to the Crown that could do irreparable harm," Joanna replied in a most somber tone. As we approached Westminster, she tossed her cigarette through the window and added, "We shall shortly be able to gauge for ourselves the true gravity of the situation."

"How so?" asked I.

"By the manner in which we enter our destination."

"I am not certain I follow you."

"Be patient, dear heart."

Her words proved to be prophetic. I expected that like most visitors to Downing Street we would come through the security gate at Whitehall and gain entrance to number ten via the iconic black door, which would be watched over by two uniformed constables. But on that early afternoon we slipped into the grounds along Horse Guards Road and entered the residence through a French door overlooking a walled garden. It was obvious that our presence was to remain undisclosed. Walking into the foyer one could not help but feel the immense power contained within the hallowed structure, which only intensified the gravitas of our visit. A look of reverence crossed my father's face, but Joanna's expression stayed placid as she gazed briefly at the hanging portraits of previous prime ministers. The surroundings were no doubt of interest to her, but she had swept away any emotion which was her custom when about to match wits with the best of villains.

A prim secretary of middle years, with gray streaks throughout her hair, awaited our arrival and, nodding to us in greeting, led us down a wide, elegant corridor to a closed door, against which she rapped her knuckles lightly. On hearing a commanding voice say, "Come," we were allowed entrance into the White Drawing Room.

CHAPTER TWO

10 Downing Street

Standing near a blazing fireplace were three men who continued their conversation despite our presence. Sir Charles Bradberry turned to us and held up a finger, indicating they would join us momentarily. The commissioner seemed to have aged since we last encountered him, now appearing somewhat thinner, with his broad shoulders more hunched and his hair and mustache taking on the color of pewter. By contrast, the man to whom he was speaking was much younger, in his mid-thirties at most, with an angular figure and dark hair combed close to the scalp. But most remarkable was his skin that was quite pale, much like a person who spent every living hour indoors so as to avoid any contact with the rays of the sun. A colorful Persian carpet covered most of the floor and seemed to accentuate the man's pallidness.

The commissioner came over to perform the introductions, beginning with the prime minister who in fact needed no introduction. Harold Lloyd-Jackson was surely the most recognizable individual in all England, with his picture appearing so often in newspapers throughout the British Isles. He was far better looking than his photographs gave him credit for, with his wavy blond hair, deep blue eyes, and a strong jawline which projected the image of unchallenged authority. But his attractive appearance was marred by the dark circles beneath his eyes, no doubt the result of stress and never-ending worry.

"Thank you for coming on such short notice," he said warmly, nodding to the three of us, but his gaze quickly directed itself to Joanna. "I am afraid we are facing a looming disaster, for Prince Harry has gone missing without reason. He has not been seen nor heard from in over two days."

The prime minister's words hung in the air, for they brought with them the gravest of implications. "The beloved prince, third in line to the throne, has vanished into thin air and there is deep suspicion he has been abducted by the Germans. Recent decoded messages from their spies in London to U-boats in the English Channel spoke of a captured asset which will bring great embarrassment to the Crown and immeasurable joy to the Kaiser. MI5 now believes that the Huns were referring to the prince, and that they plan to transport him to Berlin at the earliest possible moment."

"We obviously cannot allow this to occur, for the end result would be an unmitigated calamity," Lloyd-Jackson added. "We would very much appreciate your assistance in bringing this matter to a rapid and successful resolution."

"I require details," Joanna stated without inflection. "All and any questions related to the prince have to be answered truthfully, regardless of their sensitivity."

"I shall be happy to do so," said Roger Mallsby, the pale, younger man who had been introduced as Prince Harry's private secretary. "However, there can be no inquiries regarding His Majesty or the workings within Buckingham Palace."

"There will be no exceptions," Joanna insisted. "And what you refuse to answer, others will. Which is the very last thing you wish to happen, for it will only lengthen our investigation and may well place the prince's life in even more jeopardy."

Mallsby stared briefly at my wife, obviously unaccustomed to taking orders from a person considered to be of lesser rank. But given the circumstances, he quickly regrouped. "I shall provide all the information I have at my disposal."

"Let us start with the last time you were in the company of the prince."

"It began just after breakfast at the palace when he asked if all was in order for his horse ride at Hyde Park," Mallsby replied. "It was his custom to partake of such rides twice a week."

"Which days?"

"Tuesdays and Fridays without fail, unless there was a royal duty which superseded all other activities."

"I take it the rides had to be scheduled in advance?"

"Usually the day before, and the stable master was always most accommodating."

"So the prince departed midmorning from the Royal Mews on the day he went missing?"

"No, madam. He preferred to employ the Lancaster Gate stable at the northwest corner of Hyde Park, where he would mount Ben, a spirited bay of gentle nature, for a ride through the leafy trails in that area of the park."

"He was of course accompanied on these rides."

"By a palace guard, and at times by the stable dog Daisy who is quite fond of His Royal Highness."

"Please describe in detail the prince's journey from Buckingham Palace to the Lancaster Gate stable, with precise times of departure and arrival, and in particular any stops or pauses along the way."

"We departed the palace at ten sharp in a royal limousine, with myself at Prince Harry's side," Mallsby narrated. "The ride was uninterrupted, and we arrived at the stable ten minutes later to find Ben saddled and bridled, as was the horse to be ridden by the palace guard who had arrived earlier to ensure that all was secure and in readiness for His Royal Highness's visit. Off they went without delay whilst I remained in the limousine reviewing Prince Harry's rather busy schedule for the remainder of the day."

The private secretary took a deep breath and slowly exhaled, as if preparing himself for the unpleasant memory. "It was near eleven when the nightmare began to unfold before our very eyes. Ben, the spirited bay, returned to the stable riderless, at full gallop. The entire stable went into crisis mode, all fearing that the prince had been thrown and lay badly injured on the wet ground, for it had rained earlier in the morning. For better or worse, this was not to be the case."

"Was there any evidence that Ben had been hurt or gone lame?" Joanna asked at once.

"That was our first thought as well, but the stable master could find no signs of lameness, nor were there any cuts or abrasions detected which would have indicated the horse had taken a tumble or had in any way been injured," Mallsby elaborated. "It was then that His Highness's guard galloped in to inform us of the altogether strange happening. Approximately twenty minutes into the ride, Prince Harry pulled up to inform the guard he was about to dismount to answer a call of nature. His Highness held on to the reins of Ben and led the animal into a nearby forested area. Some minutes passed without the prince reappearing, so the guard went in to investigate and could find no trace of the prince or his horse. They had vanished. The palace guard hurried back to the stable to sound the alarm."

Joanna quickly absorbed the new information, then asked, "Are there other riding or walking paths attached to the wooded area where the prince dismounted?"

"Several are in the near vicinity which the guard looked into," Mallsby replied. "But they were vacant, with neither rider nor walker to be seen. The search required a number of minutes which explained the brief delay before the guard raced back to the stable."

"In addition, Scotland Yard carefully combed the area's riding paths, seeking out witnesses to the prince's exit, but none could be found," Sir Charles chimed in. "The trail upon which the prince and his escort rode was searched from stable to the point of disappearance, and all that was uncovered was for the most part rubbish."

"What exactly did this rubbish include?" Joanna probed.

"Cigarette stubs, various wrappings, and other scraps of paper," the commissioner detailed. "There were also a small length of rope and bits of leather which were considered to be of no consequence."

"When was the search of the riding trail conducted?"

"Yesterday morning, which was a day after the prince's disappearance."

"Why was so much time allowed to lapse before Scotland Yard was notified?"

"That is best answered by Prince Harry's private secretary."

Mallsby uttered a brief grumble, like a man about to disclose information meant to be kept out of the public's view. "His Royal Highness has been known to vanish on occasion without notice for a rendezvous with one of his many lady friends."

"Are you referring to romantic trysts?" Joanna asked straightforwardly.

The private secretary's pale face showed a hint of a blush. "I am," said he, without further explanation.

"How long do these visits usually last?"

"Never more than a day."

"Which suggests that His Highness's disappearance did not involve an undisclosed assignation."

"So it would appear."

"Now, according to the stated sequence of events, the prince went missing two days ago, and Scotland Yard was brought in only yesterday when the investigation began," Joanna calculated. "Correct?"

"Correct."

"Who ordered such a prolonged delay?"

"His Majesty himself, for he was in hopes of the prince reappearing within twenty-four hours of his disappearance as he had done in the past," Mallsby replied. "When he did not, Scotland Yard was called in, but alas, to no avail. It was then decided, with His Majesty's permission, to involve the daughter of Sherlock Holmes and the Watsons, who are known to solve the most difficult of cases, with discretion, I might add."

"All of you have been remiss in not coming to me sooner," Joanna said severely to the group. "You start me on this investigation with a serious handicap. It is inconceivable, for example, that the riding path or stable would have yielded nothing to an expert observer. But I fear that over the past days, whatever clues were present have now vanished or have been disturbed in such a fashion to be of little value."

"Although of no apparent value, the scarce evidence collected is available for your inspection," Sir Charles offered.

"A clue of even the smallest significance would be most welcomed," said she, and returned to the private secretary. "And that includes the romantic trysts the prince participated in. I shall require the names of every known companion and if possible their whereabouts."

Mallsby hesitated noticeably before replying, "I can give you limited information which should suffice."

"Again, you waste my time," Joanna admonished. "For it is

I, not you, who will determine what evidence suffices and what does not. So, without exception, you will be good enough to provide me with every detail of these assignations, including names, places, frequency, and duration."

"But some of those involved are ladies of high standing, and a few are married," he protested. "Surely, those must be protected."

"I am not in the business of protecting reputations or marriages, Mr. Mallsby. And as far as ladies of standing are concerned, they should have realized that when one plays with fire, there is every real chance of getting burned."

The prime minister interjected, "But a moment ago you stated that such assignations are unlikely to be the reason for the prince's disappearance."

"Unlikely because, according to the private secretary, these absences last no longer than a day, and the prince's absence now exceeds two days. But that does not exclude its possibility, for additional time would have elapsed if the prince had somehow sustained an injury or suffered an induced stupor." Joanna gave the matter more thought before quickly coming back to the private secretary. "Was the prince known to have used drugs during his romantic trysts?"

"Not to my knowledge," Mallsby answered promptly.

"Which does not exclude its use," Joanna apprised. "Please keep in mind that cocaine can heighten sensual arousal and at times cause the individual to take undue risks. And opiates can induce stupor which lingers as long as the drug continues to be consumed, and could account for a prolonged absence."

"His Highness showed no evidence of such use when he returned to the palace after his absences," Mallsby said hurriedly, in a voice which made one wonder if he was attempting to cover for the prince. "I can assure you I was never asked to supply him with any intoxicants."

"Nevertheless, it remains a possibility which requires follow up," Joanna persisted, and watched for a reaction from the private secretary, which was not forthcoming.

The prime minister sighed under his breath at the dire situation, which required immediate resolution, with none in sight. "Although unpleasant, I would much prefer that outcome to the one I fear most, namely, that the prince is now being held captive by German agents. That of course would be a most disheartening development, particularly when coupled with the recent setback the Allied forces have suffered in France. Such a public pronouncement would be a terrible blow to our people."

"I am afraid that remains a very real possibility as well, Prime Minister."

"This matter must be brought to an end quickly without even a moment's delay," Lloyd-Jackson demanded and, turning to the commissioner, issued an order of the highest priority. "Any and all resources of His Majesty's government shall be made available to this investigation, including every branch of Scotland Yard, MI5, and the Secret Intelligence Service. There are to be no exceptions."

"Understood, Prime Minister. Vernon Carter-Smith has been notified and is currently returning from Edinburgh."

His name drew our immediate attention, for he was the most secretive of men, who was rarely seen and about whom little was known. Capt. Vernon Carter-Smith was director of MI5 and said to be co-founder of its SIS branch, which was in large measure responsible for the recent capture of a nest of German spies in Croydon, all of whom were promptly hanged at the Tower of London.

"And any progress will be reported immediately to this office," Lloyd-Jackson was saying.

"It will be, on an hourly basis if required."

The prime minister returned to Joanna and asked, "Where will you begin?"

"With the evidence at hand."

"But there is only rubbish from Hyde Park which appears valueless."

"I should like to determine that for myself," Joanna responded, before looking to the prince's private secretary. "Please be good enough to accompany the commissioner back to Scotland Yard."

A puzzled expression crossed Mallsby's face. "For what purpose, may I ask?"

"To tell me what pieces of rubbish belonged to Prince Harry and which did not."

The meeting was adjourned with the briefest of nods and on a less than hopeful note. We hurried down the wide, elegant corridor and passed through a French door to our waiting limousine, with its chauffeur reaching to open the rear door for us. I turned my attention to the line of official limousines backed up behind ours with their motors running, no doubt delayed entrance because of the critical meeting we had just attended. As we drove in silence along Horse Guards Road, the splendor of St. James's Park came into view, with its luscious lawn now covered with glistening white snow, upon which there were strolling couples who were bundled up and enjoying the Christmas-like weather, unaware of the crisis their country may soon be facing. The bucolic picture vanished as we turned for the security gate.

"A tangled web of a problem," my father remarked. "And much to our disadvantage we have no clues to guide us."

"There are clues, Watson, which are waiting to be uncovered," Joanna assured him.

"But the investigation thus far has not yielded any," he argued mildly. "Even a most careful search of the riding path in Hyde Park came up with only rubbish."

Joanna gave my father a sly smile. "And who led this most careful search you spoke of?"

"Why, no doubt Inspector Lestrade."

"Ah yes, the ever conscientious inspector who keeps his nose to the grindstone," she remarked. "You may have noticed that Lestrade's skills as a detective are coming along nicely, for he now demonstrates on occasion the ability to see beyond the obvious, which places him a cut above his colleagues at Scotland Yard. Nevertheless, he has yet to apply scientific techniques to his findings, and I suspect these applications will be most helpful in the case before us."

"So I take it that the proficient Lestrade is at this point stymied as well."

"In all likelihood, for I am afraid he has overlooked a subtle clue which might allow him to see beyond the obvious."

My father furrowed his brow in thought. "I, too, can detect no such clue, other than perhaps the clear impression that the prince's disappearance was carried out in a smooth and unnoticed manner."

"Bravo, Watson! For you have mentioned a most important feature of this vanishing," Joanna praised. "It was accomplished in a perfect fashion."

"Is there an underlying meaning here?"

"It tells us the disappearance was planned," Joanna replied, leaning back and closing her eyes in thought. "The question is by whom?"

"And to what end?"

"You show me the who and I will show you the end."

Chapter Three

The Clues

The restricted section at Scotland Yard consisted of a large, rectangular-shaped room whose walls were lined with locked cabinets and shelves weighed down with scientific texts. Off to the side were small tables upon which rested bottles of reagents, cutting instruments, and an antiquated microscope. There were no desks or chairs, other than small stools which were pushed off to the corners. In the center of the room was a long, black workbench upon which lay the items gathered at the site of the prince's disappearance.

"Is this the entirety of your findings?" Joanna asked, peering down at the litter on the evidence table. "Surely, your search should have uncovered more."

"I am afraid this is the entire lot," Inspector Lestrade replied. "We were placed at a disadvantage, for the riding paths are swept twice a day, with the rubbish deposited in a large bin and quickly disposed of."

"Was the area where the prince brought his mount to a halt located and thoroughly gone over?"

"It was indeed, madam, for the palace guard who accompanied

Prince Harry remembered the precise location because there was a bench and an adjoining path nearby. He led us into the woods where we found the clearing that contained the rubbish you see before you. We assumed that was the area the prince chose to answer the call of nature."

"Please be good enough to describe the clearing," Joanna requested. "I am particularly interested in its dimensions and the nearby paths."

Lestrade extracted a thick notepad from an inner pocket of his jacket and rapidly thumbed through its pages. "The clearing was circular in nature, with a circumference of approximately twenty-five feet. The surrounding foliage was quite thick and led to a walking path, and beyond that more woods and yet another riding trail."

"And the floor of the circle itself?"

"It consisted of short grass which was wet from the earlier rain, with no signs that a struggle had taken place."

"Were there footprints to be seen?"

Lestrade shook his head in response. "None were visible."

Joanna returned to the evidence table and slowly walked its length, stopping periodically to study each individual item. Back and forth she went, dwelling on the cigarette stubs with obvious interest before moving on to a badly faded matchbook cover, then to various wrappings and a small, crushed package, and finally to a short stretch of rope. She held up the rope to examine it with her magnifying glass under the bright, overhead light. "Was this item examined for blood?"

"None was seen," Lestrade answered. "However, the rope was quite wet from the rain which might have washed it clean."

The commissioner asked quickly, "What is the significance of blood on the rope?"

"It might indicate the prince struggled mightily before being bound and hurried away," Joanna explained. "Being tied with a rough rope can cause deep abrasions that bleed."

"So you believe His Royal Highness was taken prisoner?"

"All I can state at this point was that some individual was waiting for the prince to appear," said she. "And that individual knew the prince would show up at a given time, and was willing to wait a minimum of half an hour for him to make his arrival."

"How do you come by this?" Sir Charles asked at once. "What evidence allows you to reach such a precise conclusion?"

"The number of identical cigarette stubs smoked to their very last," Joanna elucidated. "I counted five such stubs and knowing that it requires six minutes to smoke a cigarette, I can accurately conclude that the individual stood watch for at least thirty minutes. In reality, even more time must have passed since it is unlikely the individual did not pause some minutes before lighting his next cigarette."

"Could there have been two smokers to account for so many stubs?" my father asked.

"An excellent question, Watson, but no, for the evidence indicates there was a single individual in waiting," Joanna replied, now holding up a single cigarette end to the light. "You will notice that this stub, like the others, has been smoked to the very last and is flattened to the same degree, with black dirt ingrained into it. These features indicate a man of habit, who smoked each cigarette to the very end before crushing it beneath his foot with equal pressure." She gave the matter more thought before asking, "By the way, Inspector, was there a pattern in which the cigarette stubs were discarded?"

"They were all off to the side of the clearing."

"So this personage was quite neat, which denotes yet another feature of habit."

"What makes you so certain that the prince himself did not leave the cigarette stubs behind?" Lestrade wondered aloud.

"Because he was not gone long enough to smoke five cigarettes," she replied.

"And His Royal Highness did not smoke," Mallsby inter-jected. "He detested cigarettes because of the unpleasant odor they left on the smoker's clothes."

"It is also clear that the person in waiting was a chain-smoker and addicted to nicotine, for there was a crushed, empty package of Player's Navy Cut and a matchbook without matches mixed in with the stubs. Had he not exhausted his supply of cigarettes and matches, he might have smoked even more." Joanna carefully examined the badly faded matchbook cover whose colors had run away from the paper backing. She moved her magnifying glass back and forth in an attempt to decipher any markings. "I can make out an *r* and an *o,* followed by a large empty space, then an *a* and an *m*. It is obviously some type of advertisement."

"There also appears to be a short, written word inside the matchbook cover," Lestrade added, again referring to his notepad. "It consists entirely of capitalized, block letters, starting with an *M,* followed by *O, R,* and finally *G,* which spells MORG. There is a blurred letter or two at the very end. The only word in the dictionary which might fit is *morgue,* and that makes no sense here."

Sir Charles's brow went up. "Could it be a woman's name?"

"Such as, sir?" Lestrade queried.

"Such as Morgane, with a few of the letters faded or washed away," he replied. "It comes to mind because that was the name of my dear departed mother."

"Very good, sir," Lestrade congratulated, with a firm nod. "Might it be that a woman was actually waiting for Prince Harry or could it have been a messenger sent by one of the prince's ladies who carried the name Morgane?"

"Another rendezvous, then?" Sir Charles speculated.

"It would all fit nicely, Commissioner."

"What say you, Joanna?" asked my father.

"One must be cautious when inserting letters for those which have faded out, and reaching a conclusion on that basis," she warned. "It is a dangerous game to play."

"But it gives us a possible trail to follow, does it not?" Lestrade inquired, hoping for a positive response.

"You are setting a target predicated on an assumption," she replied. "It is best we await more definitive, reliable clues."

"But we have none."

"They will come," Joanna assured. "For our culprit is already making mistakes, and he will make more."

"But time is of the essence," Sir Charles pressed.

"Then let us not waste that precious commodity by taking the wrong track."

"Surely, no harm can come by checking the name Morgane against the list of His Royal Highness's known acquaintances."

"There were none that I know of," Mallsby volunteered.

"Nevertheless, make inquiries with the prince's friends and determine if there is a Morgane in his past."

"A clue unanswered is a clue left behind," Lestrade said sagely.

"Quite right," Sir Charles agreed.

"I prefer to take a different approach," Joanna proposed. "And with your permission, I should like to carry the cigarette stubs, matchbook cover, and piece of rope back to my Baker Street laboratory for further study."

"It would be most unusual for all evidence to be removed from the confines of Scotland Yard," Lestrade stated authoritatively.

"The alternative is to let the items lie here and gather dust," she contended.

"Take them," Sir Charles commanded. "And pray tell inform us of any significant findings."

Joanna gathered up the requested items and placed them in a large manila envelope from a nearby shelf. Whilst sealing the container, she turned to Mallsby and said, "Your presence will no longer be needed, but I would like you to contact the palace guard who accompanied the prince on his ride and have him meet us at the Lancaster Gate stable within the hour."

"That will require permission."

"Then obtain it and have him at the stable without fail."

After signing out for the evidence, we entered a motor vehicle provided by Scotland Yard and drove through the busy streets of Westminster, then drove down the Mall and over to Park Lane which bordered Hyde Park. Despite the unseasonable cold weather, colorful, blooming flowers were in full view, but they barely caught our attention, for our minds and moods were elsewhere. We had no clues of value, and with each passing day the crisis surrounding the missing prince deepened. I focused on the two possibilities mentioned thus far which would account for His Royal Highness's disappearance. Was he off on one of his romantic trysts or was he being held captive by German agents? Or was it a combination of the two? Could he have been lured into an assignation where the capture occurred? Most likely, it was a combination of the two events which transpired, for that would explain the prince's planned disappearance and his prolonged absence. But I was unaware of any evidence which would allow one to reach such an important conclusion. Perhaps there were clues in the offing I failed to see.

Breaking the silence, I asked my wife, "Earlier you spoke of clues to come. Where do you expect to find them, pray tell?"

"In the manila envelope I removed from Scotland Yard," she replied, and left it at that.

CHAPTER FOUR

The Lancaster Gate Stables

We strode toward the entrance of the Lancaster Gate stables accompanied by Inspector Lestrade, for his presence would be needed if another search of the premises was deemed necessary. The entire area was quiet, with neither horse nor person to be seen.

"I expected to find reporters from the newspapers hounding the stable hands," said Joanna.

"With the assistance of Buckingham Palace, the prince's disappearance remains cloaked in secrecy," Lestrade explained.

"How was this accomplished?"

"The palace released a notice stating that Prince Harry suffered a tumble whilst riding and, although bruised, found his way to a close friend's home in Knightsbridge where he was resting comfortably. The prince was expected to return to his royal duties in the near future."

"What of the stable hands? Surely, they will talk and gossip."

"They were shown the bulletin from Buckingham Palace, and had no difficulty believing the prince was safe and sound. Nevertheless, they were instructed in the strongest manner not to speak of the incident, for it would cause unneeded worry to His Majesty's people."

"Even with these precautions, the sad news will soon be disclosed, unwittingly or not."

"Of that, we are aware."

We entered the noiseless stable, with its high, steepled ceiling and polished wooden stalls. Not a soul was to be seen. Most of the stalls were vacant, but in those few which were occupied the horses put their heads and necks out to view us. On the neatly swept floor was a border collie who eyed us warily, as if attempting to measure our intent. The hound let out a sharp, but nonthreatening bark that alerted a caretaker who promptly appeared from the most distant stall. He was the stable master, Lestrade whispered to us, and appropriately named Walter Grooms. Comfortably attired in a cap and long leather jacket, he was a wiry man of average height, with steel-gray hair and a confident stride. The horses in their stalls watched his every step.

"How may I be of service, Inspector?" Grooms asked, his eyes darting back and forth amongst the visitors before settling on Joanna.

"Scotland Yard wishes to investigate Prince Harry's use of your stables further," Lestrade replied. "To that end we have enlisted the assistance of Mrs. Joanna Watson, who you will no doubt recognize as the daughter of Sherlock Holmes."

The stable master's face turned to worry. "I can assure you, Inspector, there was no wrongdoing on our part," he said defensively.

"That is not the purpose of our visit, as Mrs. Watson will shortly inform you."

"Very good, sir," Grooms replied, averting his eyes and now obviously intimidated by our presence.

"I know you must be quite busy, this being the end of a long day, with most of your horses still out on the trails," Joanna said in a warm voice.

"They will be returning shortly, ma'am."

"Before the sun goes down, no doubt."

"Which is a must, for there is a strict regulation against night riding in Hyde Park."

"Will they be fed then?"

The stable master nodded. "After being brushed and washed down, ma'am."

"Are they always given grassy hay?"

"That is their main course."

"Now, I must ask you to settle a wager for me, if you would, in regards to the feeding of your horses."

"Of course, ma'am," Grooms said, his interest aroused. "May I know of the wager?"

"My husband believes that horses can be fed at random and will gauge their own intake. I am of the opinion that they must be allowed to eat on a regular basis, with a closely measured meal size. Otherwise, their digestive systems may go awry."

"You win, ma'am, for horses have small stomachs and are creatures of habit," Grooms stated, now clearly in his element. "They are to be fed three times a day at specific times, with a given amount of grassy hay. If you go off the timing, they become quite unhappy."

"So it would appear that horses have a body clock."

"As far as their stomachs are concerned."

"Most interesting."

"I must say, ma'am, that you seem to know horses. Are you a rider?"

"On occasion."

"Then we shall be happy to welcome you here at Lancaster Gate stables when your schedule permits."

"Thank you for your kind invitation."

I could not help but marvel inwardly at my wife's ability to put witnesses at ease, particularly those from the working class, who as a rule were reluctant to speak with authorities, for it might somehow involve them in the misdeed. Delve into their occupation, Joanna had recommended, for it elevates their status and provides a subject which they believe they know far more than you. Now the stable master was informing her of the best horse for her to ride, should she choose to do so.

"I would suggest Ben, who can be spirited yet most gentle depending on who is in the saddle."

"I will make note of that," she said graciously.

My father and I exchanged knowing glances, for we were aware that Joanna, like her father, had a distaste for horses. According to a well-read chronicle, the Great Detective had been quoted on the subject as saying, "Horses are dangerous at both ends and crafty in the middle. Why would I want anything with a mind of its own bobbing about between my legs?" I suppressed a smile at the quote.

"Thank you for the information which will make me a guinea richer," Joanna said good-naturedly before her voice took on a more serious tone, as she began to fabricate a story to explain our presence at the stables, for as noted earlier the public had been informed that the prince, although bruised, was in safe hands. "But let us return to the purpose of our visit. Unbeknownst to most, there have been recent sightings of strangers at several stables throughout the greater London area. In one instance, a stranger was overheard speaking a foreign language. Scotland Yard was called, but the man had vanished before their arrival. This being wartime, such an incident was of obvious concern."

Lestrade nodded at the fabrication with a solemn expression.

"Was he thought to be a bloody Hun?" Grooms growled at the possibility.

"That could not be determined," Joanna continued on. "But

I believe you can see the implication, for the last thing we would wish is for a foreign agent to be in the vicinity of a member of the royal family. With that in mind, I must ask if you have seen any strangers lurking about your stable."

"Nary a one," Grooms replied promptly. "And should such an individual approach the stable, our good dog Daisy would sound the alert, as she did recently when a slacker drew near for a handout."

"I understand that Daisy and Prince Harry are quite good friends."

"They are indeed, and so are His Royal Highness and Ben who took to each other from the very start," the stable master added. "The friendship between them was sealed by the treats Prince Harry brought along. After the rides, he rewards Ben with an apple, which the horse eagerly looks forward to receiving."

Our collective spines stiffened at the mention of an apple, for all of England was under strict food-rationing, with even flour and milk in short supply. Fruits of any kind were difficult to come by, and those which were found were far too expensive for most. But then again, here we were dealing with royalty, which tend to maintain its privileges regardless of the times.

"And Daisy is always given a dog biscuit, whether she accompanies the prince on his ride or not," Grooms was saying. "But on His Royal Highness's last outing, Daisy was not allowed to run along with Ben, for she was acting a bit oddly."

"How so?"

"On most occasions when the prince approaches, Daisy yelps happily and wags her tail in anticipation. But on the last visit, the hound began to bark and scamper around the prince in a most annoying manner. For that reason, I placed Daisy in a stall and fed her a few scraps to calm her down."

"She must have been disappointed when Prince Harry did not return," Joanna surmised.

"I did not notice, ma'am, for my attention had to be focused on other, more important matters."

"Indeed, much more important," she agreed. "Your comments have been quite helpful, and I know you shall remain on the lookout for any strangers who lurk about the stable."

"I will keep a sharp eye out."

Daisy abruptly arose and froze in a crouched position, all the while pointing her nose at the entrance. The hound began to yelp pleasantly, with its tail wagging, which made me wonder if Prince Harry was about to miraculously reappear. But my hopes were quickly dashed when in walked a rather dapper man who was attired in a dark suit accented by a maroon tie. His posture and gait spoke of a military background. He introduced himself as Sergeant Ethan Adams, the personal guard to Prince Harry.

"I was told my presence was needed at the stable," he reported. "How may I be of service?"

"We require a step-by-step description of the prince's activities from the moment he arrived at Lancaster Gate stables until the end of his ride," said Joanna. "Leave out no detail, even if you believe it to be minor and of little consequence."

"His Royal Highness's limousine drove up at precisely ten after ten, with the prince looking forward to his ride. Ben, the bay he favored, had been saddled and bridled, and immediately sensed the royal arrival, with a welcoming neigh. We started off at a slow trot, as usual, then increased the gait a bit more once we determined the trail ahead was clear."

"I take it Prince Harry was in good spirits?" Joanna inquired.

"Particularly so, for it provided him a moment to relax before his rather heavy schedule that day."

"Did the riding path remain vacant?"

"Completely," Adams replied, and gave the stable master an appreciative nod. "Grooms here keep the other horses in their stalls whilst we ride, so as to avoid gawkers who might upset Prince Harry's moment of relaxation. Our only encounter was with the occasional red squirrel running across the path in search of a safe spot, I suspect."

"Pray continue."

"We had traveled approximately a mile when the prince brought Ben to a halt and requested a pause to answer a call of nature, which was not unusual. Again, I must stress the riding trail was entirely vacant."

My father asked, "How many stops were made on a customary ride in Hyde Park?"

"At least two, sir, and on occasion more," the palace guard answered, then continued. "It was at this point that the prince steered Ben into a wooded area, well away from any public view. Several minutes passed and when Prince Harry did not reappear, I entered the woods and found no sign of him or the horse."

"Had he in fact relieved himself?" Joanna queried.

"It was impossible to tell, for the grass was quite wet from an earlier rain."

"Did anything appear peculiar or out of place in the clearing?"

"I did not notice, ma'am, for I was completely occupied in my search for the prince."

"Entirely understandable," Joanna said in a neutral tone, but I could tell from the set of her jaw that she was disappointed, for here was the opportunity to observe the evidence before it was disturbed by the rain and other forces of nature.

"I should have made that observation," Adams berated himself.

"Do not be too hard on yourself, Sergeant, for you are trained to guard and protect, whilst detectives often have an innate ability to observe in a fashion which allows them to see what others overlook."

Adams furrowed his brow in thought, then quickly raised a

hand. "I did search for possible witnesses on the adjacent paths, but could find none."

"Were there any strangers lurking about?"

The palace guard shook his head in response. "All of the nearby trails and paths were vacant."

"Entirely so?"

"As far as the eye could see."

"Thank you, Sergeant," Joanna said, with a gesture of dismissal. "You have been most helpful."

After the palace guard departed, Joanna turned to the stable master and said in a most commanding voice, "You are not to mention a word of my visit to anyone. It is to be kept strictly confidential. Do you understand?"

"Not a word will be spoken, ma'am," Grooms pledged, then hesitated like a man wishing to speak, but not certain he should. Finally, his curiosity overcame him. "Ma'am, I know it is not my place to ask, but is it possible the prince's tumble was not accidental?"

"Why do you inquire?"

"Because there are clever ways to make a horse tumble."

"Your point is well taken," Joanna said, then lowered her voice. "Suffice it to say there are those who would wish harm on the royal family, and thus any accident which befalls them has to be carefully investigated."

"The bloody Huns," Grooms muttered under his breath.

"And so you must be on the lookout for strangers prowling about."

"I shall, ma'am."

"And not a word to anyone, for there are ears everywhere."

"My lips are sealed, ma'am."

On that note we followed the palace guard from the stable, with Lestrade offering us a ride to Baker Street, which we declined and chose instead to visit a nearby café for tea and a brief respite. We remained silent on our stroll until we reached Bays-water Road where the loud traffic would drown out the sound of our voices to any passersby.

"What say you, Watson?" Joanna asked.

"I say His Royal Highness has prostatitis, which accounts for his frequent calls to relieve himself," my father replied. "It is a disorder common to promiscuous men and is often the result of a bacterial infection."

"Which fits the prince's lifestyle," I noted.

"An important observation," said Joanna. "But it tells us a great deal more than simply the prince's sexual behavior."

"What, pray tell?" my father asked, with a quizzical look.

"That the prince's disappearance was beyond any question planned."

"I am afraid that conclusion goes way beyond me."

"Allow me to draw your attention to the frequency of his calls of nature," she explained. "According to the palace guard, there were at least two and often more stops on their rides through Hyde Park."

My father gave the matter more consideration. "Perhaps bouncing up and down on a hard saddle irritated the prostate gland even more."

"You are missing the most important point, Watson," Joanna went on. "If the prince did in fact make two or three stops on each outing and the locations of such stops no doubt varied, how would a possible abductor know which of the stops to wait at on any given day? Certainly one cannot envision a group of abductors spreading out through the woods and waiting for the prince's appearance."

"But someone *was* waiting at a particular place for Prince Harry," I noted.

"Exactly right, dear heart," my wife concurred. "Thus we can rightfully deduce that someone knew the prince would visit that very spot, and he had to be informed beforehand to do so."

"And the informant had to be His Royal Highness, for he was the only one who knew precisely where and when the stop would occur," I thought aloud. "So his disappearance had to be planned well in advance."

"No doubt for one of his romantic trysts," my father concluded.

"Perhaps," Joanna said, unconvinced. "But there is another feature which remains bothersome and states otherwise."

"Which is?"

"The activity of the border collie," she elucidated. "You will recall the hound's unusual behavior when Prince Harry arrived at the stable. She barked excitedly and ran in circles around him, which was not a happy greeting. It was the manner in which border collies respond to an approaching threat. They circle the flock or intended victims to draw them in closer and thus make them easier to protect. Dear Daisy was attempting to protect His Royal Highness."

"So there must have been danger awaiting the prince on his ride," I deduced.

Joanna nodded slowly as her mind went elsewhere for a moment. "Border collies have a keen sense for impending danger, perhaps the keenest of all canines."

"Are you saying that this behavior excluded the possibility of a romantic tryst?"

"Not if the supposed rendezvous involved danger," said she as we entered a crowded café.

CHAPTER FIVE

The Message

On our arrival at 221b Baker Street, we were met at the base of the staircase by Miss Hudson and an appetizing aroma of exotic food cooked in her kitchen.

Joanna sniffed the air before pronouncing, "I smell roast duck."

Miss Hudson smiled happily. "It is indeed, Mrs. Watson. Would you care to guess what the main side dish will be?"

"It will be basmati rice."

Our landlady sighed, feigning exasperation. "How do you perform such magic?"

"By simple deduction," Joanna replied. "The duck you are roasting carries the aroma of spices unique to India. Thus I think in all probability you stopped by the Indian store on nearby Edgware Road to purchase the somewhat expensive spices and the owner offered to sell you a secreted bag of basmati rice as a reward for your long patronage of his shop."

"Is there no surprising you?"

"Oh, but there is, my dear Miss Hudson, for the surprise

comes when you somehow manage to surpass the deliciousness of one repast after another."

"Thank you for that kind compliment," said Miss Hudson, with a blush crossing her face.

"Not at all," Joanna went on. "But I do have one request of you. Please allow us an hour of complete solitude without interruption, for we have most important experiments to perform."

"You shall not hear a whisper, but before you retire to your rooms, permit me to introduce a visitor to our residence," said she, and led the way into the kitchen where Toby Two, a half-spaniel mix with the keenest nose in all London, awaited us.

"Well, well," Joanna beamed as the hound came over to have its head scratched. "What brings her back to us?"

"My chum Bertie had to return to the Hebrides for yet another funeral and asked if I would be good enough to look after his dog as I have done in the past."

Our collective minds went back to an earlier adventure in which we first encountered Bertie, who had to travel to the Hebrides to attend an aunt's funeral and requested Miss Hudson care for his dog Dolly, a giant Alsatian, in his absence. The alert hound befriended us and less than a week later saved our lives from a deadly assassin, but lost hers in that violent effort. In the very same adventure, we had later called upon Toby Two to assist us in tracking a kidnapper which she did successfully. During her time with us, the owner of the kennel where she resided suffered a massive stroke, and Joanna arranged for Toby Two to be adopted by Bertie who was delighted to have such a fine, new companion.

"An uncle had passed on, you see, and left Bertie a grandfather clock which must be shipped to London," Miss Hudson continued on. "He expects to be away a week or so."

"We are more than happy to have Toby Two with us once again," Joanna said warmly.

"Perhaps she will be of assistance in your current case which is of considerable interest to you."

"Of considerable interest, you say?"

"Why, of course. Why else would the Watsons hurry off with the briefest of words, omit lunch, and return in the late afternoon to immediately conduct experiments?"

"What brings you to the conclusion we omitted lunch?"

"Your heightened appetite which you demonstrated by your most unusual attention to the preparation of the food about to be served for dinner."

Joanna nodded, with a pleasing smile. "I must say, Miss Hudson, that your power of deduction is coming along nicely."

"It is the company I keep."

Up the stairs we went to our parlor where the air had a chill to it, for the temperature had begun to drop precipitously outside, with the shattered window from the earlier explosion letting in the cold. Whilst I started a fire, Joanna hurriedly cleared her laboratory bench of test tubes, flasks, and Bunsen burners before replacing them with small bottles of clear solutions. Next, she meticulously cleaned the lenses of our Zeiss microscope and her magnifying glass before adjusting the strong beam from a table lamp and switching off the light from the above chandelier. At her request, I closed the thick curtains to shut out the fading sunlight. Only then did she empty the large manila envelope of the items of evidence collected in Hyde Park.

"Let us begin with the short length of rope," said she, and carefully examined it with a magnifying glass under a bright light. "The ends were cut with a sharp blade that showed no signs of rust. And there is no discoloration, red or maroon, to indicate the presence of blood."

Next, she rubbed a sheet of clear, white paper against the rope with vigor, but again could detect no discoloration from residual blood. Then strands of rope were placed under a microscope to search for scattered red blood cells which may have been embedded in the fibers. "No blood thus far," Joanna declared. "But now let us go to the far more sensitive guaiacum test."

"But I must say that Holmes considered that test to be rather clumsy and insensitive," my father recalled.

"I am aware of his derision, yet I along with others have found the guaiacum test to be both sensitive and specific when done with the freshest of ingredients." She opened a small vial and, using a dropper, covered the length of rope with the clear solution and waited. "If blood is present, it will turn a deep blue color."

We moved in closer to the workbench and watched for a full minute. There was no change in color to be seen.

"Perhaps the rope was not part of the crime scene and had been discarded by an earlier rider," I pondered.

"And left in the exact clearing the prince had chosen to answer the call of nature?" Joanna countered, with a shake of her head. "No, that does not fit, for it was found in the proximity of the other items, all of which were pushed aside."

"But what purpose could it serve?"

"That remains to be determined, but one possibility is that the short rope was used as a whip to deliver a blow to Ben's rump and send him on his way back to the stable."

"Why go to the bother?"

"One would not wish for a riderless horse to be roaming about Hyde Park and drawing the attention of more than a few. That could result in quite a stir, with many questions raised, which Prince Harry would hope to avoid. Allow me again to draw your attention to the obvious fact that the prince's disappearance was planned, and did not include bringing troubles to Buckingham Palace."

"But troubles were sure to come," I argued.

"Not if his departure was meant to be short-lived," said Joanna, and let the words hang in the air before continuing her investigation. "Now we should move on to the cigarette stubs which may be more revealing."

She held each of the five stubs up to the light and studied them intently with her magnifying glass. Back and forth she went on the individual stubs, paying particular attention to the unburned ends. I wondered if she was searching for a label or a brand which might tell us the class of the individual who lay in wait for the prince. But I quickly discarded that idea, for such a brand on the cigarette would have in all likelihood been burned away. But then again, what could she be searching for?

"No lipstick, which indicates the smoker was a male," she said finally.

"Or a woman sans makeup," I ventured.

"Tsk, tsk!" she responded playfully. "In this instance, dear heart, you must think like a woman which would completely remove that possibility."

"How so?"

"No woman would ever leave home without makeup applied, of which lipstick would be an essential component, for a lady's mouth is often the very first thing a man studies on a female's face."

"Why the mouth?"

"Because it contains the lips, which is the most expressive feature we possess," she answered, before waving away the consideration. "All the same, we can predict with certainty that the individual awaiting the prince was a male who happens to be addicted to nicotine and is neat by habit. Perhaps the remaining items will tell us more."

Joanna briefly studied the small strip of shined leather and tossed it aside, saying, "This scrap is of no value, for it could have come from the saddle or stirrup or even the prince's boot, particularly if his dismount was rushed."

"Could His Royal Highness have been roughly pulled off his mount?" my father wondered.

"By a single person who would have to hold the horse steady while jerking the prince out of his saddle?" she asked. "Most un-likely, and besides, the prince would dismount by himself, for that was no doubt part of the plan."

Her gaze now went to the faded matchbook cover which had for the most part been decolorized by the rain. The few printed letters that remained were difficult to decipher and required Joanna to repeatedly move her magnifying glass up and down before commenting. "I can make out the letters *r* and *o,* followed by a large space, then an *a* and *m.* They have a somewhat greenish hue that indicates the ink used may well have been ingrained, which would account for their persistence despite the rain. These find-ings point to the letters being part of an advertisement."

"Does that have relevance?" asked I.

"We shall know more once we can read the remaining letters."

"And how does one go about making the invisible visible?"

"It is simple enough," said she. "Please darken the room by turning off the light and placing a chair in front of the fireplace."

My father and I quickly performed the tasks before hurry-ing back to the workbench. The parlor became so dim that only our moving shadows could be seen. "Done," I called out. "What next?"

"Gather around and observe."

Joanna reached for a small, handheld lamp and switched it on, which caused it to emit brilliant blue rays. "This is a Wood's lamp that discharges ultraviolet light, which has the capacity to interact with iron gall ink."

"Do all inks contain iron gall?" my father asked.

"On rare occasions some are water-based, so the odds are in our favor."

We leaned forward as Joanna directed the ultraviolet light

to the matchbook cover, and in an instant bright letters were reflected in the darkness. They read

The Rose and Lamb

Beneath the clear lettering was a picture of a lamb and within it the word *pub,* and under the lamb in small letters the name *Whitechapel.*

"A pub in Whitechapel," said Joanna. "Not the most chic of neighborhoods."

Which was an obvious understatement, thought I, for Whitechapel was one of the poorest neighborhoods in all London. It was plagued by pollution, disease, and virtually every criminal activity known to man. We were quite familiar with the district, as it was home to Jack the Ripper whom we pursued only months ago in a most harrowing affair.

"It would appear our man in waiting spent time in the seediest of neighborhoods, which raises the question: What would the good prince have in common with such a character and what could be their association?" Joanna asked.

"Surely, not one that sent Prince Harry off on one of his romantic trysts," said my father.

"Do not discount that possibility, Watson," she reminded. "Recall the gentlemen drifters in our chase for Jack the Ripper."

My father nodded at the remembrance of the thrill-seeking gentlemen who would leave their respectable homes and family for an evening to enter a forbidden world of low-life pubs and cheap, anonymous sex.

"But certainly this lot would not include a member of the royal family," my father dissented.

"The term *royalty* is not synonymous with sainthood," Joanna quipped.

Her attention went to the scribbled note inside the faded

matchbook cover which contained the faint, partial word *MORG,* and ended with several, indecipherable letters. It made no sense. The commissioner had surmised it represented a woman's name, Morgane, which seemed a long shot.

"It, too, appears to be written in ink, so let us see what the Wood's lamp will turn up for us." Joanna shined the inner surface of the matchbook with ultraviolet light and the word *MORGEN* appeared in poor handwriting.

"Perhaps it is the name of the man involved or the place to which the prince is to be taken," I ventured.

"Or the last name of a woman," my father suggested.

"It is neither," Joanna informed. "Were you fluent in the enemy's language, you would instantly recognize the word *morgen* is German for *tomorrow.*"

My father's head came up abruptly. "Are you telling us the Germans are involved?"

"What other conclusion could one reach?" she replied, searching the matchbook cover for more information, but none could be found.

"But most assuredly Prince Harry would not be consorting with the enemy."

"Not knowingly, one would hope."

"Could this man be a British citizen who immigrated from Germany some years ago and held on to his native tongue?"

"And perhaps held on to his allegiance to the Kaiser as well," Joanna retorted. "A number of possibilities remain open at this juncture."

"But which do you favor?" my father pressed.

"All of them until we have more evidence to lead us to the truth," said Joanna, and returned her focus to the matchbook cover. "But why write the word *morgen?*"

My father furrowed his brow in thought, repeating the word

softly under his breath. "Is he reminding himself that tomorrow is the day he is to meet with Prince Harry?"

"He would need no reminder for such an important event," she replied at once. "That date would certainly be ingrained in his brain."

"But he must have written the note inside his own match-book," I interjected. "For what other purpose would he do so?"

My wife smiled at us mischievously. "You are both assuming the man waiting for the prince wrote the note."

"Who else would bother to scribble the German word for *tomorrow*?" I asked.

"Consider the matchbook containing the word," she instructed. "In particular, what was its origin?"

"A pub in Whitechapel," I responded.

"And what do you make of that?"

The answer came to me immediately. "Someone at or associated with that pub must have written it."

"Not simply someone, but the person issuing the command," Joanna concluded. "And it was placed in that specific matchbook cover to demonstrate the order was authentic."

"It fits well," my father agreed. "But there is little evidence to back up your construct."

"At this juncture in the investigation evidence is scarce, so we have little choice but to gather up the few clues we have at our disposal and envision a framework which may or may not be true," said she. "There will be no easy answers or quick fixes here. With this in mind, let us docket the information we have and pick out additional clues to fill in the blank spaces."

"And how do we uncover this much-needed information?"

"By putting ourselves in the stead of the individual who constructed this maze and follow his footsteps."

Joanna reached for the crushed, empty cigarette package

and shined the Wood's lamp on each of its surfaces, but could find no additional hidden messages. With the lights turned back on, she examined the packet closely with a magnifying glass before sniffing at its opening. "You will note that it is dry and was obviously protected from the rain, perhaps because it lay beneath the partially coiled rope. This dryness allowed the packet to retain a faint but distinct aroma of Player's Navy Cut tobacco."

"Which would be expected," I thought aloud.

"But there may be more as well, for in addition I can detect another faint scent that carries a somewhat sweet trait," she went on. "Keep in mind that the human hand touches virtually everything an individual comes in contact with. If a gentleman touches the wrist of a perfumed woman, the fragrance will remain on his hand. If he reaches for a duck bone from one of Miss Hudson's exotic dishes, the aroma will remain on his fingers. Present a dog with your outstretched hand, palm down, and the hound will eagerly sniff at it and process a hundred different scents in a matter of seconds. It will inform the canine of what habits you have, which foods you have recently ingested, and where your travels have taken you, along with a dozen other identifying features. In essence, the hands tell all."

"What is your point?" asked my father.

"We shall have Toby Two, the keenest nose in all London, take a whiff of the discarded package and see what she makes of it," Joanna replied.

"She will easily detect the aroma of stale tobacco despite its exposure to the elements," I predicted.

"Ah, yes, but what else?" my wife queried.

"I am having difficulty following you," my father admitted. "I should think the relatively strong aroma of tobacco will distract the hound from any fainter scents which may be present."

"Let us fetch Toby Two and allow her to clarify."

I hurried down the stairs and came back with the spaniel-mix, who seemed to enjoy the exercise of scampering up to our parlor where she quickly moved to Joanna's side and stared up at my wife, as if awaiting instructions. I noticed that the items of evidence had now been moved onto the floor, with the cigarette stubs crowded together, and separated by ten feet or so from the crushed package.

Joanna led Toby Two to the cigarette stubs and waited for her to sniff them, which she promptly did. The hound showed no signs of excitement and little interest in the stubs. Next, the dog was guided to the crushed package, where it had a totally different reaction. She deeply sniffed at the package over and over again, tail wagging, with an occasional yelp at a new finding.

"Toby Two is taking longer because there is much more to process, you see," Joanna elucidated. "It is impossible to accurately tell how many scents she is detecting, but suffice it to say the number exceeds a few, all of which originated from the individual awaiting Prince Harry. I can also safely predict that her excitement is not the result of detecting stale tobacco, for she quickly ignored the old cigarette stubs."

"Are you of the belief that the crushed package contained items other than cigarettes?" I asked.

"Of course it did."

"But what, then?"

"Additional scents which were not present on the cigarettes."

"From what source?"

"Why, from the hands of the German-speaking individual who stood in waiting."

My father interrupted abruptly, "Now you have me confused, dear Joanna, for it is clear this individual touched the cigarette stubs and the package, and thus should have left the same scent on both."

"Very good, Watson, but now I must ask you to use your

imagination and count the number of times the individual actually touched the package versus the times he touched a single cigarette."

My father gave the matter considerable thought, as he counted silently to himself. "He would have held a single cigarette once for no more than six minutes."

"And the package?"

My father again counted to himself. "At least twenty times, for that is the number of cigarettes a package holds."

"Then add to that the number of times he touched the package while purchasing it or perhaps offering a cigarette to others, and then he embedded yet more scents whilst forcefully crushing the package in his hand before discarding it," Joanna enumerated.

"But what could have possibly left such a lingering aroma?"

"Something with which he had a great deal of contact."

"Such as?"

"That is to be determined."

"What a confusing tangle we are faced with," said I. "And all centering around a prince planning his own disappearance on a ride through Hyde Park."

Joanna strolled over to the shelf that held a Persian slipper, from which she extracted a Turkish cigarette. She carefully lighted it and began to pace the floor of our parlor, with Toby Two following each of her footsteps. My wife stopped briefly to look down at the items of evidence once again, then, taking another deep puff, began to pace once more, leaving a trail of pale, white smoke behind her. She continued on, mumbling to herself and lost in deep thought before pausing at the fireplace to toss away her cigarette.

"A confusing tangle it is, for this case is not simply a ride through Hyde Park to conveniently allow for the good prince to disappear," Joanna concluded. "Everything points to a criminal activity which I am convinced His Royal Highness was not aware of."

"Criminal activity, you say!" my father blurted out.

"Oh, yes, if you consider all the evidence we have at our disposal," said she, and counted off the reasons. "We have a border collie sensing danger for a prince who is about to vanish. Then there is an unknown culprit in waiting, who is associated with a pub in Whitechapel, the crime capital of London. And now we have a German in the mix, who is commanded to act tomorrow. There is a crime underway here and I fear the prince's life is in danger."

My father slowly nodded his agreement. "Thus we can exclude the possibility of a romantic tryst."

"To the contrary, it might well be an essential prerequisite."

"In what capacity?"

"To serve as a lure."

CHAPTER SIX

The Scent

The following morning I returned to my desk at St. Bartholomew's Hospital, where I served as director of pathology, and found a heavy schedule awaiting me. There was a lecture to be given, a committee meeting on contagion to attend, a slide review with resident trainees, and preparation of a talk on cardiac trauma to be presented at the Royal Society. Fortunately, as things stood, these tasks could be completed by mid-afternoon when I could hurry back to 221b Baker Street and rejoin the most important investigation into the disappearance of Prince Harry. An early-morning phone call from Scotland Yard informed us that the prince remained missing which was causing even greater worry to the royal family.

My ever-efficient secretary, Rose, looked in quietly which indicated there were more chores at hand. "Sir, your wife called and asked me to remind you to pick up the items from the chemist that she requested. Shall I send a messenger over?"

"I think not," said I. "The items have to be carefully prepared and I must make certain it is done so."

"Very well," she continued. "And a moment before your arrival,

Dr. Quinn asked that you stop by his laboratory at your earliest convenience, for there is need of a second opinion."

"Then I shall attend to that matter first."

"And finally, Dr. Rudd called twice," she reported. "I must say he sounded somewhat agitated."

"Which is par for the course."

Rose suppressed a smile.

Hurrying down a vacant corridor, I quickly connected Quinn's request to Rudd's multiple phone calls. Dr. Jonathan Quinn was the newest member of the pathology department, having assumed his position as an instructor only months earlier. He brought with him an excellent résumé, having trained at Oxford Hospital under the tutelage of Sir George Herbert, a superb pathologist and renowned specialist in gynecologic malignancies. Sir George's brilliance had apparently rubbed off on Quinn, for he was exceptionally knowledgeable in the pathology of such disorders. But there was another obvious feature Quinn possessed which did not work to his advantage, and that was his youthful appearance. He was slight of frame, with rosy cheeks and auburn-colored hair, which gave him a barely noticeable beard. Although in his early thirties, he could easily pass for a man in his mid-twenties. Unfortunately, his boyish look was often equated to inexperience, and thus the multiple phone calls from Dr. Thaddeus Rudd, whose patient in all likelihood had a diagnosis based on Quinn's reading of a surgical specimen. Rudd would want that diagnosis dismissed and replaced with a more optimistic one. The chief surgeon's demand for a second opinion was quite common, but rarely of consequence.

My thoughts were interrupted by the approach of William Benson, a head orderly and longtime, valued employee who kept everything shipshape and running smoothly in the department.

"Good morning to you, sir," he greeted me, with not a hint of warmth.

"And to you, Benson," I replied. "I see where we have a rather quiet day ahead, for no autopsies are scheduled."

"Aye, sir, but I am afraid that is about to change."

"Oh?"

"Ollie brought in a patient who he predicts will not make it through the day," Benson went on. "In bad shape, she was, with terrible stomach pain, shaking chills, and a high fever. The doctor who examined her could barely find a pulse."

I nodded at Ollie's appraisal, for the ambulance driver, whose true name was Eddie Oliver, had a knack from his considerable experience for accurately predicting the time of demise in patients he carried in his vehicle. "She was moribund, then."

"From the moment he picked her up in Whitechapel," said Benson, nodding back in a somewhat peculiar fashion. His head seemed to move side to side rather than up and down, for his cervical spine had been badly damaged in a childhood accident. "She was cold as ice, although still breathing according to Ollie."

"Keep me informed."

"I shall, sir."

"Carry on, then."

It required only a moment for me to mentally arrange for the precautions which would be needed should an autopsy on the obviously infected woman come to be. Gowns and gloves would be a must for all participating. As I walked on, my mind went back to Jonathan Quinn who no doubt felt embarrassed yet again when a second opinion was demanded solely based on his youthful appearance. But with time, he will age as we all do, and lines will come to his face and gray to his hair, and he will finally be recognized for the skills he possessed. I entered the pathology laboratory and found not only Jonathan Quinn, but an obviously irritated Thaddeus Rudd by his side.

"How can I be of service, Mr. Rudd?" I asked, using the term *Mister,* which surgeons preferred.

"I require a careful review and a second opinion, for I have doubts on the diagnosis given," Rudd replied and moved in front of Quinn, blocking my view of the young pathologist.

"Please give me the clinical particulars."

"Can you simply not read the bloody slide?"

"No, I cannot," I answered. "We have a protocol we follow before giving a second opinion, and I must insist you adhere to it."

"Very well," Rudd said begrudgingly and began to pace the laboratory, head down, hands clasped behind his back. The technicians stood at a distance, for not only was the surgeon a large man, but his face carried an angry scowl which his thick beard could not hide. "The patient involved is a young barmaid who was admitted semicomatose, with severe abdominal pain and high fever, indicating the presence of sepsis. A diagnosis of a ruptured appendix was made, but her condition was initially so unstable that surgery was impermissible. At the earliest hour this morning, however, she improved after administration of intravenous fluids and was rushed to the operating room where an inflamed appendix was removed. The specimen was submitted to pathology for routine confirmation. Imagine my surprise and, I must add, disbelief, when I was told there was no inflammation present."

"No inflammation whatsoever?" I asked.

"None," Quinn responded. "Nor was a perforation or rupture detected."

"Nonsense!" Rudd blurted out. "There was pus around the nearby cecum, a sure sign the appendix had ruptured."

"If you would like, we can review the gross specimen and the slides once again and have additional sections of the appendix studied under even higher magnification," I offered.

"I insist and I want it done today," Rudd demanded. "And the study is to be done by you and not by some junior pathologist."

The term *junior pathologist* was meant to demean Quinn, who hung his head to avoid Rudd's angry stare.

"The report will be on your desk before the day is out," said I.

"It had better be," Rudd growled, and stormed out of the laboratory.

"What an insufferable man," Quinn remarked in a quiet voice.

"But a highly skilled surgeon," I reminded. "And thus his boorish behavior is tolerated. Needless to say, he wields considerable power at St. Bart's."

"So we are obliged to do a most careful review, although I can assure you my findings are correct."

"I have no doubt, but let us exclude the diagnosis of a ruptured appendix once and for all," I directed. "Are the slides of the barmaid's appendix readily available?"

Quinn pointed to a Zeiss microscope on a nearby table. "They are in a small box beside the microscope."

Seating myself on a small, metal stool, I meticulously studied a dozen slides under the highest magnification. The mucosa and submucosa on each were intact and showed no evidence of inflammation. I repeated the study to ensure my observations were accurate before turning to Quinn. "Your findings appear quite correct."

"As I knew they would be," he replied, with a confident nod.

"Nevertheless, we must eliminate the possibility of a small perforation which escaped our eye," I went on. "To this end, I would like you to take a length of the small intestine surrounding the appendix and apply the dye methylene blue to its inner mucosa and determine if it seeps through to the outer surface, which it will not do unless a perforation is present."

"That should provide all with an answer that is unchallengeable," Quinn chimed in enthusiastically.

"And save the stained specimen so it can be shown to Mr. Rudd."

"With pleasure."

I dashed out of the pathology laboratory, completely confident in Quinn's skills, but the correctness of his diagnosis did not bode well for the patient, for the absence of a perforation meant the source of sepsis remained in the barmaid's abdomen, making her chances of survival nil. Glancing at my timepiece, I decided to pick up Joanna's request from the chemist, so as not to let it slip my mind. She seemed very keen indeed on her requests for minuscule amounts of morphine and cocaine in their purified, undiluted forms. Up the stairs I went, wondering what possible use these drugs could have in our investigation into the disappearance of Prince Harry. There was no evidence that he nor the individual waiting for him in Hyde Park had employed either agent.

On my arrival at the chemist's window, I was greeted by Mr. Solomon Ross, a man of small frame who was neatly attired in a tie and short, white laboratory jacket.

"Ah, I have your prescriptions ready," said the head chemist as he reached for two small vials. "I must admit, Dr. Watson, that your order for such minute doses of cocaine and morphine stirred my imagination. Certainly, they were not to be used for human consumption."

"We plan to employ the drugs in experiments being carried out in mice which require only small amounts."

"Regarding tolerance or addiction, might I ask?"

"Both."

"Let us hope for worthwhile results, then."

"That is my expectation," said I, remembering that my dear wife always had a most excellent reason for performing the strangest of experiments.

It was much later in the afternoon when I hurried back to 221b Baker Street, for my work at St. Bart's had consumed far more time than I anticipated. I was concerned that my tardiness would delay our investigation, but this was not to be the case. On my arrival, Joanna was dashing in through the front entrance, with an airtight container secured in both hands.

"Ideal timing," she declared, taking the stairs two at a time and leading the way into our nicely warmed parlor. "I presume you have the necessary prescriptions."

"Morphine and cocaine in the exact doses you requested," said I.

"Excellent!" She reached for the two labeled vials and, after briefly examining them, turned to my father. "Now, Watson, I would ask you to light your pipe with Arcadia Mixture and fill the air with its pleasant aroma. As you are performing this enjoyable task, John will be good enough to stroll down to Miss Hudson's kitchen, and wait five minutes before returning with Toby Two."

Back down the stairs I went, attempting to put together the odd pieces of this experiment. In an enclosed space there was to be air permeated with tobacco smoke, small vials of morphine and cocaine, and an airtight container holding an unknown substance, all of which were to be sampled by the keen nose of Toby Two. But to what end? The answer was beyond me.

On entering the kitchen, I found Miss Hudson at her oven, basting a goose with a spicy recipe that ensured a crispy skin. Toby Two was nearby, mesmerized by the delicious smell and watching every move our dear landlady made.

"I trust the hound has not been too much of a bother," said I.

"Not at all," she replied. "I gave her a lamb bone to chew on earlier which of course required all of her attention."

"Which has now returned to your oven for the moment."

"Where it will remain, but if she becomes uneasy, I will pitch her a dog biscuit that will occupy her completely. Dogs, you see, are concerned only with what is presently at hand, whilst the future is of little concern to them. And that no doubt is the key to their happiness."

"But Dolly, the sweet Alsatian, sensed future danger which saved our lives."

"Ah, but to Dolly, the danger was immediate, which made it part of her present."

"Well put, Miss Hudson," said I. "I did not know you were so informed on the habits of dogs."

"I wish I were, but the bits of knowledge I do have come from my chum Bertie, who is truly an expert on the behavior of dogs."

As Miss Hudson began to apply more of her crispy-skin recipe, my mind returned to Joanna's experiment and what specific scent she expected Toby Two to detect and what role it might play in our investigation. How a single aroma could lead to Prince Harry totally escaped me. I glanced over to the hound and wondered if she had somehow been primed to detect a unique scent.

"Has Toby Two been given access to our parlor in my absence?" I asked.

"Oh, no, sir, for Mrs. Watson instructed me to keep the hound occupied and not allow her upstairs," Miss Hudson replied. "She was quite specific for Toby Two to remain in the kitchen."

"Well then, her confinement is about to come to an end, for my dear wife now wishes to enjoy the dog's company." I turned to Toby Two and, with a gentle wave, commanded, "Come, girl."

The hound slowly rose to her feet, apparently somewhat reluctant to leave the comfortable surroundings, but once I departed she followed and happily scampered up the stairs. On entering our parlor she went directly to Joanna and was rewarded with a lump of sugar, which she eagerly chewed before looking up at my wife for yet another treat.

"Later," said Joanna, "for now you have work to do."

She led Toby Two to the far side of the parlor where the

crushed cigarette package lay on the floor, and allowed the dog to give the item a thorough sniff. The hound remained over the package for ten seconds or so, apparently reacquainting herself with previously detected scents, then looked up at Joanna.

"There are multiple scents in that container, two of which I myself could identify despite their faintness," my wife commented. "One was that of stale tobacco, the other an almost imperceptible sweet aroma which defied definition."

With that description, she and Toby Two moved ten feet away to a gathering of the discarded cigarette stubs which Toby Two whiffed at casually, showing little interest.

"She was able to detect only stale tobacco, which was identical to that in the package and thus aroused little curiosity," said Joanna. "The smoke from Watson's pipe did not distract her, which I assumed would be the case. Thus we can safely say her keen nose is as sharp as ever."

Next, the hound was directed to a small slip of paper on the floor, which was several feet away from the cigarette stubs. Toby Two gave it the briefest of sniffs and turned away. "That paper holds a small amount of morphine, which is entirely odorless and merits no attention," Joanna told us, now pointing the dog to another slip of paper which was several yards away from the other items.

Toby Two spent a bit more time at the second slip, for it contained a substance that aroused her curiosity, but only briefly. Once more she gazed up at my wife, as if waiting for further instructions. But on this occasion Joanna had no need to direct the hound, for it sampled the air and suddenly dashed over to a third, final slip of paper only a few feet away and eagerly put her nose to it, with her body and tail straight as an arrow.

"Found something interesting, did you?" Joanna queried.

Only seconds passed before Toby Two, without instruction, raced over to the crushed cigarette package and yelped at it in an effort to gain my wife's attention. Joanna ignored the dog as it continued to yelp and run back and forth between the crushed package and the final slip of paper.

"Does anyone wish to hazard a guess as to what scent is present in both the cigarette package and the third slip of paper?" Joanna asked.

I thought back to my wife's earlier evaluation of the crushed package in which she detected two faint but separate scents. One was that of faded, stale tobacco, the other carried the trace of a sweet, unidentifiable aroma. "It must have been the second, sweet smell you noticed."

"Very good, John," said she. "It was the second, faint scent, which seemed vaguely familiar, but I could not place it. As my esteemed father once remarked, 'It is the uncommon clues which are most often the most important.' But how, I wondered, were we to connect a sweet aroma to the disappearance of a prince? It continued to escape me until I recalled the notion that Prince Harry's prolonged absence might have been induced by a head injury or perhaps a drug-induced stupor. That was the reason for my asking the private secretary whether His Royal Highness partook of intoxicants."

"Which he did not," my father remembered.

"Assuming the secretary was telling the truth."

"Why would he not?"

"To cover up a fact that neither the prince nor the royal family would wish known," said Joanna. "With that in mind, Watson, pray tell which intoxicants could result in a prolonged stupor?"

My father easily counted off the possibilities. "An alcohol-binge, repeated morphine injections, and an overdose of opium or cocaine."

"Those were the very same intoxicants that crossed my mind," said she. "So I spent most of the day searching through the appropriate texts to determine which of the agents possessed a sweet aroma. Interestingly, only opium and cocaine fell into that category, and that was the purpose of the experiment I just performed. The most excellent nose of Toby Two identified the source of the sweet fragrance in the crushed cigarette package. It was the smoke from burnt opium which I placed on the third slip of paper."

I nodded at once. "I, too, now recall that particular aroma when we visited the opium den in one of our earlier cases."

"As did I," Joanna noted.

"But it was not Prince Harry who was using the drug," my father argued. "It was the individual in waiting at the clearing in Hyde Park."

"Precisely, my dear Watson, for with this most important clue in hand we can now say that the game is truly afoot."

"How so?"

"It will lead us to the very clever mastermind behind this crime."

CHAPTER SEVEN

The Morrison Syndicate

Miss Hudson's goose would have to await its presence on our dinner table, for we had one more important visit to make that evening. All it required was a single phone call for Joanna to arrange a meeting with Mr. Freddie Morrison, the head of London's most notorious crime syndicate whose tentacles reached out from a rather plain, working-class pub. My father would be unable to join us, for his arthritic knee was acting up and limiting his activity.

"It is a dangerous neighborhood that you are about to enter," he warned, with his leg resting on a cushioned footstool. "Perhaps you should bring along Lestrade."

"If we involve Scotland Yard, our host will clam up quicker than a wink, for they have the power to search and arrest, which we lack," said Joanna. "Moreover, Freddie Morrison rules the entire district with an iron fist, and I can assure you the word has gone out that we are not to be harmed."

"And you trust such a word?"

"I do."

"Pray tell why?"

"Because it is in his best interest to do so."

"Nevertheless, I wish I could join you, with my trusted Webley close at hand."

"Please do not concern yourself with our safety, for we shall be fine and shortly return to enjoy Miss Hudson's goose with you by our side."

On that note, which I must say my father did not find comforting, we departed Baker Street in the taxi waiting at our doorstep, and traveled through the unilluminated streets of London. The buildings and residences along the way were darkened, and even the lampposts turned off, so as not to present a lighted target should the German bomber return in a surprise raid. But in reality these precautions were of limited value, for the Huns often dropped incendiary bombs prior to the actual raid itself, which lit up London like a giant fire. An ambulance sped by us, its alarm ringing. It did not have its lights on.

As we rode south along quiet streets, I could not help but wonder why we were visiting Mr. Freddie Morrison, for his syndicate was known to be involved in the profitable ventures of extortion, prostitution, drugs, and contract killings. But by far, the greatest profit came from the sale of highly priced, ill-gotten items, such as masterpieces, which needed to be placed on the black market. The syndicate was willing to act as an intermediary for a 20 percent commission that at times exceeded ten thousand pounds. With all this in mind, kidnapping was not on their agenda, particularly one involving a royal prince, which would find the perpetrator facing a lifelong prison sentence.

We crossed the Thames and entered the industrialized section of South London, which was even darker than Central London. There were no lights to be seen whatsoever, neither on the streets or surrounding buildings nor in the massive factories themselves. All remained silent until the taxi slowed and approached our destination, upon which the driver turned to us and asked, "Shall I wait for you, madam?"

"Yes, and you should park next to the tobacco shop on the opposite side of the street."

Our taxi arrived at the front entrance of the darkened Angel pub, which for all the world appeared to be a simple, neighborhood drinking establishment. But sights can be deceiving, for behind its doors emanated some of London's most notorious and violent crimes.

We alighted from the taxi and walked down a narrow alleyway which was littered with trash and carried the aroma of spoiled garbage. In the dimness just ahead of us, a burly man wearing a leather jacket over a turtleneck sweater stood guard.

He carefully measured us and, without a word, opened the door to a busy kitchen and led the way in. The scene within seemed identical to that of our last visit. Several cooks were preparing dishes of shepherd's pie and Welsh rarebit, whilst two slightly built Asians were washing and drying plates, and speaking in a totally incomprehensible language. Once again we were ignored, with no one even bothering to glance in our direction. On entering the pub itself we were guided through a noisy, rowdy crowd of merrymakers, most of whom were drinking from large, glass tankards. An obviously intoxicated man staggered toward us for a closer look and was roughly pushed aside, with a stern warning from our guard. We reached the end of a long bar where a door on our right was opened by yet another guard, and we were ushered into a rather plain office that was filled with cigar smoke. From behind an uncluttered desk, a heavyset man attired in a nicely tailored suit motioned us to the two chairs in front of him. He was well groomed in every way, but his general appearance was marred by a deep scar that ran from his left ear to his upper cheek.

"I was assured that I am not being investigated for any crime," said he in a voice that demanded a reply. "Does that assurance stand?"

"It does," Joanna responded as the guard departed and closed the door behind him.

"I should like it in writing."

"Don't be absurd, Mr. Morrison, for if that was the purpose of this visit, you would be speaking to Scotland Yard and not me."

"If you attempt to associate me with any criminal activity, I shall only answer in the presence of my barrister," Morrison went on. "You may count on that, madam."

"Please let me know when your rantings are done so we can get to the business at hand."

"Which is?"

"Information on a pub in Whitechapel called The Rose and Lamb."

"I know nothing of it."

"That is your first false statement."

Morrison stared back, as if to stand by his words.

"Shall we begin again?"

"My response will be the same even if you bring Scotland Yard along with you."

"If I am forced to return, it will be with the SIS."

Morrison's face turned to worry at the mention of the Secret Intelligence Service, who were known to deal harshly with those attempting to harm the Crown. "Do not tell me we are dealing with treason again. For if that is the case, I can assure you I am in no way involved."

Joanna uttered a sigh of impatience. "Mr. Morrison, I am here only for information which I believe you can provide. Any crimes which you may or may not have committed are of no concern to me. Suffice it to say, you inhabit and control a world

I am very much aware of, and I have powerful, influential associates that you no doubt wish to avoid. With these connections in mind, let us establish a truce and get on with the matters at hand."

"Truces are unheard of on my side of the street, madam, for they are for the most part made to be broken."

"Then make an exception, for in the end we shall both benefit from it."

A faint smile crossed Morrison's face. "Are we to be colleagues, then?"

"For the time being."

"And will this alliance be written in the clever chronicles written by your husband?"

"Of course, but fear not, for it will only enhance the extraordinary power you wield," she replied. "Readers will assume you have influence on both sides of the street."

The syndicate boss gave the offer further consideration before nodding slowly. "It could be quite useful."

"Then let us proceed," Joanna continued on. "I require the name of the owner of the aforementioned pub in Whitechapel."

"Nathaniel Day, but most consider that to be an alias."

"Do you know him?"

"Our paths have crossed."

"Are you aware of what criminal activities he might be involved in?"

"Only from a reliable source who no doubt would wish to remain anonymous."

"Please list them."

Morrison tilted his chair back and furrowed his brow, as if in deep thought. "Allow me to again stress that my information is not firsthand."

"We are on a limited schedule, and I would like you to answer questions without deflection," said Joanna. "In order to absolve yourself of any association, you may use a third person narrative. Now, name Mr. Nathaniel Day's activities without exception."

"I was told he was involved rather heavily in extortion, prostitution, and drugs, although altogether he is considered a minor player. It is also believed he carries on a highly profitable trade in abortions."

"Surely, he does not perform those acts himself."

Morrison shook his head. "They are said to be performed by his sister-in-law whose name is Dorothea. She is supposedly quite talented and is in great demand."

"Are such services not offered at other pubs as well?"

"Very few indeed, for those convicted will serve a very harsh imprisonment, and if the woman happens to die, a death sentence may be in the doer's future."

"Thus the risk far outweighs the profit."

"So it would seem, despite the high fees charged."

"Let us return to Mr. Day's drug trade," Joanna continued on. "Which intoxicants would be available to those patronizing The Rose and Lamb?"

"The usual," Morrison replied offhandedly. "Cocaine, heroin, and morphine."

"Does he deal with opium, as well?"

"The Chinese have that trade pretty much to themselves, for they control the opium dens where the drug is cheap and readily available. It is a virtual monopoly for them in that no one can compete with their prices."

"Is there any one Chinese individual who controls the opium trade you speak of?"

Morrison nodded. "A bloody smart Chinaman named Ah Sing who knows where every puff of opium is being inhaled and by whom. I am told he actually keeps record books on individual preferences."

"That clever, is he?"

"And some."

"Ah Sing, you say?"

"Ah Sing," Morrison repeated.

"Do you know him?"

"Never had the pleasure."

But Joanna had, I thought to myself, recalling a case from several years back, in which we visited the Chinese den owner and gained valuable information. My wife was now asking questions to test Morrison's truthfulness. "Does Ah Sing own more than one den?"

The syndicate boss smiled humorlessly. "If you find an opium den that he does not own, it will be the only one."

"I am surprised others have not attempted to take over Ah Sing's monopoly."

"Oh, it has been tried, madam, by those who wished they hadn't."

"So Ah Sing is not a man to be trifled with."

"Not unless you are willing to pay the consequences."

"Well put," Joanna said. "And now I have one final set of questions that deal with the sale of precious items on the black market."

Morrison stiffened in his chair, now instantly on guard. "I am not involved in such transactions," he lied with a straight face.

"Come, come, Mr. Morrison. Here we are such close colleagues and you are already straying off the path of the righteous," Joanna said without condemnation.

The syndicate boss muffled a laugh. "Oh, madam, you truly outdo yourself."

"It is a habit I possess," Joanna quipped. "Now, back to those who sell precious items on the black market."

"I have heard stories, again from reliable sources."

"That is the information I am most interested in, and in particular how it might relate to Mr. Nathaniel Day and his pub in Whitechapel."

Morrison shook his head vigorously. "He himself could never handle such a transaction, for he has neither the skill nor connections which would be required."

"But he might seek out an intermediary who possessed those requirements."

"He well might."

"Have you heard of any such transactions taking place recently?"

Morrison hesitated in an apparent attempt to choose his words more carefully. "A story similar to that has been floating around."

"I need particulars," Joanna pressed.

"The source was told that a painting by a young French impressionist was being offered, but what interest it generated quickly disappeared when its origin was revealed."

"And that origin?"

"I will only say that the offeror was somehow connected to the royal family."

"Who remains unknown."

"Sometimes, madam, it is best not to know."

"Indeed it is," said Joanna, arising from her chair. "I trust I will not be visited by Scotland Yard or the SIS?"

"Your trust is well placed."

We departed the Angel pub via the same door used to make our entrance, then hurried past the burly guard and down the alleyway, for a light rain was beginning to fall. Our taxi driver saw our approach and started his motor.

"Someone close to the royal family needed money," I concluded.

"And someone near the royal family was addicted to nicotine and opium," Joanna noted.

"Surely, not the prince."

"What makes you so certain?"

"The prince's private secretary said the prince was neither a smoker nor a user of drugs."

"The prince's secretary said a lot of things, all of which now have to be challenged and verified."

We ran for our taxi as the light rain turned into a downpour.

CHAPTER EIGHT

The Ransom Note

We received yet another important telephone call the next morning, but this call came from Scotland Yard rather than 10 Downing Street. Inspector Lestrade informed us that a handwritten ransom note for the release of Prince Harry had been received the night before. Our immediate presence was requested by the commissioner.

"Handwritten, you say?" Joanna asked at once.

"In block letters, according to Lestrade," I replied.

"Excellent!" my wife declared, arising from our breakfast table. She hurried over to her workbench and swept all of the Hyde Park evidence into its large manila envelope before reaching for her Wood's lamp. "Watson, is your doctor's satchel available?"

"It is safely tucked away in my room," said he.

"Please fetch it and empty its contents to make room for the Wood's lamp."

"Lestrade did not mention faded letters on the ransom note," I recalled.

"The lamp is to serve another purpose," said Joanna.

Much to the later chagrin of Miss Hudson, our fine repast

was left unfinished, for the race was now on to find the prince before his abductors denied us of his presence one way or another. My father's knee had responded nicely to the application of heat and salicylate cream, and he was more than eager to rejoin the investigation. I watched his gait in my peripheral vision and could detect no evidence of a limp, for his step now had a definite bounce to it.

At the entrance to 221b Baker Street we hailed a taxi and rode to Scotland Yard, with one question weighing heavily on my mind, as well as on my father's, for it was he who asked, "Why the delay in sending the ransom note?"

"I can think of at least two good reasons," Joanna responded. "The most obvious is that a prolonged delay would increase the royal family's worry and make them even more anxious to pay whatever ransom is demanded. The second, and perhaps more likely, is that the abductors required more time to secure the prince from any possible view."

"So you believe they would seek a locale outside of London," I concluded.

"And out of the reach of Scotland Yard," my father added.

"A distinct possibility," Joanna said without inflection.

"But there are more than a few hiding places in our crowded city where Prince Harry could be secured and never noticed," I proposed. "Such a task could be easily accomplished by those familiar with our dark streets."

"You are assuming the abductors are Londoners, are you not?" Joanna queried.

"Who else?"

"Allow me to again draw your attention to the inside of the matchbook cover, upon which the word *morgen* is inscribed."

"The Germans!" my father and I bellowed out simultaneously.

Our words seemed to hang in the air at the dreadful possibility that enemy agents could prance into London and abduct a member of the royal family with such apparent ease. I quickly turned to my wife. "Are you convinced the Germans are involved?"

"They must be, with the only question being to what degree."

"What a coup it would be for the bloody Huns," my father said unhappily. "Can you begin to envision the Germans parading young Prince Harry up and down the major avenues of Berlin? It would deliver a most demoralizing blow to the British people, particularly when coupled with the disheartening news from the front where our losses continue to mount daily."

"But we have no solid evidence to back up that contention," I argued mildly.

"Yet I must say there is a definitive clue which seems to point in that direction," my father noted.

"So it would appear," Joanna said, unconvinced.

"Do you not find that an important observation?"

"I find it disconcerting, Watson."

"How so?"

"As my father was once quoted as saying, 'There is nothing more deceptive than an obvious fact.'"

We alighted from our taxi at the entrance to Scotland Yard and hurried into the commissioner's office where Inspector Lestrade and Sir Charles awaited us. A bright light shined down on a single sheet of paper atop the commissioner's desk, and next to it a set of rubber gloves.

"The ransom note was examined for fingerprints and a watermark, neither of which were found," Sir Charles informed, pointing to the sheet of paper.

Joanna put on the rubber gloves and, holding the note up to the light, carefully examined it with her magnifying glass. "It is quite inexpensive paper which could have a thousand untraceable origins. The ink is also commonplace, I believe."

"Thus it appears to hold no clues," the commissioner gathered.

"Appearances can be deceiving, Sir Charles," said she as we huddled around the desk to view the ransom note. It read:

RANSOM DEMAND FOR HRH TOMORROW
AT 3:15 BY PHONE
PREPARE THE ROYAL FAMILY

"We can safely predict the call will come to Scotland Yard and not Buckingham Palace," the commissioner stated.

"No doubt," Joanna agreed.

"But why the phone rather than a written note?"

"Because in all likelihood the demand will be lengthy, with emphasis on how and where the transaction is to occur."

Sir Charles gazed down at the ransom note and studied its wordage before asking, "It has a most peculiar ending which tells us to prepare the royal family. Do you believe their demand will be that excessive?"

"That, commissioner, is a certainty," Joanna replied. "But what?"

"A large sum of pounds sterling, I would presume."

"Or some royal possession, with a value beyond price."

"Such as?"

"A few sketches of Leonardo da Vinci would be worth millions and easily sold on the black market," she answered. "But these are all guesses which serve no purpose and only detract. Let us return to the note itself, for it contains a most important clue."

"Which is?"

"It was written by the same individual who awaited the prince to relieve himself in the clearing at Hyde Park," Joanna replied and, turning to my father, requested, "Be good enough, Watson, to remove the Wood's lamp from your doctor's satchel and plug in its electrical cord."

Sir Charles squinted his eyes, clearly bewildered. "Are you saying a hidden individual lay in wait for Prince Harry?"

"I am," Joanna said as she reached for the Wood's lamp.

"Who?"

"Someone with ties to Germany."

"What!"

"All will shortly become clear." Joanna emptied the large manila envelope onto the desk and separated the faded matchbook cover from the other items before having the lights switched off. Next, she opened the matchbook cover and shined the light from the Wood's lamp onto the inside of the cover where the letters *MORGEN* were written. In an instant the ultraviolet rays were absorbed by the hidden ink and the word *MORGEN* appeared.

"*Morgen* is the German word for *tomorrow*," she defined, then detailed the significance of the five discarded cigarette stubs and the crushed cigarette package in the clearing, all of which indicated the same individual had spent thirty minutes or more waiting in place for the prince who was obviously expected to show up at that particular location."

"And what of the short length of rope?" Lestrade asked, pointing to the item.

"I suspect it was used to deliver a blow to the horse's rump and send him back to the stable once Prince Harry had dismounted."

"So his departure was planned, with the aid of a German accomplice," Sir Charles deduced. "But why?"

"That is to be determined."

The commissioner worriedly tapped a finger against his chin before asking, "Are you implying that our prince is somehow involved with a German agent?"

"So it would seem."

"That is a most serious charge to make, and one which requires much more evidence than a word within a matchbook cover."

"I am afraid that evidence is at hand, for the individual who wrote the word *morgen* is the same individual who composed the ransom note."

Sir Charles furrowed his brow in thought. "Based on the fact that both were written in block letters?"

"No, commissioner, it is based on the shape of the *R*s and *E*s in the messages," Joanna explained, and placed the opened matchbook cover next to the ransom sheet. "You will note the shape of the *R* in both, in which the end of the *R* has an upward curve. Also, pay attention to the *E,* in which the top ends in a downward curve. These characteristics are present in both the matchbook word and in the ransom note. Since these uncommon variations are involuntarily made in one's handwriting and are done out of habit, we can say beyond a doubt they were written by the same individual."

"A bloody Hun!" the commissioner spat out the words. "It is most difficult to believe our Prince Harry is associated with an enemy agent."

"He may be doing so unwittingly," Joanna suggested.

"But the damage could still be done."

Joanna closed the matchbook cover and, turning it faceup, shined the ultraviolet light upon its faded cover. The advertisement for The Rose and Lamb pub in Whitechapel was clearly revealed.

"Ah, The Rose and Lamb," Lestrade recalled. "It is a rather dreadful establishment in the center of Whitechapel. One cannot go much lower, as evidenced by the seediest of characters who frequent there."

"I take it the pub is the seat of known criminal activities," said the commissioner.

"Quite so, sir, with most of it dealing with drugs and prostitution," Lestrade replied. "But major crimes are not on their menu."

"Nevertheless, such a disreputable pub would be worth looking into."

"I would be most careful here," my wife cautioned. "As the inspector noted, any association with a prince of England would be far beyond their reach. And if by chance there was some sort of involvement, the sudden appearance of Scotland Yard would force them into deep cover or send them on the run, and any possible clue would be lost."

Sir Charles nodded in agreement. "The clever fox always manages to disappear at the approach of the hounds. But on the other hand, we cannot disregard the pub altogether despite its low status. We must keep in mind the German word was written in one of the matchbook covers, which is the only telling clue we have at this point." He gave the matter more thought, then abruptly turned to Lestrade. "Inspector, I would think we have more than a few snitches in that district."

"Quite a few, sir, most of whom would happily sell their mother for a guinea."

"Then you should make inquiries in a most discreet manner to learn if there have been any whispers about a German or royal connection," the commissioner directed. "Use only your best men and in particular those who know the most reliable of snitches."

"It will be done on the quiet, sir," Lestrade assured.

Sir Charles came back to Joanna, the worry clearly on his face. "Time is now even more of the essence, for I fear for the prince's life."

"As do I."

"I must be told if there are any other avenues we have overlooked that merit investigation," he said in a most urgent tone.

"It may well involve the royal family or those very close to it," Joanna warned.

"There are to be no exceptions."

"So be it," said she. "It is imperative that we have the names of all the prince's known female companions, particularly those he spent the night with on more than one occasion. I will require date, place, and duration. To this end, a meeting must be arranged with Mr. Roger Mallsby, the prince's private secretary, tomorrow afternoon. He is to bring along a written, detailed list of the aforementioned companions who were involved in a romantic tryst which necessitated a secret rendezvous."

"Where should this meeting take place?" Sir Charles asked.

"In Inspector Lestrade's office, for even those associated with the royal family realize the penalty of perjury while being questioned by Scotland Yard."

"It will be done."

We departed from the commissioner's office and hurried out the front entrance, not speaking until we were well clear of Scotland Yard. The footpath was crowded with strolling people during the lunch hour, so I waited until we reached a quiet place, free of those who might overhear, and stated, "I noticed that you omitted the finding of the opium scent in the crushed package."

"I did so with a purpose," Joanna said.

"Pray tell for what purpose?"

"To prevent Scotland Yard from bungling the most important clue we are about to follow."

"Which is?"

"The trail left behind by the German, of course," she replied, and hailed a passing taxi.

CHAPTER NINE

The Barmaid

I hurried into my office at St. Bart's just past noon and was greeted by my secretary who held up a pathology report awaiting my signature, alongside that of Jonathan Quinn's.

"The stenography pool has delivered the transcript on Mr. Rudd's patient," said she.

I quickly read the report which clearly stated that the appendix showed only minimal inflammation and that no rupture could be detected, which confirmed the misdiagnosis by Mr. Rudd who was now in the process of seeking a second opinion on the surgical specimens. To make the situation even more uncomfortable for the surgeon, the young barmaid had expired in the early-morning hours and now lay cold as ice on an autopsy table. Perhaps now we would learn the true cause of the woman's misery and demise.

I applied my signature and handed the document back to my secretary. "Are there other matters which require my attention?"

"You may wish to speak with Mr. Quinn who earlier this morning requested the name of our best microbiologist at St.

Bart's," she replied. "I gave him the name of Dr. Adam Sharpe, whom I know you favor."

"Did he mention the need for the referral?"

"Only that it involved a strange bacteria."

"Of what type?"

"He did not say."

I moved quickly down the corridor, spurred on by Quinn's description of a strange bacteria, which by itself carried a dangerous connotation, for those were the microorganisms that tended to be the most contagious and inflict the most tissue damage. If the infected individual had been an inpatient at St. Bart's, which was the most likely case, the identity of the bacteria would have to be rapidly determined and measures put in place to prevent its spread. The last bout of contagion, which began on the surgery ward, resulted in a dozen deaths and double that number of prolonged hospitalizations.

On entering the pathology laboratory, I found Jonathan Quinn standing over a large sink whilst vigorously scrubbing his arms. The aroma of a strong disinfectant filled the air which indicated precautionary measures against the infecting agent were already underway.

"What type of microorganism are we dealing with?" I asked.

"It is not the usual staphylococcus or streptococcus, but rather a Gram-negative bacteria," Quinn replied as he dried his hands and arms with a clean towel.

"*Pseudomonas* or *E. coli*, then?"

"The former, Dr. Sharpe believes, for he was able to detect a sweet, grape-like aroma, which is characteristic of that microorganism."

"And its source?"

"The poor barmaid who now carries the diagnosis of an abortion gone wrong," the young pathologist answered. "Which may explain Mr. Rudd's misdiagnosis. With the patient in such a precarious condition, he had no choice but to enter and exit without performing a thorough exploration of the abdomen."

"Perhaps, but in his haste he missed the opportunity to save that young woman's life or at least spared her some of her misery."

Quinn nodded slowly. "She must have suffered terribly with her ongoing and widespread sepsis, all of which originated from a punctured uterus."

"And what of the fetus?"

"A little over two months in age, with facial features just beginning to form."

"Sad."

"Quite."

Glancing at the wall clock, I said, "I must be on my way, for a lecture podium awaits my presence. Please let me know once the microorganism has been conclusively identified."

"I shall."

I hurried down the corridor, hoping against hope that the infecting agent could be limited to a single patient. During the barmaid's hospitalization she had been examined or touched by a considerable number of personnel, including doctors, sisters, aides, and orderlies, most of whom could have spread the bacteria to every corner of St. Bart's. Moreover, specimens from the patient, which were surely infected, had been held and studied by a dozen or more laboratory technicians and their assistants. All in all, it seemed the chances of containing an outbreak seemed small indeed.

My thoughts were interrupted by Benson, the head orderly, who rushed over, pushing an empty gurney which he brought to an abrupt stop. The sheet that lay atop it was spotless.

"A good afternoon to you, sir," he greeted me, with his usual lack of warmth.

"And to you, Benson."

"I was wondering if I should remove the remains of the barmaid from the autopsy room."

"I see no need to delay unless there is something you wish for me to see."

Benson shrugged his shoulders indifferently. "Nothing unusual here, for we have yet another Whitechapel lass gone astray and had a bad abortion."

My jaw must have dropped at the obvious connection between the features just mentioned by the head orderly. A *barmaid* from *Whitechapel* had undergone an illegal *abortion*. The Rose and Lamb pub immediately came to mind, where the owner's sister-in-law ran an abortion service.

Benson stared at my stunned expression and asked, "Is there something amiss, sir?"

I gathered myself quickly and narrowed my eyes, as if in deep thought. "I seem to recall a similar case some time ago. If my memory serves me correctly, it, too, involved a barmaid who worked at a pub whose name escapes me."

The head orderly reached for a rather thick chart that lay on the gurney and hurriedly thumbed through its pages. "Ah, here it is," said he, and handed me the chart, for Benson could not read, but recognized the admission sheet on all patients admitted to St. Bart's.

"She was employed at The Rose and Lamb," I read aloud slowly, to give the impression the name was unfamiliar to me. "I shall have my secretary review our files to determine if there was a similar case at this pub."

"Very good, sir," Benson said, obviously uninterested.

On placing the chart back on the gurney, I commented, "I see that she was admitted for care, which would be most unusual, for those with the earnings of a barmaid could never afford the expense of a hospital stay."

"Unless she had a very well-to-do sponsor, sir."

Or one with considerable influence at St. Bartholomew's, I thought silently as I hurried down the corridor docketing this information, but unaware of how relevant the tragic death of a barmaid would soon become.

CHAPTER TEN

Ah Sing

My long day had not yet come to an end, for there was one last visit to make which would hopefully bring to light an important piece of the puzzle facing us. At the sound of Big Ben striking the hour of eight, I found myself in the company of Joanna and my father traveling to East London for a meeting with Ah Sing, the owner of a prosperous string of opium dens, with whom we had done business in the past. According to Joanna's reliable source, the Chinaman, who also carried the alias Mr. Johnson, had a most colorful history. The Shanghai native came to our shores as a stowaway on a tramp steamer and immediately went to work cleaning brothels in Whitechapel. He was later to become a runner or messenger for the crime syndicate that owned the brothels, before graduating to the position of troubleshooter for a gang of Chinese extortionists. After being arrested on a number of occasions, he served a brief sentence at Hammersmith Prison, and upon his release became involved in the opium trade. Following the suspicious death of his business partner, Ah Sing became sole owner of a large opium den which was the foundation of his current wealth and status.

"He is not a man you wish to cross," she summed up the opium dealer's criminal past.

"But I must say he treated us with undue courtesy on our prior visit," my father remarked.

"He was also said to be quite cordial when dealing with his former partner who conveniently died and left no heirs behind," Joanna noted, which brought brief smiles to our faces.

As our taxi approached the dark district of Limehouse in East London, the driver glanced back to us over his shoulder and warned, "We are entering a most rough neighborhood, madam. Are you certain of the address?"

"I am, and you are to stay parked awaiting our return," said my wife and, sensing the driver's concern, added, "You will not be harmed, for the man we are visiting controls this area with an iron fist and will see to your safety."

We came to a stop at a storefront that had Chinese characters written on its window. Lurking about in a nearby alley, I could see shadowy figures in the dimness. I tapped the driver on his shoulder and directed his attention to the alleyway. "Your protectors," I assured him.

The driver nodded hesitantly, not fully convinced.

Joanna led the way to a thick door and rapped twice upon it. Almost immediately the door opened and a young, sharp-featured Chinese woman looked out and measured us carefully.

"Are you the famous daughter?" she asked.

"I am," Joanna replied.

"This way, then, please."

The woman, who seemed to float rather than walk with her silent footsteps, escorted us into a smoke-hazed den, where beds and mats took up most of the space. Upon them rested Englishmen, upper and lower class, all puffing on long pipes that were being held over lamps. The patrons were reclining in order to place their lengthy pipes directly over the lamps that heated the drug until it evaporated, thus allowing the smoker to inhale the vapor.

A stout Chinaman, in his middle years, hurried over to greet us. Ah Sing appeared to have aged since our last visit some years ago. His posture seemed more slumped and there was noticeable gray in the tightly braided pigtail that extended halfway down his back. He was attired in expensive Oriental garb, with a jacket of blue silk accompanied by matching hat and slippers.

Ah Sing gave my wife a respectful bow, saying, "It is an honor to see you once again, Mrs. Watson."

"Thank you for making time for us," Joanna replied.

"No bother at all," said he in perfect English, turning to my father and rendering him a bow as well, but not as deep as the one he gave to Joanna. "Ah, the inestimable associate of the late Sherlock Holmes," he welcomed, obviously pleased with my father's presence. "And beside you is your son who so resembles you and has taken the role of chronicler of the daughter's detective skills."

"I take it you have read his accounts of our mysteries."

"As has every Londoner," Ah Sing went on. "I must tell you that I was pleased to see my name displayed in *The Disappearance of Alistair Ainsworth.*"

"Did it not concern you to be mentioned as a source of information?" Joanna asked.

"Not in the least, for it was noted by people in authority who I wished to impress," he said with a hint of a smile that quickly disappeared. "Have you come for more information on yet another of your adventures?"

"That is the purpose of our visit," she replied. "Let us begin with the individuals who frequent your establishment. With your keen eye, you can no doubt readily distinguish between the various classes of your patrons."

"It presents no problem, for their attire and mannerisms tell all."

"But those can be hidden or disguised."

"Not to the sharpest of eyes."

"I am interested in your clientele of the upper class."

"That narrows the list considerably."

"It would be an individual who visits the opium den on frequent occasions."

"Are you referring to someone who is addicted?"

"Most likely."

Ah Sing gave the matter thought before answering, "There are less than a dozen who would fit into that category."

"Do any have a foreign accent?"

"Obvious or trace?"

"Both."

The Chinaman furrowed his almost lineless brow in thought once again. "Which language are you most interested in?"

"French," Joanna lied.

"None."

"Middle Eastern?"

"A young homosexual who comes in with his black lover." Joanna ignored the answer. "German?"

"They would not dare, for any such accent in this neighborhood could bring about a most unpleasant ending."

"You mentioned a couple who frequents your establishment," Joanna probed. "Are there other couples whom you can recollect?"

"Occasionally a man will enter for a pipeful with another, but they appear to be only good friends and show no evidence of addiction."

Joanna considered another possibility before asking, "Do you ever see mixed couples—man and woman—who visit your den on a regular basis?"

"Not regularly and surely not addicted, but I have observed

one such couple who visit once a week or so to enjoy a few pipefuls together."

"Do they appear upper class?"

"Oh, yes, but they attempt to hide it by wearing shabby
clothes and oversized caps which partially cover their faces," Ah
Sing described. "And she wears little makeup, with her hair bundled up under her cap."

"Lovers, would you say?"

"Beyond any doubt."

"But why go to such extremes to cover their true identity?"
Joanna asked, but her expression told me that she already knew
the answer.

"It is the behavior of secret lovers."

"Yes, that would fit," said she. "By chance, did you have an
opportunity to see their faces?"

"I did not, for they took care to isolate themselves by reserv-
ing a mat in the far corner away from the others."

"For which they would pay an additional fee, I would think."

"Of course, as one would expect for any special service."

"Did they grumble over the added cost?"

"It was not they who made the payment, but the manservant
who made the reservation for the couple, which was yet another
sign of their upper-class status. The cost seemed to be of no concern to him."

"Was it the manservant who always called and paid for the
reservation?"

"Each and every time."

"So you must have gotten a good look at him."

"He was slim and well dressed, and spoke in an articulate
manner, and thus I assumed he came from an upper level of British society." Ah Sing hesitated at length, now thinking back in
time. "There was one somewhat unusual feature to him. He was

pale beyond description. I do believe he was the whitest English-man I have ever seen. And it was made even more so by his slick, very black hair."

Roger Mallsby, the prince's private secretary! we all thought simul-taneously and did our best to keep our expressions even. It was now clear that Mallsby had been less than honest with us and we could not help but wonder how much other information he had withheld.

"Did this manservant give his name?" Joanna asked in a neu-tral tone.

"He did not, for there was no need for him to do so."

"Indeed there wasn't," said my wife, but I knew what she thinking. No name was needed, for Roger Mallsby had unwit-tingly left his calling card. She gazed over to my father and asked, "Do you have any questions, Watson?"

"I have only a few, and these relate to your customers who appear to be addicted to opium," he began. "In particular, did you notice anything peculiar about the mats they used?"

Ah Sing shrugged his shoulders. "The mats are promptly washed down to remove any debris left behind."

"Would this debris include bits of straw, such as those eaten by horses?"

I watched my wife's eyes light up, for it was an excellent question which attempted to connect the opium addict to the Lancaster Gate stables.

Ah Sing briefly paused before shaking his head. "I do not recall straw or similar items on the used mats. And had it been tracked in on the user's shoes, it would have been noted and in-stantly removed."

"What of crushed, empty cigarette packages?"

"Never, for the opium urge takes precedence over that of tobacco."

"As one might expect."

A group of sailors with Oriental features entered the den, obviously in a cheerful mood. Ah Sing waved to them and, turning back to us, asked to be excused.

"Of course," Joanna said. "And thank you for your assistance. You have been most helpful."

We walked out into a light drizzle and discovered that our taxi had departed, its driver no doubt intimidated by the sinister surroundings. The street was dark and misty, with the lamppost unlighted because of the wartime blackouts. There was no traffic, and the shadowy figures in the nearby alley had disappeared. I immediately rapped on the door to the opium den, and the young Chinese woman reappeared without delay. After hearing my request for a taxi to be called, she hurried away, but did not ask us back in from the rain. Her message was clear. Our business with Ah Sing was done.

"On the evidence thus far, it would appear the individual who waited for the prince in Hyde Park did not frequent this den," my father concluded.

"Oh, he was surely here," Joanna asserted. "For how else would Prince Harry and his aristocratic companion find their way into this particular opium den? What was the chance our good prince just happened into Ah Sing's whilst wondering about this dreadful neighborhood?"

"Perhaps he was led to the den by his private secretary?" I suggested.

"I think not," Joanna countered. "Mr. Roger Mallsby was not a customer at Ah Sing's and only made his appearance to set up the reservation and pay in advance for the visit. Keep in mind that the secretary was not royalty nor an aristocrat, and thus a class beneath the prince. I can assure you Prince Harry never socialized with Mallsby in any setting."

"Then who?"

"The German who was a heavy user of opium and no doubt

frequented Ah Sing's, where the very best mixtures of the drug were available," she replied. "His obvious association with the prince tells us he is far and away the best candidate."

"But there is no proof."

"That will come later."

In the dimness we saw a black taxi approaching, with its headlights on despite the wartime restriction. For some reason, it appeared to suddenly increase its speed as it neared.

"Is that our taxi?" I wondered aloud.

"Too quick!" Joanna shouted, and hurriedly shoved us into the doorway of the den.

The motor vehicle whizzed by, coming so close to us we could feel the heat of its exhaust. The driver made no attempt to apply the brakes and continued on at a high speed, now without lights as it disappeared into the darkness. We remained motionless and unnerved, our senses on high alert to determine if there was even more danger lurking in the black night. But the quiet returned, and we slowly ventured back into the street as our dreadful unease began to subside.

"Is anyone injured?" my father asked worriedly as he stared down the narrow street to make certain the motor vehicle was not returning for a second attempt on our lives.

"I am unhurt," Joanna replied, and took a deep breath to gather herself. "And you, John?"

"I am intact except for bruised knuckles which occurred when my hand scraped against the front door of the opium den," said I as my pulse began to slow. "Had he come an inch or two closer, that would have been the end of us."

"Thank goodness Joanna sensed danger and pushed us out of harm's way," my father noted, then turned to my wife. "Was it the speed of the vehicle or its lights that alerted you so quickly?"

"It was its time of arrival," she replied in a calm voice. "It was too rapid."

"How so?"

"The phone call for the taxi was placed only minutes ago," she deduced. "There was simply no way it could arrive in such a short period of time. The driver would have to be notified and he had to have been some distance away, for I can assure you there are no central taxi facilities in this dark neighborhood."

"Then, you must have added in its sudden increase in speed and the fact that it had its lights on."

"That, too," Joanna agreed. "And now that I put all the pieces together, I can safely say that this was a well-planned attack."

"How do you reach that conclusion, may I ask?"

"Someone followed us to Ah Sing's, then either bought off or frightened away our taxi, and replaced it with another vehicle which was driven by an assassin."

"And that assassin was hired by an individual who is deeply concerned about our involvement in the disappearance of Prince Harry," said I.

"Yes, yes," my father concurred hurriedly. "But who?"

"An individual who is far more clever than I gave him credit for," Joanna answered.

"Indeed, for despite our best efforts, this individual remains in the shadows, and our trail to Prince Harry has turned cold."

"To the contrary, Watson, the trail you mentioned is now back in our sights."

"Based on what?"

"The observation that Mr. Roger Mallsby is a bona fide liar, and everything he has told us must be discounted until proven otherwise."

Another motor vehicle appeared, moving slowly with lights turned off. We backed up against the door to the opium den and only ventured into the street when we were certain it was a genuine taxi.

Chapter Eleven

Roger Mallsby

Although virtually everyone at St. Bartholomew's knew of my association with the daughter of Sherlock Holmes, I attempted to keep separate my position as director of pathology from any ongoing criminal investigation, but on more than a few occasions the two became intertwined. And this case was such an instance. I had surreptitiously enlisted my faithful secretary, Rose, to gather information on the barmaid from The Rose and Lamb who had tragically died of a botched abortion. Being a longtime employee at the hospital, she knew coworkers in every department who could unwittingly provide the data I required.

Whilst waiting for Rose to return, I changed the dressing on my bruised knuckles which reminded me of the frightening episode we had experienced the evening before. We were later to sit in front of a cheery fire in our parlor, with brandies in hand, to settle our nerves and discuss the incident at length. Joanna and I were convinced it was a well-planned attack to either kill or badly maim us, but my father offered a different, equally logical opinion. Since there were a goodly number of pubs and opium dens in the immediate area, he proposed that the driver of the speeding vehicle may have been intoxicated by either drink or drug, and had difficulty controlling the motor vehicle as he sped by, not even noticing us. Furthermore, our own taxi driver might have departed because of the sinister surroundings. Joanna thought my father's explanation was plausible, but given the circumstances believed otherwise and implored us to exercise a high degree of vigilance, for assassins who fail in their initial attempt often return to complete their mission.

My thoughts were interrupted by Rose who slipped quietly into my office and closed the door behind her to prevent our conversation from being overheard.

"I have the information you requested," said she in a secretive voice.

"Excellent," I responded, then asked, "And I take it they all understood the reason for the needed data?"

"Oh, yes, sir," Rose assured. "They were told of the dangerous bacterial infection which had occurred in several patients, and thus the need to determine if there was any association between them."

"Did you mention the possibility that this bacteria might spread to others?"

"I did indeed, and told them that was the concern which prompted the investigation," she replied. "I stressed that the inquiry was being done on the quiet, so as not to cause unwarranted worry."

"Well done," I praised, and motioned her to have a seat on the opposite side of my desk. "Please give me all the details."

"Allow me a moment to collect my notes."

"Of course."

As Rose thumbed through the pages of an oversized notebook, I congratulated myself, pleased that my fabricated story had been received so well. I had informed my secretary that there were two patients who appeared to have been infected with a most virulent bacteria which brought about their demise. The diagnosis of a botched abortion was never alluded to.

"The first patient I inquired about was Mr. Horace Frampton," she began.

I pretended to listen, for Mr. Frampton was of little interest. He was a barrister from Surrey who was a heavy smoker, with a diagnosis of bronchogenic carcinoma that had spread throughout his frail body. At the end of his life he became infected with an unusual staphylococcal organism which brought about his death.

"Now, the second patient came from an entirely different background, being just twenty-one, and worked as a barmaid at The Rose and Lamb in Whitechapel. She, too, had a terrible infection involving most of the pelvis. Her entire hospital chart, with the exception of the death certificate, is now under review according to Annie in medical records. No reason was given."

Someone at St. Bartholomew's was most interested in the case of a criminal abortion, thought I, and wondered who that someone might be.

"Martha Ann Miller lived in rooms at 825 Prescot that is located in a better section of Whitechapel, which I am afraid doesn't say much for her living conditions," Rose noted, then added, "A most dreadful area, you see."

"Yet she apparently could afford her stay at St. Bart's," I remarked.

"That was not the case according to the admissions office," my secretary informed, turning to another page. "Her guarantor was The Rose and Lamb, which of course is the pub where she was employed."

"I am surprised admissions was willing to accept a pub in Whitechapel as the sponsor."

"They had reservations as well, and only allowed her admission when she was accompanied by a fifty-pound note."

I nodded at the answer, but the size of the required payment was extraordinary, for fifty pounds would be the equivalent of a year's salary in a lower-class pub. It was doubtful Martha Ann Miller had fifty pounds in savings and even more doubtful her pub would lend or hand her such an amount, for there was a long line of women eager to take such a position.

"Will more information be required?" Rose inquired.

"The data you have collected will do nicely," said I. "You are to be commended for your fine effort."

"I enjoyed every step of it," she said, smiling at the compliment. "And would not hesitate to do so again."

"I shall keep that in mind should the need arise."

"Then back to my desk I go," Rose said, pushing her chair away.

"And please remember to keep my schedule clear from two o'clock on, for I have a most important meeting at Scotland Yard."

"What if Mr. Rudd barges in yet again and demands to know your whereabouts?"

"Tell him the truth," said I, wondering what the ill-mannered surgeon's response would be.

"Forgive my tardiness," Roger Mallsby apologized. "My duties at the palace consumed more time than I anticipated."

"Not to worry, for we arrived only moments ago," said Joanna. "I take it you have brought a complete list of the prince's companions over the past three months."

"I have it here," he replied, and showed us a very thin folder. "The list is far shorter than one would have surmised."

"Does it include the name of the woman who frequently accompanied Prince Harry to his favorite opium den?" she asked tersely.

Mallsby stiffened in his chair, his jaw dropping for a moment. "I—I beg your pardon?"

"Does-it-include-the-name-of-the-woman-who-frequently-accompanied-Prince-Harry-to-his-favorite-opium-den?" Joanna repeated, pronouncing each word in a distinct fashion.

The private secretary swallowed audibly, but made no response.

"Do you not recall making the reservations and paying for each of their visits?"

"I have no idea what you are speaking of," Mallsby said, trying to regain his composure.

"Ah, but you do, for we have a witness who will attest to your presence," my wife pressed, arising from her chair to light one of her Turkish cigarettes. She began to pace slowly around Inspector Lestrade's office, with her every step being followed by Mallsby's eyes. "You have been here less than a minute and you have already lied once. Lie again and you will be charged with obstruction of justice."

"Perhaps I should contact my barrister," the private secretary said, but there was no conviction in his voice.

"You have every right to do so," Lestrade interjected. "But should you misinform or in any manner be complicit in the disappearance of Prince Harry, you no doubt will lose your position at Buckingham Palace and may well find yourself confined to one of His Majesty's most uncomfortable prisons."

"Which would be an unpleasant ending for a man of your station," Joanna added. "And of course your family name would be forever ruined."

All resistance departed from Mallsby's face. "I was only attempting to protect the prince."

"And in the process cost us valuable time," Joanna admonished. "So you will now answer our questions without equivocation, giving us every detail no matter how unsavory. Understood?"

"Yes, madam."

"Let us begin with how you became aware of Ah Sing's opium den."

"I was told by a barmaid who was an occasional companion to the prince."

"He enjoyed the low life, did he?"

"Now and then."

"Did the prince himself ever visit the drinking establishment where the barmaid was employed?"

"Only once, for he found The Rose and Lamb too sordid for his taste."

I made every effort to keep my expression even at the mention of The Rose and Lamb, the place of employment of the barmaid with the botched abortion. And now Prince Harry was in the mix!

"So, was it you who guided the prince to that particular pub?" Joanna was asking.

"It was not me, madam, but a gentleman drifter who happened to be an acquaintance of the prince."

"Do you know the name of the acquaintance?"

"I do not."

"Do you yourself ever frequent The Rose and Lamb?"

"Never."

"Then how did you come to know the barmaid who worked there?"

"The prince was quite taken by Martha Ann and directed me to find her suitable rooms in Whitechapel where he could visit when the urge arose."

I could not help but interrupt, "Are you referring to her flat at 825 Prescot Street?"

Joanna stopped pacing and stared at me, obviously surprised I possessed that information.

Mallsby nodded without hesitation. "I met her there once at which time she signed the lease and I made the payment for one year in advance."

"And she just happened to mention Ah Sing's opium den?" Joanna queried and went back to pacing.

"It was Prince Harry who asked me to inquire, for he believed a barmaid would know the best of the dens."

"Which he was to later visit with his secret lover," my wife asserted.

"On a number of occasions."

"Be precise."

"At least five that I know of."

"Was it the barmaid Martha Ann who accompanied the prince to Ah Sing's?"

"No, madam. It was Lady Spenser who was by his side in the opium den."

That admission was totally unexpected, for Lady Charlotte Spenser stood high up on the social scale. Her husband was a high-ranking naval officer who was noted for his gallantry, and who spent considerable time at sea away from home. Moreover, it was widely known that Commander Spenser had married late in life to a beautiful noblewoman far younger than he.

"For how long were the prince and Lady Spenser secret lovers?" Joanna asked, breaking the silence.

"At least two months."

"Is that approximation based on a particular event?"

"It is based on the first time I made the arrangement at Ah Sing's."

"Very good," Joanna approved, obviously docketing the information for future use. "Let us return to the barmaid Martha Ann for the moment. When she signed the lease on the flat, she must have been required to supply her full name."

"It was Martha Ann Miller."

"And pray tell did Martha Ann Miller have personal experience at Ah Sing's?"

"I asked her that very same question, wanting as much information as possible before recommending the den to Prince

Harry. I had no reason to disbelieve her when she stated she had only visited Ah Sing's on two occasions, both times with a rowdy fellow she met at the pub."

"Rowdy, you say?"

"She described him as quite rough in a number of ways, and in addition had a foreign accent which made her wary of him."

"She never went out with him again, then?"

Mallsby shrugged his shoulders. "I would doubt it, for she was soon to have the comforts given to her by the prince."

"Did the barmaid mention what type of foreign accent this rowdy fellow possessed?"

"Only that it was foreign."

"Not German, then?"

Mallsby shrugged his shoulders once again. "There was no mention of it being so. You might wish to question her on that matter."

"A worthy suggestion," Joanna noted, not yet aware that Martha Ann Miller lay stone dead in the hospital morgue as a result of a botched abortion. "Let us now turn our attention to the list of companions you brought along."

Mallsby opened the thin folder and gave my wife a single sheet of paper which appeared to contain only handwritten names. She studied the list carefully, reading over it twice and on each occasion counting silently to herself. "I see that Lady Spenser is the only companion to have been with the prince on multiple occasions."

"That is correct, madam."

"Did you serve as an intermediary on all of these visits?"

"To the best of my knowledge."

"I have one final question," Joanna said as she crushed out her cigarette. "Did you have any inkling of a plan for the prince to disappear?"

"No, madam, I most assuredly did not."

"Think back," she requested. "Did the prince bring along any items, such as toiletries, which could indicate he was prepared for an absence?"

Whilst Mallsby searched his memory, Lestrade pointed to his timepiece, reminding us of the phone call from the ransomer which was scheduled to occur in less than ten minutes.

"Yes or no?" Joanna demanded.

"None come to mind."

"Very well," said she. "You may take your leave."

Mallsby nodded hurriedly and literally dashed for the door, but Joanna interrupted his exit with yet another final question. "I neglected to make one last inquiry. Of all the names on the list, which of the women had an affectionate nickname?"

"The prince often referred to Lady Charlotte Spenser as Lollie."

"Lollie," Joanna repeated softly, then gave the prince's private secretary a wave of dismissal. "You may go."

Once the door closed, my father turned to Joanna and asked, "Do you believe his words?"

"For the most part, but there is one portion of his story which needs to be verified," my wife replied and handed the list of companions to Inspector Lestrade. "Excluding Lady Spenser, please be good enough to have Scotland Yard discreetly investigate the remaining names on the list. They should pay singular attention to their social proclivities and unusual indulgences with the prince."

"Are you referring to the hidden pleasures?" Lestrade asked tactfully.

"I am referring to those in particular."

"I have female officers who are remarkably talented at uncovering this sort of behavior."

"Excellent, for females have an instinct for knowing where to

dig," Joanna said, reaching for the door. "You must also obtain
an immediate search warrant for the flat at 825 Prescot Street."

"To what end, may I ask?"

"To determine the barmaid's role in the disappearance of
Prince Harry."

CHAPTER TWELVE

The Sovereign Orb

The time scheduled for the ransom phone call came and went. It was now twenty after three and our worry was to increase with each passing minute. The commissioner was pacing the floor in his office, pausing intermittently to stare at the telephone on his desk, as if commanding it to ring.

"I fear they may have already disposed of Prince Harry," said he.

"That would be most unlikely, Sir Charles, for they have a highly prized commodity in their hands, for which they will demand an extraordinary fee," Joanna contended.

"I suspect it will be bundles and bundles of hundred-pound notes."

My wife shook her head at the notion. "That would take up far too much space. We must keep in mind that the ransom has to be carried away by the individual."

"Could they not stow their treasure in a motor vehicle?"

"That could be followed, even in the busy streets of London."

"What, then?"

"As I mentioned before, a masterpiece from the royal collection would do nicely."

"But that, too, would be sizeable, would it not?"

"Not necessarily, for a precious Rembrandt or Vermeer could be removed from its frame, then rolled up and be well concealed under a raincoat."

"He could also be followed."

Joanna shook her head once more. "A skillful dodger would lose your tracker in the blink of an eye."

The phone rang loudly. All in the room stared at it for a brief moment.

"Do not forget to demand proof of life," Joanna instructed hurriedly.

"They may not allow him to talk," Sir Charles said in a rush as the phone rang a second time.

"Demand they do so."

"And if they refuse?"

"Then have them ask the prince what the word *Lollie* means."

The commissioner quickly picked up the receiver at the end of the third ring. "Yes?

"Speaking," said he.

"Before I listen to your demands, I must have proof that Prince Harry remains alive," he went on. "Otherwise, we cannot do business."

Sir Charles listened intently before insisting, "We must speak with him to assure he is well and unharmed.

"I am sorry, but our connection is poor. Did you say the prince was being held away from the phone and thus is unable to speak with us?"

The commissioner nodded the caller's response for our benefit, then proposed, "I have an alternate plan which I believe you will agree to. Mention the word *Lollie,* L-O-L-L-I-E, to His Royal Highness and inform us of his response."

And on that request, Sir Charles replaced the receiver into its cradle. "They will call back."

"They are being most careful," my father noted.

"They are also being very skillful, for I can assure you that Prince Harry is quite near the caller, who refuses to allow the prince to talk for fear he might offer a clue as to his location," said Joanna, turning to the commissioner. "Did you hear any unusual background noise behind the caller's voice?"

"There was nothing in particular," Sir Charles replied. "What type of noise were you referring to?"

"Those made by horns or motor vehicles or even carriages being pulled along cobblestone streets."

"None of those were heard, but I must remind you that most of the cobblestone streets in London have now been paved over with asphalt."

"Which would make the sound of a cobblestone street quite informative," said Joanna.

The phone rang once again.

"As I stated a moment ago, Prince Harry was nearby the caller, which accounts for their rapid response," Joanna deduced. "Remember to keep your ears pricked, Commissioner."

Sir Charles picked up the receiver at the start of the second ring. "Yes?"

Then he nodded slowly. "That is the correct answer. Now tell us of your demands."

Joanna shook her head immediately and waved her hands far apart before whispering, "Prolong the conversation as long as possible."

"Hold for a moment whilst I reach for my notepad," the commissioner told the caller. "I wish to write down the exact words of any demands so they can be followed to the letter."

He paused a full ten seconds, then returned to the abductor. "You may proceed with your demands.

"What!" Sir Charles bellowed out in awestruck surprise.

There was another long pause before he shouted into the receiver, "You cannot be serious!"

Apparently, the caller was, for he must have repeated the demand, to which the commissioner slowly acquiesced. "The Sovereign's Orb," he said solemnly. "You will trade the prince for the Sovereign's Orb."

There was stunned silence in the office, for the totally unexpected demand was for a priceless item from the crown jewels. We were all aware of the Sovereign's Orb, for it was pictured in the newspapers during the coronation of King George V. It consisted of a hollow gold sphere, surrounded by a band of emeralds, rubies, and diamonds, which the new king held in his right hand as part of the coronation ceremony. It was beyond value.

Sir Charles quickly gathered himself. "Of course, such a demand will have to be agreed upon by His Majesty himself."

His listened carefully, then replied, "I cannot speak for His Majesty." There was yet another long pause before he spoke again. "Two days should suffice, but an extra day might be needed if the king and his counselors wish to make a counteroffer."

Sir Charles hurriedly placed a hand over the receiver and reported in a whisper, "They are arguing, and someone in the room is shouting out the number nine. And now I believe I hear the sound of a foghorn.

"Yes, yes, I am here," he said into the receiver, and listened intently before nodding. "Then, two and a half days it will be."

The commissioner went back to his notepad. "Please speak slowly for who and how the item is to be delivered. Let us begin with the individual assigned to meet with your representative and exchange the item for Prince Harry."

The caller's response brought an astonished look to Sir Charles's face. He swallowed away his surprise and asked, "The daughter of Sherlock Holmes, you say?"

The commissioner nodded at the reply. "In that case, we shall have to contact Mrs. Watson and solicit her participation."

The receiver nearly dropped from Sir Charles's hand, as yet another look of astonishment crossed his face. He placed the receiver into its cradle, obviously bewildered, then turned to my wife. "The caller knew you were in my office, Mrs. Watson. When I mentioned that I would have to confer with you, he replied that I should simply gaze over my desk where you were standing." He shook his head again, searching for an answer. "How could he have possibly known?"

"By a number of different ways, but the simplest explanation is that we were followed to Scotland Yard," said she. "And the caller correctly surmised my presence would be requested for the ransomer's phone call, which he knew was to be directed to the commissioner's office."

"Or perhaps there is a traitor in our group," my father suggested.

"Whom did you have in mind, Watson?" Joanna asked.

"Mr. Roger Mallsby, the private secretary, who has had his nose in every aspect of Prince Harry's disappearance."

"And what is he to gain for being a turncoat?"

"Perhaps he is a Hun worshipper underneath it all, or it could be that he was bought off."

"Both are possible, for greed is known to subvert loyalty, particularly in those with a bend in that direction," Joanna agreed mildly. "But at this juncture, we are guessing without evidence, which is a bad habit that too often leads one down the wrong track. Thus we should turn our attention to what we know, beginning with the barmaid Martha Ann Miller. Other than her meetings with the prince at the flat he set up for her, this devil-may-care lass moved about in the lowest circles, which included the rough, rowdy character at The Rose and Lamb. It was also he who directed her to the merits of Ah Sing's, which she in turn passed on to Roger Mallsby and then on to the prince. We also know that in all likelihood this rather unpleasant fellow was German, because of The Rose and Lamb's matchbook cover discovered at the site of Prince Harry's disappearance. Recall the word *morgen* written within its cover, which is German for tomorrow. Now, with all this information, what role do you believe he played in the abduction?"

"Most likely, he was a messenger or intermediary, I would think," Sir Charles surmised.

"Oh, no, Commissioner, his involvement goes much deeper than that," Joanna asserted. "He may in fact be one of the principal planners."

"May I ask how you reached that conclusion?"

"From the phone call you just participated in," she replied. "You will recall the number nine being shouted out during an argument in the background when you asked for a time extension of one day. It was not the number nine that you heard, but the identical sounding German word *nein* which means *no*. Thus we can conclude the caller was asking for a delay of an extra day, to which an individual in charge replied *no*. So it is the German associated with the barmaid we must track, for it is he who will lead us to the prince."

"Pray tell how can we hope to accomplish that?"

"By the clues left behind," said Joanna. "Now, let us move to the sound of the foghorn you heard, Commissioner. Was it in the distance or nearby?"

"It was not close."

"It is possible that the sound originated from the Thames which is miles away from us, and thus of little help."

"But it would indicate the prince is being held in London."

"Not necessarily, for the call could have come from any number of large ports along the English Channel."

"From Dover to Folkstone," my father added.

"And beyond," Joanna went on. "That is why I requested Sir Charles to prolong the phone call as much as possible. Big Ben has quarter bells which chime every fifteen minutes. Had the commissioner heard those familiar sounds, we could have said with certainty that the prince remains in London proper."

"We seem to be making such little progress," Sir Charles said unhappily. "And time is so short."

"Three days to be exact," my wife predicted. "You of course noted that they refused the extra day delay you requested to allow for three days' time to carry out the ransom demand. But they would only give you an additional half day, which gives two and a half days to deliver. All of which tells us they have a schedule to meet and plan to depart in three days."

"Why is the extra half day so important?"

"It is most likely needed for them to travel to the site of their departure."

"By sea, then?"

"That is how the Germans would leave."

"With their precious ransom in hand," Sir Charles said glumly.

"And perhaps Prince Harry as well," Joanna warned.

"Would they dare?"

"Of course," she said, with certainty. "Why not strike a double blow if the opportunity presents itself?"

"A double blow," the commissioner murmured under his breath, shaking his head in disgust. "No doubt His Majesty will be reluctant to part with the Sovereign Orb."

"He may have no choice."

"It will be a treasure gone, lost forever," Sir Charles continued on. "Whoever thought that a crown jewel would ever be used in such a fashion?"

"But it could also have yet another use?"

"Such as?"

"A lure," Joanna replied. "It could serve as a perfect lure, if we play our cards correctly."

The door to the commissioner's office opened after a brief rap and a young detective hurried in to give Inspector Lestrade an official-appearing envelope. "The search warrant for 825 Prescot Street, sir."

"Excellent," said Joanna, and started for the door. "Let's make haste, and hope that the mastermind has not yet removed important clues from the barmaid's flat."

"Do you believe he is that clever?" my father asked.

"He is a most formidable foe, Watson, and to underestimate him would be a grave mistake."

"Perhaps you give him too much credit."

"I think not, for this clever devil is always a step or two ahead of us and is thus able to predict our next move. Moreover, the clues he leaves behind are subtle and meant to be overlooked by Scotland Yard."

"Are you saying these clues are intended for you and you alone to discover?"

"Precisely."

"But why would he wish to match wits with you, the famous daughter?"

"Because he is convinced he can outwit me, and has continued to do so in a most admirable fashion."

My father nodded slowly at the obvious conclusion. "Which indicates he must possess the keenest of criminal minds."

"And that, my dear Watson, is what makes him so formidable."

CHAPTER THIRTEEN

The Barmaid's Flat

On our ride to Prescot Street, I had no choice but to describe the findings of a botched abortion on the corpse of Martha Ann Miller. I was reluctant to do so because of the presence of Inspector Lestrade, who would insist that the pub where the barmaid worked be thoroughly investigated. All clues, from the matchbook cover at the abduction site to the criminal abortion, pointed to the lower-class drinking establishment.

"What induced you to inquire about the barmaid's address?" asked Joanna.

"When I learned from the head orderly that the woman was employed by The Rose and Lamb, I gathered as much as possible on the victim," I replied.

"Well done," my wife praised. "Was there additional information of merit?"

"Only that her admission to St. Bartholomew's was allowed because she was sponsored by The Rose and Lamb, along with an accompanying fifty-pound note."

"All for a barmaid, eh?"

"So it would appear."

"Pubs at that level do not act as guarantors for their employees," my father noted. "And in particular not for a serving girl."

"Nor would someone as young as she have fifty pounds at her immediate disposal," Joanna added. "There is someone else behind this dreadful business."

"We will find out soon enough," said Lestrade as we approached the district of Whitechapel. "Every inch of that pub will be searched, and everyone employed within will be lined up and questioned. And if there is even a hint of someone's involvement in the disappearance of Prince Harry, they will be further questioned under the brightest lights at Scotland Yard."

"It might be wise to delay your investigation, Inspector, until we have more substantial clues in hand," Joanna suggested. "At the present time, all of our evidence is circumstantial at best and would never stand at an official inquiry. Moreover, we would not wish for the abductors of Prince Harry to learn that we are aware of the pub's connection to this treacherous crime, which would only serve to put them on greater alert. Let them believe for now that we continue to flail about in the dark. The moment to strike will come later."

Lestrade nodded slowly as he assimilated my wife's advice. "Your point is well taken, for up to this juncture I have instructed our detectives to stay well clear of the pub and its patrons, so the neighborhood remains unaware of our suspicions. In this rather seedy area, the presence of Scotland Yard would be quickly noticed and cause the perpetrators to scatter. Thus, we have no plans to rush in. Nevertheless, I shall be obliged to bring the proposed timing of such a search to the commissioner's attention."

"As you should," Joanna concurred, knowing full well that Sir Charles would see the merits of such a delay.

Our Scotland Yard motor vehicle entered Whitechapel, which was one of London's poorest districts, but the impoverished area had not escaped the fury of German bombs. Turning onto a wide avenue, we passed buildings that lay in ruins, with only their scorched walls left standing. Then we came upon houses that had been reduced to smoldering piles of masonry which were strewn on the footpaths and made them impassable. Just ahead was an elderly couple seated on boxes and staring in disbelief at the blackened rubble of their all but destroyed home.

"Where will they live?" Joanna asked in a soft voice. "Where will they find rest?"

"Only God knows," said I.

We finally arrived at 825 Prescot Street which was a sturdy two-story building, with its façade consisting of aged but well-kept red bricks. The windowsills on the first floor held colorful flower beds, and the frames themselves had been recently painted. It was obvious that my secretary, Rose, had misjudged the scale of the barmaid's address.

Standing at the doorstep was a diminutive, nicely attired man whose gray-gold hair curled at the collar. He introduced himself as Neville Simms, the leasing agent for the building.

Inspector Lestrade handed the agent a search warrant. "You are to immediately open the door to the flat belonging to Martha Ann Miller."

"Is there a problem I should be aware of?" Simms asked.

"Just open the door," Lestrade said brusquely.

"Of course, sir," the agent said obediently, and led the way into the building.

The barmaid's flat was on the ground floor, as one might expect, in that visitors such as the prince would wish to come and leave at all hours and not be seen by other tenants. The corridor was relatively wide and revealed flats on both sides. I counted a total of four on the ground floor.

As the leasing agent reached for a key and opened the door to the barmaid's flat, Joanna stepped in front of him to prevent his entry.

"I have a few questions for you," said she. "First off, did you ever see this tenant?"

"No, madam, only the gentleman who let the apartment for her."

"Were you given a prior address?"

"That is not a requirement for letting."

"Once she moved in, did you ever inspect her flat?"

"There was no need."

"Did her neighbors ever meet her?"

"Only Mrs. Dempsey, a widow who occupies the flat across from hers," Simms replied. "She keeps an eye out on the premises, for which she receives a small consideration on her rent."

"And she no doubt serves as a lookout for any unusual happenings."

"Indeed she does."

"Did she report any such happenings for the new tenant?"

"None of any consequence, other than the occasional male caller who arrived at a late hour."

"Did she recognize the caller?"

"No, madam."

"Very good," said she. "You are to remain in the hallway in the event additional information is needed."

We entered the flat, closing the door behind us, and found ourselves in a small parlor which was remarkably neat. Two well-worn chairs were positioned equidistant from the front of a stone fireplace that was free of ashes. Off to the side was a short stack of logs, each placed directly against one another, with no splinters of wood or debris on the nearby floor. A small lamp table held an ashtray that was filled with used cigarette stubs, and atop them a crushed, empty package of Player's Navy Cut.

"She appeared to have been a heavy smoker," Lestrade noted, lifting the ashtray to determine if anything was beneath it.

Joanna shook her head at the notion. "The unkempt ashtray

is entirely out of place in such a neat parlor. Allow me to draw your attention to the otherwise neatness which surrounds us. Even the fireplace stokers are sparkling clean, and the flower beds on the windowsill well looked after. This is not a woman who would tolerate a badly soiled ashtray." My wife walked over to the curtains and sniffed them at length. "You should also note that there is no odor of stale tobacco embedded in the curtains, which would certainly be present if the barmaid was a heavy smoker and addicted to nicotine. Thus these Player's Navy Cut stubs in all likelihood belonged to our German abductor."

"Could they have come from another male caller?" my father queried.

"That is a possibility, Watson, which I believe can be undone by Toby Two who will sample the crushed package and determine if the German left behind his characteristic taint of opium."

A small kitchen near the curtains revealed nothing of interest except for the refrigerator which contained items far too costly for a barmaid to afford. There were expensive chocolates and various appetizers and cheeses from Fortnum & Mason where only the wealthy shopped.

"She lived in style, one must say," I remarked.

"For which she may have paid a dear price," Joanna said, and guided us into the bedroom where we were met by a most disturbing site. The bed was unmade, and in the center of its top sheet was a pool of caked blood. I could also detect the aroma of necrotic human tissue.

"She bled here from the botched abortion," said I. "You will also note the lingering odor of dead tissue which fits in with that diagnosis."

Joanna raised the sheet from the mattress to determine how much blood had seeped through. Another large spot came into view, indicating a significant hemorrhage. "The bleeding was substantial, but not nearly enough to bring about exsanguination."

"But it was surely the start of her slow, painful death."

"Which I suspect the German witnessed."

I nodded at my wife's conclusion. "The cigarettes."

She nodded back, as she turned the pillows, looking for hidden items. "Quite so, John. He waited in the parlor, smoking one cigarette after another, waiting for her to breathe her last. He departed only when convinced there was little life remaining."

"How did she make it to the hospital, then?" asked Lestrade.

"She must have had another visitor who found her dire condition," Joanna surmised.

"Certainly not Prince Harry," the inspector said. "The time sequence does not fit."

"But he could have been responsible for her pregnancy," Joanna prompted, but when there was no response she added, "and arranged for the abortion."

"And ordered someone he trusted to come around and check on the poor girl," my father concluded.

"And who might that someone be?"

"Roger Mallsby, the prince's private secretary."

"We need to question him again," Joanna said, with a gesture to Lestrade. "Please set up the meeting at your earliest convenience."

My wife searched a spotless bathroom which revealed a bottle of tablets labeled FEMALE PILLS which promised a miscarriage, but never truly worked. She next went through a bedroom closet that held far more clothes than one might expect for a barmaid. More than a few of the dresses had sale tags that indicated they were purchased at Selfridges, a luxury department store. In the inner pocket of a tweed jacket was a five-pound note.

"Well kept, she was," Joanna commented. "By someone of wealth and taste."

"Do you place Prince Harry at the top of that list?" my father asked.

"I would simply place him on the list until we have further evidence," she replied. "But keep in mind we must continue to focus on the German, for he is the key to the puzzle."

"But he is obviously connected to the prince."

"We must keep that in mind as well," Joanna said, and, on returning to the closet, removed multiple sale tags from the clothes purchased for the barmaid. She gave the tags a final study before handing them to Lestrade. "Be good enough, Inspector, to have Scotland Yard track these down and see if the purchaser can be identified."

We departed the flat, with instructions to the leasing agent that no one other than Scotland Yard was to be allowed entry. Furthermore, he was to make himself available on short notice to immediately reopen the flat for officials who supplied him with a search warrant.

Twilight was turning to darkness as we stepped out into a foggy evening that had a chill to the air. The lampposts were some distance away, and thus the only illumination was provided by the lights on the passing motor vehicles and a single light over the doorway.

"I have one final question, madam," Lestrade queried. "Assuming there was a late-night visitor, how did he arrange for admission to St. Bartholomew's?"

"A very good question which I have given some thought to," Joanna responded. "I can assure you he did not accompany the ambulance to the hospital. In all likelihood he fabricated that the pub would serve as a sponsor, and sealed the arrangement with a substantial deposit of fifty pounds. The ambulance driver and the admissions officer at St. Bart's did not argue in view of the patient's extremis condition."

"Would the visitor not be concerned that the ambulance driver might pocket the fifty-pound note?"

"The driver may have been tempted, but desisted, for such a theft would undoubtedly cost him his position."

"I should ask the ambulance driver if he can recall the late-night visitor," I offered.

"That might be of help, John, but I suspect their conversation was brief and the visitor may have disguised himself, or at a minimum remained in the shadows."

At that moment I felt a heavy drop of what I initially thought was rain striking my hat. But as I raised my hand, I detected small pebbles dropping from above.

"I believe the brick façade may be crumbling a bit," said I as yet another piece of stone hit the footpath, then came another that was even larger.

My father reacted immediately and shoved the three of us back into the doorstep and against the door itself, shielding us with his own body. An instant later a huge rock the size of a football smashed into the footpath and split into a dozen jagged pieces. "Cover your heads!" he shouted whilst more chunks of brick rained down.

The driver of the Scotland Yard limousine hurriedly alighted from the vehicle and began firing multiple shots at a dark figure on the roof of the building. The hail of huge bricks stopped.

Lestrade and the driver ran for the stairs inside the structure, weapons drawn, in hopes of capturing the assailant. We remained pressed against the door, with our heads covered whilst hoping the attack was over. A full minute passed before the inspector called down the all clear from the roof.

I breathed a sigh of relief before noting, "That was so close. Just one of those missiles could have inflicted a deadly skull fracture."

"He knew we would be here," Joanna said, stepping out onto the footpath for a closer view of the sizeable bricks. "And he waited for the most opportune moment."

"Do you believe it was the German?" asked I.

"He would be my candidate of choice," she replied. "What say you, Watson?"

"It was Moriarty," my father said in a solemn voice.

"What!" my wife and I bellowed out simultaneously, for my father was referring to Professor Moriarty who Sherlock Holmes once designated as the Napoleon of crime, the evil mastermind who was every bit as cunning and clever as the Great Detective himself.

"But Moriarty is dead," Joanna countered. "He was killed in the struggle with my father at the Falls of Reichenbach."

"It cannot be him," I agreed. "Dead men do not throw bricks."

"He has come back in another form to seek revenge," said my father.

"And pray tell what is this other form?"

"His younger brother, Colonel James Moriarty."

CHAPTER FOURTEEN

The Moriartys

"What caused you to believe that Professor Moriarty's brother was behind the attempt on our lives?" Joanna asked, adding a third log to the fire in our parlor, for the outside chill had suddenly deepened.

"The manner in which it occurred," my father replied. "And this was not his first try, but his second."

My wife nodded, now recalling the speeding vehicle which narrowly missed us as we departed Ah Sing's opium den. "Moreover, both attempts were remarkably similar to those visited on my father."

"Precisely, my dear Joanna. The initial attack on Holmes happened just as he was turning a street corner, alone and on a dark night. A carriage suddenly rushed toward him, and he was barely able to step out of the way in time. Thus, the initial attempt on our lives was done in an identical fashion, except the instrument was a motor vehicle rather than a carriage. The second try on Holmes's life was far too close for comfort. He was walking along a footpath when a large brick fell from the roof of a house, missing him by only inches."

"Much like the one we just experienced on departing the building on Prescot Street," I noted.

"It was in every way identical, which brought to mind the second attack on Holmes," my father went on. "It was this rapid remembrance which prompted my immediate response that pushed all out of danger."

"Which no doubt saved our lives," Joanna said gratefully.

"It is most heartening to be of use despite one's advancing years," my father said, downplaying the heroic act with a gentle smile which quickly left his face. "But now, there will be a third attempt on your life, Joanna, just as there was on your father's."

"A thug armed with a billy club," she recalled.

"Who will appear out of nowhere," my father added to the event. "Fortunately, Holmes, despite his relatively thin appearance, was able to overcome his assailant and deliver him to the police. You see, unbeknownst to most, Sherlock Holmes was skilled in the self-defense art of Bartitsu, which originated in Japan as a combination of boxing, jujitsu, and cane fighting. It was the latter talent that rendered his assailant senseless."

"Bartitsu," Joanna repeated softly to herself. "How might I learn more about this marvelous art?"

"By reading the story entitled *The Adventure of the Empty House,* in which Holmes revealed to me that he also used this form of Japanese wrestling to subdue Moriarty during their struggle at the Reichenbach Falls."

I refilled our glasses with a fine Madeira before asking, "But, pray tell, how could you have possibly known that a younger brother of Professor Moriarty remained involved in his dead sibling's criminal activities?"

"From a letter Holmes wrote to me only months prior to his death, in which he told of Colonel James Moriarty's several attempts to seek revenge for his brother's demise."

"May we please see the letter?" Joanna implored.

"As soon as Miss Hudson can recover it from our storeroom," my father replied. "It is hidden away in a box which I labeled PERSONAL REMEMBRANCES. Our ever-diligent landlady will find it in due time."

My wife strolled over to the Persian slipper holding her Turkish cigarettes and, after lighting one, began to pace the floor, muttering to herself. "I knew it! I was aware of it from the onset, but I did not pursue it and allowed the obvious to pass unexplained."

"What was so obvious?" asked I.

"The clues which were lined up so nicely for us to follow," she elucidated. "We were cleverly led to locations where our assassinations could be carried out. Just put your mind to it. First, there was the crushed empty package of Player's Navy Cut, from which the mastermind predicted we would detect the scent of opium and that would eventually lead us to Ah Sing's where the initial attack on our lives occurred. And of course he left behind a matchbook cover that would reveal an advertisement from The Rose and Lamb in Whitechapel where the barmaid was employed."

"But how could he have predicted you would use ultraviolet light to bring out the faded, rain-damaged advertisement?"

"Because he fancies himself every bit as clever as I am, if not more so," Joanna responded. "He placed himself in my stead and was thus able to foresee our next moves, including the visit to the barmaid's flat."

"Are you convinced he actually set up the girl's abortion?" my father asked incredulously.

"No, I am not, but I can assure you he was aware of it, for he sent his German associate to visit the barmaid's flat and report back to him immediately. Then he had a lookout posted to inform him of our arrival at 825 Prescot Street, at which point the second attempt on our lives was to occur."

My father nodded at Joanna's assessment. "I recall your comment early on in the investigation that the order of appearance of the clues was disconcerting."

"They were too plainly laid out, but I neglected to make much of it," she admonished herself. "I allowed the observation to slip by."

"Do you believe he is leading us in circles?"

"He is attempting to."

"To what end?"

"To guide us away from Prince Harry whose abduction he no doubt planned."

"For whom he will collect an extraordinarily valuable ransom."

"There is more to it than that."

"But can you draw any conclusions?"

"Only that Colonel James Moriarty is every bit as clever as his dead brother."

Following a brief rap on the door, Miss Hudson entered, carrying a dust-covered box and announcing, "It was tucked away under a stack of Mr. Holmes's reference books."

"Well done, Miss Hudson," my father praised, walking over to inspect the contents of the box. He lifted its lid, but had to briefly step back to avoid the particles of thick dust which flew into the air. "Ah, yes! And I see the letter is atop and untouched over the years."

"I shall be on my way, then, for a beef roast awaits my attention."

Once the door closed, my father returned to his overstuffed chair and momentarily studied the letter, which no doubt rekindled old, warm memories. "My very last contact with the dearest of friends," he said nostalgically.

"Please read it to us, Watson, slowly, so we can measure each word."

My father cleared his throat and began the recitation in a firm, clear voice.

My dear Watson,

I write these last lines not only to bid you a fond farewell, but to warn you of an approaching danger which may be close at hand. Over the past months there have occurred several attempts on my life which I believe are the workings of a Moriarty. Not the Professor Moriarty we were so familiar with, but rather his equally evil younger brother, Colonel James Moriarty. Surely, you remember him as one of the two brothers Moriarty possessed, the other being a stationmaster in the west of England. My investigation into this matter revealed there is only one brother, the nefarious colonel, who cleverly established a ghost sibling to throw any pursuers with an arrest warrant off of his trail.

It was this colonel who wished to bring my life to a premature end in the peaceful South Downs of England. Less than a week ago, the second such attack took place. While enjoying a leisurely stroll, I was accosted by a thug wielding a cosh who exclaimed, "This is a present from the Professor!" You no doubt recall a similar incident that occurred many years ago in London. Fortunately, on this occasion, as on the prior one, I possessed my walking cane and, using the martial art of Bartitsu, delivered a crushing blow to the thug's skull just below the bridge of the nose. It is there that the blood supply is most generous and the bone thickness unimpressive. The end result was a massive hemorrhage which left the thug in a semicomatose state for several days before he entered the world of the severely brain damaged. But I suspect that Moriarty will not be dissuaded and will send another to do his repulsive work. If he is unsuccessful, I fear he will go after the daughter I had never seen.

*You are no doubt surprised that she occupies a portion
of my thoughts which I assure you are not paternal, for I am
incapable of such an emotion. But I do take satisfaction from
protecting the innocent, and the opportunity to again thwart a
Moriarty is one I cannot resist. Now, to the best of my knowledge Irene Adler gave birth to a daughter named Joanna, for
whom you were good enough to arrange an adoption following
the mother's death which occurred shortly after giving birth. I
must admit that I lost all interest, but knowing you, my dear
Watson, I was certain you would keep an occasional eye on
the child to see that she was cared for appropriately and that
the trust fund we established for her was not misused. So I am
afraid it again falls upon you to look after her well-being, for if
Moriarty is unable to inflict his revenge on me, he will certainly
attempt to do so on my daughter. No need to say, Scotland
Yard should not be called in for protection, for they will bumble
about and quickly be outwitted by the vengeful colonel. You
must use your well-stocked brain and steady hand to win the
day. And if you can devise a means to do away with the last of
the Moriartys, so much the better.*

*Pray give my greetings to your son who I have learned will
soon enter Oxford, and believe me to be, my dear fellow,*

Very sincerely yours,
Sherlock Holmes

We sat in absolute silence, for it was as if this long-dead
Sherlock Holmes was actually talking to us in our parlor at 221b
Baker Street. How keen he was to know that my father would
keep a careful eye on the adopted Joanna, and how his dear Watson could be depended on to protect the daughter Holmes had
never seen. And to my surprise, there was a touch of warmth for
Joanna if one were to read between the lines of the letter.

"Thus," my father broke the silence, "beyond any doubt, another Moriarty means to harm another Holmes."

"We should do everything in our power to protect her," I asserted.

"And we shall," my father vowed.

"He wishes you to kill Colonel Moriarty," Joanna said without inflection, but she reached for my hand and gave it a gentle, reassuring squeeze, for she knew I would worry about my father confronting such a clever, powerful foe.

"Much as Holmes did to the older brother at the Falls of Reichenbach," I noted.

"So be it," said my father, adjusting the shoulder holster that held his Webley revolver. "Given the opportunity, I will not hesitate."

"Unfortunately, we have so little to go on, which gives Moriarty the advantage," I stated the obvious.

"He will most likely follow in his brother's footsteps," Joanna predicted. "The assailant will approach me unexpectedly, with a billy club in hand. One well-delivered blow will split open the thickest portion of the skull and bring with it certain death."

"How will you protect yourself, then?" asked I. "Your skills in jujitsu alone will not suffice."

"I shall do as my father did in his letter, and carry a walking cane wherever I go," Joanna responded, then added, "And preferably one with a heavy head."

"I can place a sturdy oak cane at your disposal," my father offered. "It has quite a thick handle which will suit your purpose well."

"Excellent," said Joanna, who seemed lost in thought for a moment before coming back to me. "And now, with me protected, let us turn our attention to our major quest, which is tracking the German. Please keep in mind that he is the key to the puzzle."

"But it is Moriarty who is the key," I argued.

My wife shook her head at once. "Moriarty is the lock, the German is the key. The two go hand in hand. There is an obvious connection between them, namely the barmaid who underwent a botched abortion."

My father's brow went up. "Are you of the opinion that Moriarty used the German to actually set up the abortion?"

"Either the colonel knew it was to be performed or somehow became involved in setting it up." Joanna hurried over to the Persian slipper and extracted yet another Turkish cigarette, which she lighted from the one she was smoking, and began again to pace the floor of our parlor. "Let us fit together all the pieces of this puzzle we have collected thus far. The barmaid had an abortion and became ill because it went badly. We know the German was aware because he sat in the poor girl's flat smoking cigarettes and watching her slowly die. He eventually left the flat and reported back to Moriarty who devised the second attempt to kill or permanently maim us. Is everyone on board thus far?"

My father and I nodded in the affirmative.

"Then, pray tell, how did Moriarty learn of the abortion? There are only two possibilities. Either he planned it, or was later told about it by the individual who did in fact plan it. Now tell me, which do you favor?"

"It was Moriarty from the start, for he was directing the German at every step, including the abortion, and which clues to leave behind for us," my father declared.

"Bravo, Watson! You are truly outdoing yourself," said Joanna. "The German was in all likelihood simply a pawn, being told what to do. And the final piece of the puzzle strongly suggests that the good Prince Harry was also a pawn, who was trapped by Moriarty via the abortion setup."

"So you believe that Prince Harry was intimately involved in Martha Ann Miller's abortion?"

"It fits, particularly when you think back to the comfortable flat he rented for her, and how he showered her with gifts of fine clothing and gourmet foods. He was obviously quite fond of her, you see."

"Are you of the opinion that Prince Harry both impregnated the barmaid and arranged for her abortion?" asked I.

"I am, but I have doubts he would have it done by a clumsy abortionist."

"But who, then?"

"Someone who is quite skilled in that procedure," Joanna responded. "Tell me, John, did you yourself perform the autopsy on the barmaid?"

"It was done by my young associate, Jonathan Quinn, who I assure you is well trained," I replied.

"How well trained?"

"He studied under Sir George Herbert at Oxford prior to joining our staff last year."

"With that background, I suspect he has limited experience with botched abortions."

"No doubt, but the case of the barmaid was straightforward, with an induced rupture of the uterus."

"What I wish to know is was there other evidence to show that the procedure was performed by an unskilled abortionist?"

"He made no mention of it."

"Which does not exclude its presence."

"And if it were?"

"It would indicate the abortion was done on the cheap, as one would expect of a barmaid on a very limited income," Joanna explained. "But what if the abortion was carried out by a professional, with no scrapes on the cervical opening of the uterus, and the curettage itself done in a skilled manner?"

"Yet we would still have to contend with the uterine rupture," I argued mildly.

"Which at times occurs in the best of hands."

"I fail to see the point you are making."

"We must connect the dots here," Joanna informed. "First and foremost, we have a wealthy prince showering gifts on an attractive woman to whom he has taken a genuine liking. If she was to become pregnant, do you believe he would leave her on her own to find a cheap abortionist, or would he seek out a skilled professional to do the task?"

"Obviously the latter," I answered.

"Who makes a tragic error, and the poor girl is rushed to a prominent hospital accompanied by a fifty-pound note which allows for her admission."

My father's eyes widened as he reached the very same conclusion as I. "The good, but gullible Prince Harry has been used. Once the girl required an abortion, Moriarty devised an ingenious plan to lure the prince into a trap where he was captured, and for which His Majesty will have to pay a huge ransom to have his son freed."

"It is even possible that this skilled abortionist might be associated with St. Bartholomew's and somehow managed to facilitate her admission," I surmised.

Joanna smiled mischievously. "My, my, the Watsons are coming along so nicely. But there remain pieces of this puzzle which need to be brought to light. With this in mind, what should our next step be?"

"We have to determine if a skilled abortionist was in play here," I replied. "To that end, I shall carefully reexamine the autopsy findings on the barmaid first thing in the morning."

My father shook his head slowly, a frown now on his face. "It is difficult to believe an individual at St. Bart's was involved in this dreadful manner. To do so requires a stretch of one's imagination."

"As does the involvement of a prince who happens to be third in line of succession to the throne," Joanna added.

There was a brief rap on the door, which announced the arrival of Miss Hudson and a platter holding juicy slices of roast beef. An appetizing aroma soon filled the air.

In a low voice, Joanna turned to my father and asked, "Tell me, Watson, did the third attack on Sherlock Holmes occur during the day or night?"

"During the day," he replied. "The other two attempts happened in the dark of the night."

My wife tossed her cigarette into the fire and watched it incinerate. "Which unfortunately informs us that the final attempt on my life can come about at any time and any place."

"And that works much to his advantage," my father said concernedly. "I am afraid he will plan your demise with great precision."

"Much as his brother did for my father at the Falls of Reichenbach, and in the end no doubt regretted doing so."

"In a fierce, physical struggle, do you consider yourself Holmes's equal?"

"We shall find out soon enough."

After a very long day and satisfying late dinner, we retired to our rooms for much needed sleep. Yet, rather than change into her night clothes, Joanna seated herself in front of the large bedroom mirror and began applying a thick, white cream to the edges of her cheeks.

"Are you having problems with your skin?" I inquired.

"One of considerable bother," she replied.

"Shall we have my father take a look? He is quite knowledgeable in such disorders."

"It is not the diagnosis which eludes me, but its cure."

"And the diagnosis?"

"Deepening crow's-feet which are becoming more and more obvious."

I studied my wife's lovely face, with its highest cheekbones and perfectly contoured lips, and could see no change from the day I first met her. "They are hardly noticeable."

"Not to my eye."

"Does the skin cream help?"

"Very little I am afraid, but I have been assured by others that *Her Ladyship's Special Emollient* works wonders."

"How long have you been using it?"

"Almost three months."

"With such minimal result, why continue to apply it?"

"It is the triumph of hope over experience."

"May I suggest that a long, deep sleep might be of greater value?"

"I shall give that thought, but only after we have finished our business with Moriarty."

"Which requires you to pace the floor of our parlor night after night?"

"So it would seem."

I leaned down to kiss the back of her neck before commenting, "Your crow's-feet are barely visible."

Joanna smiled up at me. "You are biased, and thus your opinion is not reliable."

"Guilty on all counts," I confessed. "But do try not to stay up through the early-morning hours."

"I may have no choice, for I must reexamine all of Moriarty's prior moves if I am to predict what his next one will be."

"And thus prepare us for it."

"It is more to it than that, dear heart," said she. "I believe there is a pattern to these moves and, once deciphered, it will tell us the final destination of this most strange road we are traveling."

"A very strange road indeed," I agreed.

On that note, I retired for the night and slept soundly with-out interruption. Upon awakening early the following morning, I discovered my wife's side of the bed to be empty. Slipping on a robe, I hurried into a smoke-filled parlor and watched Joanna pace back and forth, with her head down as she puffed on a Turkish cigarette. She paid scant attention to my presence. Apparently, the final destination Moriarty had so skillfully plotted had continued to escape her.

CHAPTER FIFTEEN

A Repeat Autopsy

On my arrival at St. Bartholomew's later that morning, I found yet another stack of paperwork awaiting my attention, but only the top sheet demanded my immediate action. A note from Adam Sharpe indicated the infecting organism was in fact *Pseudomonas aeruginosa* which probably originated in the patient's bladder. Her urine was heavily infected with this bacteria as well, and Sharpe wondered if the abortionist had accidentally punctured both the uterus and bladder which created a route between the two and allowed the *Pseudomonas* to contaminate the uterine wall. He also noted that there had been no further cases of infection with this microorganism, and thus no evidence at this juncture for a spreading contagion at St. Bart's.

A bullet had been dodged, thought I, as I hurried down the corridor, now with two reasons to review the autopsy on Martha Ann Miller. The first, which was primarily of academic interest, was to uncover the source of the *Pseudomonas* that had brought about the patient's sepsis. The second was to examine the endometrium of the uterus and determine if the attempted abortion had been performed by an unskilled hand or by a professional without even a hint of morals. Up ahead, I saw Benson, the head orderly, who had the remarkable ability to present himself the moment he was needed.

"Ah, Mr. Benson, do you have a moment?"

"Of course, sir," he replied, with his characteristic crooked nod. "How may I be of service?"

"It has been brought to my attention that we shall have to reexamine the corpse of Martha Ann Miller."

"May I ask why, sir?"

"She is the victim of a botched abortion, which of course is a criminal offense that has been brought to the attention of Scotland Yard."

"Will there be an inquiry?"

"That is to be determined."

"Shall I notify Dr. Quinn?"

"I will do it."

"Very good," said Benson, shaking his head which seemed off center. "But I must say there has been considerable interest in this particular corpse."

"How so?"

"Well, first off, as you know, sir, if a body goes unclaimed it is either sent to the medical school to be used as a cadaver for study or transported to a potter's field for burial. As we were making preparations for such a journey, the body was suddenly claimed for appropriate burial by a group called The Friends of Martha Ann Miller. They of course were required to name the funeral home making the arrangements."

"Which was?"

"Ferguson's in Whitechapel."

"Have you ever heard of them?"

"No, sir, I have not. But knowing the area, I am certain there are quite a number of such houses which are kept quite busy."

"Indeed, for Whitechapel has a well-deserved reputation for a high rate of violent death."

"Which our autopsy tables can bear witness to."

"When is the body scheduled for transfer?"

"At noon, sir."

"Then we must proceed with haste."

"I will have her set up shortly, sir," Benson assured. "Shall I notify Mr. Rudd as well?"

"I did not know he was involved," said I, keeping my voice even.

"Oh, yes, sir. He has shown a keen interest, for he was the surgeon who operated on the girl once her blood pressure stabilized. He, along with others, had made a presumptive diagnosis of ruptured appendix, which of course was not the case."

"He must have been quite unhappy that he had missed the diagnosis."

"Not particularly so, sir. He seemed most curious about the terrible infection which caused her death," Benson replied, before lowering his voice. "Apparently, there are questions being asked around the hospital on this very same matter."

"I see," said I, wondering if my secretary Rose's questioning of her coworkers had reached the ears of others. "In answer to your question, there is no need to notify Mr. Rudd of our reexamining of Martha Ann Miller."

"Very good, sir."

I continued on my way through the pathology department to meet with Jonathan Quinn and tell him of the need to restudy the corpse of the barmaid. I would have to choose my words carefully, so as not to convey the impression that the initial autopsy was not well done. No simple matter, that, thought I. But it was the interest of Thaddeus Rudd in the death of Martha Ann Miller which captivated my attention. Was it truly brought on by a missed diagnosis? Or was he concerned about the presence of a virulent bacteria that might spread throughout the hospital? Or was there a more sinister connection?

I stepped into the larger of the pathology laboratories and found Jonathan Quinn studying slides under a Zeiss microscope. He waved with one hand, whilst using the other to adjust the magnification of the microscope.

"I will be with you in a moment, sir," said he.

His use of the word *sir* caused me to feel my age, as it always did. But then again, I was a good fifteen years older than the young pathologist, and in his view that made me his definitive senior. In addition, I was director of the pathology department whilst he was its youngest member, only months out of his residency training. Thus I merited the title of *sir,* and he would have it no other way.

"An interesting case of pernicious anemia, sir," said he, arising from a metal stool. "It shows the classic findings."

"Are you referring to the peripheral blood smear or bone marrow?"

"The peripheral blood smear which is swimming in hyperlobulated leukocytes."

I nodded at his conclusion, for most leukocytes have a nucleus with two or three lobes, whilst those with pernicious anemia have as many as six lobes. It was a clear-cut diagnosis, but unfortunately there was no treatment for it, and the patient would waste away with a progressive anemia.

"Do you have time this morning to assist me in reexamining the corpse of Martha Ann Miller?" asked I.

"Of course," he replied, his face now showing worry. "Have I overlooked something?"

"I suspect not, but a botched abortion is a criminal matter, and Scotland Yard may become involved," I said, which was a half-truth. "Should there be an inquiry, certain features of the autopsy will come into question. For example, were bruises and cuts noticed in the vaginal vault?"

"I must admit that I did not examine the vaginal vault, sir," he replied unhappily.

"Neither would most pathologists," I reassured. "For now we are entering the field of forensic pathology, which combines our specialty with the law."

"I am afraid I have little experience in that area, sir."

"No one does because it is so new," I went on. "But I have more than most, and that is why Scotland Yard calls upon me at times. I would be willing to train you in that subspecialty if you wish."

"I would be delighted, sir!" he exclaimed.

"This way, then."

After donning masks and gowns, we entered the autopsy room and watched a gloved Benson put the final touches on the corpse which were necessary for autopsy. He performed these tasks effortlessly and without emotion, for the body was cold as ice and white as a sheet, although some semblance of her youthful beauty remained. Benson stepped back and handed us rubber gloves.

I examined the labia and discovered no evidence of trauma, nor were there bruises or lacerations within the vaginal vault itself. "No signs of forced entry," I remarked.

"Why is that important, sir?" Quinn asked.

"It would tell us if she was a willing participant," I answered, but more importantly the finding told me that the abortionist was not a rank amateur.

On a nearby table was the victim's uterus which had been resected out en bloc. The cervix showed a small, round opening which indicated the woman had never given birth. Again, there was no evidence of trauma. "You will note that the cervix is unabraded."

"Which suggests she offered no resistance," Quinn noted.

"Very good," said I, and opened the body of the uterus. The curettage was nicely done in an even and deliberate fashion. No anatomic parts of the aborted fetus remained. There was a single puncture wound near a Fallopian tube that was surrounded with pus. "No doubt this was the site of the infection which caused her death."

"Which indicates the abortionist can be held responsible," Quinn stated the obvious.

"No doubt."

"I find this study of forensics most exhilarating," said he, pleased with the information attached to the infected site.

I nodded, but I was thinking if he only knew the half of it. What the repeat autopsy showed was that the abortionist was quite skilled, despite the puncture, and would have commanded a considerable fee. I turned my attention to the victim's bladder, which was intact and could not have provided a route for the bacteria to enter the uterus, although splashed urine could have contaminated the abortionist's instruments.

"Have you an opinion on the welt marks, sir?" Quinn interrupted my thoughts.

"What welts?"

The young pathologist turned the corpse on its side and pointed to the multiple deep welts which covered her buttocks. Their purplish discoloration was in stark contrast to the whiteness of her surrounding skin. My God! She had been whipped severely with a thick belt.

"Could that be an allergic reaction?" Quinn inquired.

"Most unlikely," said I. "Allergic welts cause swelling, but not indentations. These welts are quite deep, which tells us she was beaten with a strop."

"Do you believe she may have been a participant in sadomasochism?" Quinn asked incredulously.

"A possibility," I replied, knowing full well that was not the case.

"But that would not have caused her death."

"No, it would not have," I said, stripping off my gloves. "We are done here, but now you must rewrite the autopsy report and include all the findings we discussed. Leave out the implications, however."

"Most instructive," Quinn murmured, more to himself than to me.

I hurried down the corridor, grumbling at the savage cruelty of the German who watched the young woman die. I suspected that he wished to speed up the abortion process and mercilessly beat the poor barmaid with a thick belt, believing, in his ignorance, that the beating would expedite expulsion of any fetal parts and no doubt bring her to death's door. And all it did was add to the poor girl's misery and pain. This sequence of events fit the findings. There would be no other reason for the welts.

I entered my office, trying to hide my fury at the German's barbaric behavior.

"There are several messages from your wife," Rose said, handing me reminder slips. "The first is for you to arrive at Scotland Yard promptly at two o'clock for a most important phone call."

I nodded at the reminder, recalling that was the exact time the abductors of Prince Harry were scheduled to phone with their further instructions.

"And you must clear your calendar in order to attend the matinee of the play which begins at five-thirty sharp."

"Please see to that, Rose."

I closed the door to my office, still wondering why Joanna had put up such little resistance to attending a play at the Duke of York's Theater on St. Martin's Lane. It was her custom to avoid all distractions when involved in a difficult case, for she insisted that her concentration and train of thought not be interrupted. But this particular play, *The Last Coronation,* had received dazzling reviews, which must have caught Joanna's eye, for she happily agreed to my father's invitation once he had purchased such excellent seats for us. Perhaps my wife did in fact need a short respite, which might freshen her brain for the difficult task of outwitting the ever clever Moriarty. I returned to the stack of papers which awaited my signature, having not the slightest notion that during the course of the coming evenings our travels would take us from the most elegant of surroundings to the lowest dregs of British society.

CHAPTER SIXTEEN

The Second Call

Once again the abductor's phone call to Scotland Yard did not arrive at the scheduled time. It was approaching ten past two and the phone had yet to ring.

"Trying to make us a bit more anxious, eh?" Lestrade suggested.

"And doing a good job at it," the commissioner noted, staring out a large window at a sunless, gloomy day.

"He is simply demonstrating that he is in control," said Joanna. "The rules we must play by will be his, and his alone."

"Are you referring to the German whose voice we heard in the background during the initial call?"

"No, Sir Charles, I am referring to the brother of the late Professor Moriarty who is the mastermind behind it all."

The commissioner turned about sharply. "Is this based on suspicion or fact?"

"Both," Joanna replied, and described at length the evidence for Col. Moriarty's involvement. "The attempts on our lives were his calling cards."

"But he meant to kill you and not simply announce his presence," Sir Charles said, giving the matter more thought.

"That was not his intent, for if he wanted us dead at those moments, we would be so," she explained. "Think back and consider each attack in detail. In the first attempt outside Ah Sing's opium den, the driver came directly at us just as we stepped off the footpath. In doing so, he gave us time to retreat into the doorway and escape harm. Had the assailant wanted us dead, he would have waited until we moved into the street to wave down the approaching motor vehicle, which would have had its lights on, so we would believe it to be our taxi. We would have made very easy targets indeed, and the hand of death would have instantly been upon us. In the second attempt outside the barmaid's flat, you will recall that my dear John felt small pebbles striking his hat from above, which again gave us prior warning before the large bricks fell. Thus we can conclude that Moriarty knew that Watson would put the pieces of the puzzle together and realize that the attacks were remarkably similar to those visited upon my father. Beyond any doubt, Moriarty was sending us his calling card and telling us he planned to avenge his brother's death."

"But why not kill you outright?" the commissioner asked. "There are a number of means by which he could render you quite dead. A marksman with a long rifle could perform the task with ease."

"You are missing the point, Sir Charles," said Joanna. "Moriarty wishes this to be a contest to the death between the two of us, much as it was between my father and his evil brother at the Falls of Reichenbach. The colonel wants it known that he annihilated the daughter of Sherlock Holmes, and thus he has the revenge he seeks for his brother's death."

"How will you deal with this threat?"

"In the same manner my father dealt with his brother."

"Which is?"

"By allowing Moriarty to underestimate me."

The phone on the commissioner's desk rang loudly.

Sir Charles picked up the receiver on the second ring. The room became instantly quiet. No one moved.

"Yes?" said he.

"Speaking," the commissioner replied. A moment later a look of surprise crossed his face before he handed the phone to Joanna. "He wishes to talk with the daughter of Sherlock Holmes."

"As I expected." My wife did not exchange amenities with the caller, but rather asked in a straightforward fashion, "How may I be of service, Colonel Moriarty?

"Yes, yes, of course I looked into your background and learned you are the younger brother of the late Professor Moriarty, whom my father described as the Napoleon of crime."

A humorless smile came and went from her face as she responded, "And you are in the process of living up to that sterling reputation, are you not?

"Ah, and even surpass it? Well, that, my fine adversary, will take some doing."

Joanna listened, then for our benefit repeated Moriarty's reply. "And near the top of your list is a rather bold plan to repay me for your brother's death. . . .

"Oh, I suspected you would eventually come my way," said she, showing no concern. "In my heart of hearts, I believe some sort of revenge was on his mind when he began his final, watery exit from this good world, with an assist from my father.

"A similar fate awaits me, you say?

"Colonel, it is a bad habit to write history before it occurs," said she, brushing off the threat. "Enough of this chatter which serves little purpose. Let us turn to the business at hand, and in particular your demands for Prince Harry's return to his family."

Joanna nodded to herself, saying, "I shall write down your

demands, so speak slowly. In addition, I will repeat your words for the benefit of others in the room. Now, let us begin.

"The exchange will take place at the painting *The Virgin of the Rocks* by Leonardo da Vinci in the National Gallery at noon sharp the day after tomorrow," she reiterated. "I am to present myself at said painting, with the Sovereign Orb in my hands. It is to be contained in a white box that has a red ribbon tied around it. When Big Ben strikes noon, I am to untie the red ribbon, so that the lid of the box can easily be lifted. But the lid is not to be removed until I am approached by a heavyset individual, with a noticeable scar across his cheek. He is to be allowed to gaze into the box and ascertain the presence of the orb."

Joanna interrupted abruptly, "No! No! I must insist on some form of protection.

"Of course, not Scotland Yard, for they are in no way to be involved in the exchange. . . . Should their presence be detected, the exchange will be called off, perhaps permanently.

"But I must insist on having a safeguard," she went on and gestured to my father. "To that end, I shall be accompanied by Dr. Watson who will remain close by. He is a quite excellent marksman who will not hesitate to place a round from his Webley into the head of your German colleague, thus preventing a grab-and-run maneuver.

"And, as a nearby backup, my husband will be armed and prepared to intervene should there be an attempt to overpower the senior Dr. Watson.

"Now, let us turn our attention to Prince Harry, and how we can be certain that he is the individual being offered for exchange.

"No, no," she responded at once. "His appearance alone will not do. Look-alikes are too easy to find or manufacture.

"Definitely not. We will not allow anyone from the royal family to participate."

Joanna paused to consider the matter further. "Here is how the identification will be accomplished. The prince will be in the National Gallery and within our sight. I will send my husband over to ask a question only the prince can answer. If all is in order, the exchange will proceed.

"Agreed, then. But inform your German associate that he is to keep both hands in full view of myself and Dr. Watson. He is of course not to be armed, and if he makes a sudden, untoward move, it will be his last.

"Not at all, Moriarty. It was not meant as a threat, but rather a precautionary statement of fact."

Sir Charles reached into his pocket for a five-pound note and vigorously pointed at it, reminding Joanna to offer the abductors an alternate form of payment.

"And finally," she continued on. "His Majesty is most reluctant to part with the Sovereign Orb for obvious reasons. He wonders if you would be willing to accept a most generous offer of pounds sterling rather than the orb itself."

Joanna shook her head at the response. "Even if a sum of 100,000 pounds could be made available on short notice?"

She shook her head once more. "Then it shall be the Sovereign Orb.

"And no Scotland Yard," she restated and returned the receiver to its cradle.

"I smell a trap," Sir Charles noted promptly.

"And a well-designed one," Joanna added. "There will be too many people around the exhibits at noontime, any of whom could be used as shields or impediments."

"Or as armed adversaries," my father warned. "We are sure to be outnumbered and under-armed."

"Scotland Yard must be present," Sir Charles insisted.

"And the moment you are spotted, the exchange will come to an abrupt end," Joanna portended.

"We can have them so well disguised that even their own wives will not recognize them."

"With all due respect, Commissioner, you are underestimating the enemy, which in this instance could be a fatal mistake," said Joanna, reaching for a Turkish cigarette and lighting it as she began to pace the floor. "We must recall that my father not only named Professor Moriarty the Napoleon of crime, but also referred to him as the greatest schemer of all time and the controlling brain behind London's underworld. It would be wise for us to consider his brother much the same. With this in mind, I suspect the colonel has all the guile and cunning of the departed Professor Moriarty, who was able to match wits with my father to the very end. Believe me when I tell you he is a most formidable adversary."

"But you seem to be his equal," Sir Charles countered.

"Perhaps, but thus far he remains one step ahead and I fear he will remain so."

"It appears you have strong doubts that he plans to live up to the proposed exchange."

"When it comes to the Moriartys, expect the worst, for that is when they are at their very best."

"Surely, you are not suggesting that we call off the exchange."

"Do that and we place Prince Harry in even more jeopardy."

"But he has such an obvious advantage."

"So it would seem."

"How, then, can we possibly succeed?"

"By removing his advantage," said she, crushing out her cigarette and taking my father's arm as we departed.

CHAPTER SEVENTEEN

The Duke of York's Theater

As we waited for the curtain to rise, I took the opportunity to once more glance at the auditorium's Victorian décor, with its numerous cherubs and dragons painted in glorious colors. I could not help but wonder if the depictions mirrored the life experience of Prince Harry, in which the dragons represented his current terrifying ordeal as a captive of the Huns, whilst the cherubs spoke of his delightful past as a playboy and beloved member of the royal family. Surely, he would be emotionally traumatized by his harsh captivity, for his very life was at stake, but of equal concern was the worry of long-term damage to his psyche.

The audience quieted as the curtain went up for the final act of *The Last Coronation,* a fascinating yet somewhat unsettling play, for it was centered around a small but powerful group who wished to abolish the monarchy before the new, young queen could be crowned. The drama of course was fictional, but its intent was quite real, for there was currently such a movement afoot, which seemed to be gaining traction during the harsh living standards brought on by a world war. But I must say that Penny Martin, affectionately known as Pretty Penny, was magnificent in the role of the aspiring queen. One moment she was strong and forceful, standing up to her adversaries without a flinch, whilst the next she was a frightened young girl who seemed to be buckling under the strain. Her emotional swings were moving indeed, as every whisper and change in her voice was heard and felt by an enchanted audience. All were hoping she would emerge victorious and save the crown, which of course she did. At the end of the play, a strong, vibrant Pretty Penny stood at center stage, projecting the compelling image of power and grace. In one hand she held the Sovereign Orb, in the other the royal scepter. The queen had been crowned, the monarchy saved.

As the orchestra played the concluding notes of Elgar's *Pomp and Circumstance* which signaled the end of the coronation, the audience rose and burst into a thunderous applause. The players received three well-deserved standing ovations. But the roar became deafening when Pretty Penny appeared onstage by herself. No monarch, here or elsewhere, appeared more graceful and in command.

Pretty Penny, who began as a homeless waif from Whitechapel, had stolen everyone's heart with a stunning performance that would long be remembered.

"What say you, Joanna?" my father asked as the audience slowly filed out of the theater.

"She possesses a God-given talent," she replied. "It was as if she was born for that role."

"In a manner of speaking she was, for early in life Pretty Penny learned how to survive and overcome the harshest of forces. Despite her beauty, she was not the sort to bend easily."

"But her voice," I chimed in. "It had the perfect pitch and tone for each emotion, and once uttered the words seemed to stay in the air."

"That is God's gift," Joanna reiterated. "We should send her a note and flowers at our earliest convenience."

"Oh, I think I can do better than that," said my father, with a gentle smile. "I spoke with Mr. Blackstone after purchasing the tickets and arranged for us to have a backstage visit. He of course knows of the daughter of Sherlock Holmes and believes the cast would be thrilled to meet her."

"Excellent, Father! What a splendid idea," said I.

My wife took my hand as we mounted the steps to the backstage. "I trust Pretty Penny has been told of our upcoming visit, for she may only vaguely recollect our faces from the brief encounter when we assisted in her rescue from Jack the Ripper."

"I insisted on it, for that very reason," said my father. "In addition, were she by chance to suddenly recognize our faces it would bring back horrifying memories."

"Which would be most unfortunate."

"To say the least."

We turned in to a passageway that led backstage, and stepped around a coil of misplaced rope. Ahead, we could see the actors and actresses crowded together, obviously celebrating yet another fine performance.

Roger Blackstone saw us first and, giving Pretty Penny a gentle nudge, pointed in our direction. The lovely actress dashed over to us and flew into Joanna's arms, holding her in the tightest of embraces.

"Oh, Mrs. Watson, what a pleasure to see you once again!" Pretty Penny gushed.

"And I, you," Joanna said, stepping aside so the actress could reach out to me and my father.

"Ah, the good Drs. Watson," she exclaimed, squeezing our hands warmly. "Now it is a perfect evening. And it comes to mind that I never had the opportunity to appropriately thank you for saving my life, and I do so with all my heart. I truly owe the three of you an unpayable debt."

"You are most welcome," my father said. "And we shall consider your magnificent performance tonight payment in full."

"Hear! Hear!" Joanna and I joined in.

"You do me too much honor," Pretty Penny said modestly.

"Well done and well deserved in every way," my father insisted. "And I must say I am delighted to find your spirits so high."

"Life has been good to me, Dr. Watson, and the past is little more than a distant memory which I no longer visit," she disclosed.

"Bravo!" my father congratulated.

"And please allow me to insist that the debt for the three of you saving my life remains unpaid, and will always be so. My warm feelings to the Watsons will never diminish."

"I trust these warm feelings apply to me as well," said Dr. Maxwell Anderson, who silently approached and gave Pretty Penny a tender embrace, which she returned with a smile.

"Ah, my Prince Charming has arrived," said she.

"At your service, madam," he replied.

We all enjoyed a light chuckle at the exchange, for Maxwell Anderson, an associate professor of pathology at St. Bart's, had early on been Pretty Penny's secret lover. She, at the time an actress in Whitechapel, would not have been considered a suitable companion by Anderson's aristocratic, class-conscious family. My! My! I thought to myself. How their opinion had changed since her rise to fame in the theater world.

"My family has arranged for a late-night dinner at Alexander's after the last performance tonight, and hope that you will be good enough to join us," Anderson invited her.

"I have a very busy schedule," Pretty Penny said playfully. "But I do believe I can squeeze your dinner date in."

The handsome pathologist smiled at her response. "There was a time when I worried how my family would react to Penny. Now, they continue to ask why I do not bring her around more."

"Ah, good taste always prevails," my father jested.

"Well put, Dr. Watson, well put indeed."

Whilst our conversation continued and turned to the evening performance, Joanna eased away from the group to have a private conversation with Roger Blackstone, a short, plump man, with silver-gray hair. His attire, which consisted of a linen suit, striped shirt, and bright red tie, was that of a showman. Whatever topic they were discussing brought no joy to the director's face, which was evidenced by repeated shakes of his head before he finally nodded. The group was now speaking of the importance of the theater remaining open despite the bombing raids, for the stage gave the public a respite and distraction from the dreary news of the war. I reluctantly agreed, but the thought of a direct hit by a bomb on a packed audience was too gruesome to even ponder. Moments later the stagehands began rearranging the trappings and furnishings for the next performance, indicating it was time to depart. Joanna rejoined us just as we were wishing one another farewell, with promises to gather again in the not-too-distant future.

When we were outside the theater and away from listening ears, I asked Joanna, "Pray tell, what was the topic of your conversation with Roger Blackstone?"

"Deception, my dear John," said she, and left it at that as our taxi approached.

CHAPTER EIGHTEEN

The Rose and Lamb

Upon entering our rooms, Toby Two instantly recognized us despite our disguises, for to canines it was their acute sense of smell rather than their eyesight which allowed them to quickly identify individuals they had encountered previously. Prior to the hound's entrance, Joanna had placed the slip of paper containing a trace of opium at the far end of the parlor, whilst hiding the crushed cigarette package from the barmaid's flat under her workbench. She guided Toby Two over to the slip of paper and set her to work. The hound gave the bit of paper a careful sniff, then darted over to the crushed package and yelped with delight.

"It would appear our German foe has left his mark behind yet again for us to find," said Joanna.

"Why does he bother to lead us on?" I asked.

"It is not he, but Moriarty who is orchestrating this cat-and-mouse game," Joanna replied. "The German is but a pawn we must follow if we hope to rescue Prince Harry."

"A pawn perhaps, but one who is behind every aspect of this most puzzling case," my father noted. "It was he who was present at the site of the prince's abduction and who later appeared to be intimately involved in the barmaid's tragic abortion and death."

"It is all Moriarty, the master schemer, who is moving his pawn in such a fashion that we have no choice but to follow," said she. "And time is of the essence, for in less than forty-eight hours the supposed exchange is scheduled to occur."

"Certainly, the strictest precautions will be applied to ensure we receive the prince for the Sovereign Orb," my father advanced. "Our adversaries must be aware of their impediments."

"Trust Moriarty at your own peril," Joanna warned. "Please keep in mind that his singular objective is to avenge his brother's death."

"Which means in the end he plans to outwit and destroy you, much as what your father did to Professor Moriarty."

"Precisely, my dear Watson, and my goal is to see to it that he ends up in the good earth next to his brother," my wife spoke with determination. "So let us put the finishing touches on our disguises and begin the process."

The process, which was the term my wife used for the bold moves we were about to undertake, would start with tonight's visit to The Rose and Lamb. Like our earlier appearances at another lower-class pub in Whitechapel, she would be disguised as an Unfortunate, with tattered, soiled clothing, and unshined walking boots. Her sandy blond hair was now covered by an unkempt brown wig which showed patches of gray. She had used red lipstick to give her face a stern, yet appealing expression. But on this occasion she had placed a small pillow between her abdomen and dress, giving her the appearance of a woman who was several months pregnant. She also applied additional rouge to her cheeks which produced the glow of pregnancy. And, as a final touch, Joanna left her ragged sweater unbuttoned and opened, so the bulge in her abdomen would be noticed by the most casual of observers. I, on the other hand, would be dressed in a tweed suit and a finely woven wool cap which gave me a professorial look. That was the impression I wished to show, for I was to be introduced, if necessary, as a lecturer in anatomy at a nearby college. My wig was heavily grayed, as was my thick mustache and pointed goatee. Unlike our earlier visit to a Whitechapel pub, my father would not be joining us, for much to his displeasure his arthritic knee was flaring up a bit, which caused a slight, but noticeable limp. We thought it best he rest the leg and apply healing cream and heat in hopes the inflammation would soon subside, for he had a most important role to play in the exchange which would take place at the National Gallery.

We departed from our rooms and hired a taxi to take us to the Whitechapel Underground Station, where we would casually stroll in and purchase tickets back to Baker Street, then turn about and walk the short distance to The Rose and Lamb. This maneuver was necessary, for patrons at that pub rarely arrived by coach or taxi, and if they did it would cause immediate suspicion of who you were and what your intent was. Whilst Joanna practiced her Cockney accent, I mentally went over the details of the plan to identify and capture the German before he had the opportunity to do himself in, and thus deny the chance to interrogate him and hopefully learn of Prince Harry's whereabouts.

Joanna and I would enter the pub, which the foreign agent was known to frequent, and seek information which could help us identify him with certainty. Once we had him in our sights, we would keep a close eye on the Hun and wait for him to depart the pub, upon which Joanna would follow him to the footpath and offer the services of an Unfortunate. This act would be the signal for two Scotland Yard detectives, who were disguised as drunken vagrants, to stagger by the couple before turning and delivering solid blows to the German's head, which would render him unconscious. The body would be dragged into a nearby alley, whilst the detectives awaited the arrival of a police vehicle which had been continually circling the blocks surrounding the pub. Of course there were flaws in the plan, thought I, but time was short and risks had to be taken.

"I'll 'ave a 'arf and 'arf," my wife interrupted my musing, again practicing her Cockney accent. It was perfectly uttered and translated into, "I'll have a half and half," which was a mixture of two beers, one of which was of lesser density than the other.

"Nicely spoken," said I. "If you wished to go even lower in class, you might request a three halfpenny worth of rum."

Joanna shook her head at the suggestion. "The half and half is pricier and shows that I am with a man of means rather than the usual layabout in the pub. I should remind you not to attempt to blend in with their dialect, for the working class will quickly see you as being an outsider, pretending to be one of them. Simply speak as a lecturer in anatomy and they will accept you as such."

Our taxi drew up outside the Whitechapel Underground Station which was sparsely populated at the late hour. We walked over to the ticket booth and purchased two rides back to Baker Street, then stepped outside and, making certain we weren't being followed, strolled down Durward Street toward the pub. The footpath was strewn with litter and spoiled garbage, upon which large rats were feeding. For the moment, they seemed to be ignoring the carcass of a dead cat that gave off a most pungent odor. A motor vehicle approached and slowed as it passed by, then regained speed. In its backseat was a hunched-down figure who bore a similarity to Inspector Lestrade. Just inside the alleyway next to the pub sat two intoxicated vagrants who we assumed were disguised Scotland Yard detectives.

"All seems in place," I said in a whisper.

"Too obvious," Joanna whispered back. "The trap is too obvious."

"But it cannot be changed at the last moment."

"Unfortunately," said Joanna, and buttoned her sweater to conceal her apparent third month of pregnancy.

"Why hide your pregnant state?"

"Because it may well appeal to some prospective clients."

"Then why bother with the disguise at all?"

"It has a use, but only when employed at the opportune moment."

We entered the noisy pub arm in arm and found seats at the end of a long wooden bar that had a row of occupied stools pushed up against it. Behind the bar was an impressive, but cracked mirror that showed advertisements for a variety of beers. The pub itself was crowded, with most of the people standing in the center area, drinks in hand, and conversing loudly. The air was heavily clouded with tobacco smoke which gave off a stale aroma. Off to the side, a rough-appearing man was throwing darts at a board and cursing his bad luck.

A bearded barkeep hurried over, attracted by my fine attire, and wiped his hands on a dirty towel. He was heavyset, with scarred brows and knotted knuckles from countless fights.

"What'll you have?" he asked.

"A 'arf and 'arf for me and my chum," Joanna ordered at once, her Cockney accent impeccable.

"If you want a Guinness, it'll be pricier."

"Bring it, dearie."

Whilst waiting for our drinks, we surveyed the crowd gathered in the room under bulb-like lights. Most were working class, but a few were gentleman drifters who were surrounded by Unfortunates offering their services. It was the patrons, with their top hats and elegant dress, which failed to draw our attention, for it was most unlikely the German agent would be amongst them.

The barkeep deposited our half-and-halfs before us and said, "That'll be ten pence."

After paying, I waited for the barkeep to move away, then asked in a low voice, "Should we be looking for an individual with Teutonic features?"

"I think not," Joanna replied quietly. "For if someone had those features, with even a hint of a German accent, he would be most unwelcome here or in any other pub in England."

"So you believe he will appear to be British?"

My wife nodded in agreement. "Think as he would, John. And keep in mind that blond hair can be dyed and sharp cheekbones softened by the placement of spectacles. It is the voice which betrays more often than not."

"And its harsh tone or Germanic inflection could slip out unintentionally."

"As it does on occasion," she concurred.

"How, then, will he attempt to explain it?"

"By letting it be known that he is a refugee from any of the occupied countries where a Germanic lilt might exist."

The customer sitting next to us, who smelled of kerosene, abruptly stood and staggered toward the door, bumping into others as he made his way out. In an instant his vacant stool was occupied by a young girl, barely out of her teens, with auburn hair and a freckled nose.

"Buy a poor lass a drink," she begged of us, eyeing our expensive half-and-halfs. "And perhaps I will consider being part of your evening."

"Move your arse along, or I shall do it for you," Joanna threatened.

"Just asking," the girl said defensively. "A three halfpenny worth of rum might change my luck."

"Slim pickings tonight, eh?"

"Slim pickings every night, what with the war and all," the waif bemoaned, then studied Joanna's face for a moment. "I think I remember you."

"Do you now?"

The thin girl nodded. "You were here some months back."

"That, I was," Joanna said, seeing an opening to take advantage of. "So you visit this pub quite a bit, then."

"I did on a regular basis until me and the barkeep broke apart."

"Showered you with free drinks, did he?"

"All night long for nearly a month."

"Well then, you might be able to help me find my chum, Martha Ann Miller, who I must see."

"And what is your need to meet up with Martha Ann?"

"I came to pay back a loan," Joanna said, then toughened her voice a bit. "And what business is that of yours?"

"Because that loan will have to remain unpaid, for dear Martha has passed on."

Joanna feigned a stunned expression. "Oh, no! What happened?"

The waif cleared her throat loudly, sensing Joanna's interest in the former barmaid. "My voice box seems to have gone dry."

Joanna waved the barkeep over. "A three halfpenny worth of rum for my friend."

"Annie is good at making new friends, aren't you, luv?" the barkeep remarked, with a humorless smile.

"Bugger off," Annie said without inflection, and when he returned with her drink, she gulped it down in a single swallow. "Now, where were we?"

"Martha Ann's passing," Joanna prompted.

"Ah, yes, the poor thing had an abortion that went wrong," she recounted. "And she died in real misery, or so I was told."

"Got it done here, did she?" Joanna whispered, glancing around the pub, as if wondering whether the abortion was set up by the pub's owner.

Annie shook her head and replied softly, "The rumor is that

it was done proper, but with a terrible result nevertheless. Of course, it could have been carried out here, though."

"Was the abortionist known to her?"

The freckled waif squinted her eyes at the question. "Why all this interest?"

"Because I am in need of the same service," my wife said, and unbuttoned her ragged sweater to reveal the bulge of an early pregnancy.

"Oh, my," said Annie, studying Joanna's abdomen. "Moving right along, aren't you, dearie?"

"Much faster than I would like, and I have been told that the earlier it was taken care of, the better."

"It is said to be quite chancy at your stage."

"But I have little choice."

"Then look elsewhere unless you wish to be covered with cold earth." Annie licked at her empty glass, removing the last drop of rum. "I could surely use another, for my throat has gone dry again."

Once the second drink was served, Joanna said, "I shall heed your warning and search elsewhere, but I am an honest girl and the unpaid debt to Martha Ann gnaws at my bones. Is there a relative to whom it could be paid?"

"How much are we speaking of?"

"Ten shillings, which was a lifesaver at the time it was loaned."

"I was the closest thing she had to family," Annie said, with an eye on the money.

"Not close enough," Joanna replied tersely. "But since you were her chum, would you be going to the funeral?"

"Ha!" the Unfortunate said derisively. "Her type goes to a potter's field, not some fancy funeral home." She paused to consider the matter further before adding, "But then again, her new, well-to-do boyfriend might have decided to give her a fond send-off."

"Was he that well off?"

"Must have been, for he set her up in a nice flat, bought her expensive clothes, and even gave her spending money," she went on. "And on top of that, she told me he was a handsome devil to boot."

"She was more than pretty enough to attract the handsome type," Joanna commented.

"She attracted all types," said Annie. "Her chum before the handsome one was a rough character whose looks were nothing special. He was a refugee of some sort."

"Was he the one with the accent?"

The Unfortunate nodded. "He was from Belgium, and got out before the Germans moved in. I didn't see much in him, but Martha Ann liked him."

"The refugee must have had some features that she was keen on," Joanna probed.

"Not that I ever saw," Annie replied. "He was short and stocky, and had brown hair that was slicked down with some sort of pomade. But she found him attractive despite the scar on his cheek."

"Scar, you say?"

"A bloody big one that ran across his cheek to his ear."

Joanna pondered the apparent disfigurement. "The scar must have been thin."

"It was, and straight as well, but it still stood out."

We had our man! thought I. The Unfortunate had described a dueling scar which was made by a saber-slash to the opponent's face. They were seen as a badge of honor in Germany.

"He might know if Martha Ann had any relatives in London," Joanna queried. "Is the refugee here tonight?"

"I have not seen him, but he will no doubt be in the pub tomorrow night," Annie replied. "At eight sharp, they'll be having a dart championship which carries a prize of five pounds. Freddie will be eager to take part, for he is an expert at throwing darts."

Joanna and I exchanged quick, knowing glances, for Freddie was close enough to the German name Friedreich, and thus the foreign agent would respond with ease to both.

The Unfortunates standing in the center of the room uttered sounds of glee when the door opened and a pair of gentleman drifters entered. The drifters tipped their top hats to the women who rushed over to offer their services. My jaw must have dropped, for Joanna immediately followed my line of gaze, as did Annie. The larger of the new arrivals was Thaddeus Rudd.

My wife covered our surprise by saying, "Very nicely attired are those two."

"And mean as could be, particularly the big one with the beard," the waif remarked.

"How so?" Joanna asked, signaling the barkeep to refill our informant's glass.

Annie swallowed the rum in a single gulp, and tongued the bottom of the glass for the remaining drops. "He likes to strike the girls whilst he is doing it."

"Does he cause damage?"

"Mainly bruises and blood spots, but on one occasion he broke the girl's rib, and paid dearly for it."

"Were the police called?"

"Never, for if called they would always side with the gentleman drifter."

"So then, how was the drifter made to pay for the damage he inflicted?"

"A guinea would do for the girls to put up with it."

"Did he ever take advantage of your services?"

"Only once, and that occurred after Martha Ann had dropped him off her list."

"They were a pair, then?" Joanna asked.

"Oh, they went 'round and 'round for a number of weeks."

"And she tolerated the beatings?"

Annie shrugged her answer. "Money is money, particularly during the slow times."

"I take it Martha Ann dropped him after the new, handsome chum entered her life?"

The waif nodded promptly. "She wouldn't even speak with him, which infuriated the old bastard."

"Did he threaten her?"

"In so many words, but then the barkeep stepped in and warned the bugger off," said Annie, now glaring at Rudd with obvious dislike. "Because they are big spenders that sort of behavior is put up with, but only to a point."

We waited for Rudd to turn his back to us as he struck up a conversation with a strikingly frail Unfortunate, then quickly prepared to take our leave.

"Well now, the hour is late and we must be on our way," Joanna announced, with a wide yawn.

"A parting drink for the poor lass?" the waif begged.

We gifted her with yet another, for she had been a font of information which could be put to good use.

As we made our way to the door, a barmaid carrying a tray loaded with tankards crossed our path and, with her head turned, collided into Joanna. The tray flew into the air and the drinks it was holding noisily crashed to the floor. Everyone, including the gentleman drifters, looked over to the disturbance, with most laughing at the apparent accident. But Rudd showed no merriment. His eyes seemed fixed on me in a cold stare.

I leaned down next to Joanna who, along with the barmaid, was returning the tankards to the metal tray. Whispering in my wife's ear, I said, "Rudd may have spotted us."

Joanna shook her head and whispered back, "I think not, for our disguises are far too clever."

"Yours perhaps, but not mine."

"Then cover yourself by giving the barmaid a hug and kiss, which will show that you are one of the regulars at this pub."

I quickly did so and handed her a handful of coins to make amends for the spilled drinks.

"You are a proper gentleman, you are," said the barmaid and kissed my cheek in return.

On reaching the door, I stole a glance over at Thaddeus Rudd. He was again speaking with the frail Unfortunate, apparently having lost interest in me.

"I think our disguises held up," I said sotto voce.

"Let us hope so, for it is best that Rudd be kept in the dark."

Once on the footpath, we hurried past the alleyway and ignored the detectives disguised as vagrants. The motor vehicle with Lestrade in the backseat drove by us ever so slowly and, after viewing us, disappeared into the dark night. A moment later a second vehicle came toward us and abruptly stopped, with its brakes squealing. I immediately shielded Joanna, but stepped aside when I recognized it was a taxi seeking a hire. I waved the vehicle on as my wife and I breathed sighs of relief. We hurried along our way, keeping a sharp eye out for the unexpected.

"Interesting night, eh?" Joanna asked as we approached the Whitechapel Underground Station.

"A thousand times more than you could possibly imagine," said I. "Allow me to begin by informing you that Thaddeus Rudd had shown great interest in the care of Martha Ann Miller at St. Bart's."

Joanna stopped in her tracks. "How so?"

"First, he was the attending surgeon who had operated on the barmaid once her blood pressure rose to a sustainable level. Moreover, he made the misdiagnosis of a ruptured appendix which caused the infected uterus to be left in place. Secondly, Rudd made numerous inquiries on Martha Ann Miller's autopsy, with considerable interest in the cause of infection and her death.

And finally, as you surmised, the abortion was cleanly performed, with no undue trauma, and a smooth, even curettage. It was obviously done by a skilled operator, even taking the puncture wound into account."

Joanna smiled mischievously and rubbed her hands together gleefully. "Would you be good enough to connect these three points for me?"

"Their interconnection is quite clear, and goes as follows. Thaddeus Rudd was infuriated over his lost love, then performs the abortion and purposefully punctures the uterus to cause illness and death as revenge for her leaving him."

Joanna's smile widened. "What an evil idea!"

"Do you disagree?"

"Not at all, for the very same thought crossed my mind."

"But how does Thaddeus Rudd fit into the disappearance of Prince Harry?"

"The question to be asked is not *how,* but rather *if.*"

I sighed regretfully. "Another puzzle which needs to be solved."

"Keep your eye on the prince, and the other players will come into view."

"In that regard, we have failed miserably in our effort to trap the German agent."

"Worry not, dear John, for we are about to be presented with an even better opportunity."

We dashed into the underground station to board the last train to Baker Street. A satisfied smile remained on Joanna's face.

CHAPTER NINETEEN

The Baker Street Irregulars

The following morning, just before noon, Miss Hudson briefly rapped on our door and allowed the Baker Street Irregulars to enter, which brought a smile to my father's face, for they reminded him of his exciting days with the long-dead Sherlock Holmes. There was a most interesting history behind the Irregulars which few were aware of. The Great Detective had somehow gathered up a gang of street urchins whom he employed to aid his causes. They consisted originally of a dozen or so members, who could go anywhere, see everything, and overhear anyone without being noticed. When put to the task, they had a remarkable success record. For their efforts, each was paid a shilling a day, with a guinea to whoever found the most prized clue. Since Holmes's death, most of the guttersnipes had become ill or drifted away, but their leader, Wiggins, remained and took in new recruits to replace those who had departed. At present, the entire group had dwindled down to three, which included Wiggins, Little Alfie, and Sarah The Gypsy.

"Got your message, I did, and came at my quickest," Wiggins

said in a deep Cockney accent. "That'll be two shillings for the ride over, if you please, ma'am."

Joanna handed him several coins and carefully inspected the trio, all of whom had on their best clothing, anticipating their assignment would be similar to the one given them some months ago.

"Your attire looks very good indeed," said she. "But unfortunately it is not appropriate for the mission ahead."

"We can change in a flash," Wiggins responded. "Tell us what you have in mind, ma'am."

"I require an individual to be followed."

"Easily done."

"From a pub in Whitechapel late at night."

"And the name of the pub?"

"It is called The Rose and Lamb."

Wiggins hesitated, giving the matter more consideration. In his mid-twenties, he was tall and thin, with hollow cheeks and dark eyes that continually danced around at his surroundings. "What hour are you speaking of?"

"After ten, in all likelihood."

"That might present problems."

"How so?"

"We will be dealing with deserted streets which have only unlighted lampposts, and the fog lately has been a real pea-souper."

"Five pounds says it can be done."

"Oh, I am certain it can," Wiggins said at once. "But I will need the particulars, starting with his transportation. If he arrives and leaves by motor vehicle, I shall have to make arrangements to have my good friend Georgie borrow a taxi from the garage where he serves as a security guard."

Joanna shook her head. "I do not believe he would use a

motor vehicle, for it would draw too much attention from the people in the pub. He is supposedly a refugee from Belgium, who managed to escape before the Huns took over his country. Anyone other than the gentleman drifters, who always arrive by automobile or carriage, would arouse suspicion."

"Good, good," Wiggins approved. "If he is a local, he will walk; if a visitor, he will probably take the tube."

Little Alfie stepped forward and nodded at the leader. "The Whitechapel Underground Station is only a few blocks away from The Rose and Lamb, which would be most convenient for him."

"But it provides an interchange for both the Hammersmith and District lines, as well as the London Overground," recalled Joanna, who, like her father, had extensive knowledge of the city's underground stations and the lines they served. "If he travels by tube, you will have difficulty deciding which line he plans to take."

"Difficult indeed, ma'am, for if this chap is a clever dodger he will buy a return ticket on his arrival, just in case he is held up on his way back to the station," Wiggins opined. "If he does, we cannot hope to see him or hear him make the purchase."

"There is no need to know beforehand which return ticket he buys," said Little Alfie, who despite his youthful appearance was easily the smartest of the lot. At fifteen years of age he seemed years younger, with his unkempt brown hair and short stature. Yet, from our past experience, I learned he never spoke until he had a solution to the problem. As if on cue, he added, "The way around this dilemma is to purchase tickets for all the lines, so if he returns to the underground station, we simply follow him aboard the train and depart when he does. Of course it will be a bit more expensive, but the extra tickets will allow us to never lose track of him."

"We shall be obliged to include that cost in our final charges," Wiggins reminded us.

The Wayward Prince

The Wayward Prince 165

Joanna nodded her agreement before asking, "Should he take a given line, which of you will follow?"

"Sarah The Gypsy, for she poses no threat at all," Little Alfie replied. "Girls tend to be ignored, particularly those who appear to be crippled."

Sarah smiled ever so briefly at the description, for the dark-complected, young teenager had performed convincingly with a feigned limp in one of our earlier cases. She might draw a glance from the target, but he would quickly look away and pay her no further attention. "I will keep my distance from him, whilst watching his every move from his reflection in the glass window."

"All well and good if he takes the tube," Joanna said. "But I suspect he resides in the neighborhood, for he visits The Rose and Lamb so frequently that he is known to the regulars at the pub. And on a number of occasions he departs in the company of an Unfortunate. Furthermore, he is the type who does not wish to be noticed."

"Secretive sort, eh?" Wiggins inquired.

"Quite, so he will not let a flat where neighbors would take note or might even approach him in conversation," my wife went on. "He would feel most at ease in the second-class hotels, from where he could move from one to the other without drawing attention."

"There are a goodly number of those in Whitechapel," Wiggins remarked.

"Do not concern yourself with the level of a doss-house where only the poorest would sleep," Joanna advised. "His stay will be at a medium-sized hotel which is comfortable, inexpensive, and off the main thoroughfare."

Little Alfie cleared his throat. "This secretive bloke, will he be armed?"

"In all likelihood," Joanna answered. "And please keep in mind that he is as mean as a snake and twice as deadly."

"Have you actually witnessed such behavior?" Wiggins asked, showing the first sign of concern.

"We have indeed," Joanna replied, with some gravity. "We came upon the body of a young woman who died miserably whilst he calmly smoked cigarettes and watched her to the very end."

"Is he thought to carry a knife or pistol?"

"I suspect a pistol."

"Then we shall be double cautious."

"That would be the wise move," said she. "Now, I take it you are familiar with The Rose and Lamb?"

"I know it well."

"And you are aware of its dartboard?"

"It is off to the side near the window."

"Well then, that is where your attention should be tonight, for that is when a dart championship is scheduled to occur."

"It begins promptly at eight."

Joanna gave Wiggins a sharp look. "Are you planning on participating?"

"No, ma'am, but I know of it because I saw posters advertising the match."

"Very good," Joanna continued on. "You are to sit at the bar and sip rum whilst watching the match. Your target is a short, heavyset chap who has a noticeable scar across his cheek."

"I know him, ma'am."

Joanna's eyes suddenly widened. "How so?"

"I, too, fancy a game or two at The Rose and Lamb, although I am not nearly as sharp as the Belgian."

"Are you on speaking terms?"

"Not at all, ma'am. It is only that I have watched him play, and he no doubt has seen me at the dartboard as well."

"So you are saying he would recognize you."

"In all likelihood."

Joanna's brow went up at the sudden disclosure of Wiggins's closeness to the Hun. "That presents a problem, for he is a very clever fellow and would be alert to even a hint that he is being followed."

"It can be done, ma'am, even in plain view of this clever bloke."

"How so, pray tell?"

"I shall view the championship match from a position of four rows back, drink in hand and cheering on the players. At the conclusion of the match, whilst the prize is being presented, I shall refill my glass and wait for the mark to make his exit. At that very moment, I will wander to the loo, passing a small window which faces an alleyway. I will then pause briefly to light a cigarette, which is the signal that the Belgian is on the move. If he travels toward the tube station, Little Alfie will follow; if in the opposite direction, Sarah The Gypsy will watch his every step. Once the bloke's trail is established, both of my mates will stick to him, changing positions every so often, which will confuse the cleverest of marks."

Joanna gave the plan considerable thought before asking, "From your place well back from the contestants, how will you keep a close eye on the target? As I recall, the lighting is poor in that area of the pub."

"No problem there, ma'am, for he has a most unusual tossing motion," said Wiggins, and gave a demonstration. "He brings the dart up and behind his right ear just prior to throwing it."

"Right-handed, is he?"

"That is his dominant side for sure, ma'am."

"A well-thought-out plan," Joanna approved, and turned to Little Alfie and Sarah The Gypsy. "You must be most careful, for this man is trained to survey his surroundings and detect anyone following him. Let me assure you that he can match your very best moves."

"Not to worry, ma'am," Little Alfie said, unconcerned. "Sarah has a sixth sense that tells her that she is being watched."

"I get an itch when it occurs," Sarah The Gypsy remarked, with a casual shrug. "It has never failed me."

"I think it best you do not exaggerate your limp, for he may interpret it as being feigned," Joanna cautioned.

"It is not so much the limp, but the pain on my face with each step that catches their eye." The thin waif paused to scratch absently at her armpit. "I am quite good at this, ma'am."

"Be at the top of your game, then," said my wife as Big Ben struck the noon hour. "Are there further questions before you leave?"

Wiggins cleared his throat noisily. "Perhaps we should discuss fees, ma'am."

"Ten shillings each for watching the pub and following the target," Joanna replied. "An additional pound if you can track him to his residence, and a fiver if he enters a hotel and you can pinpoint his room number."

"Have your purse ready, ma'am."

Greed was written all over their faces as they hurried out to begin their quest.

Once the door closed, my father arose from his overstuffed chair and walked about, without the slightest of limps, which indicated his knee was much improved. But there was obvious worry in his voice.

"I fear you are exposing them to extraordinary risk," said he. "If they are detected, the brutal Hun would slit their throats without a moment's hesitation."

"Even if he discovers his trackers, he will not kill them, but rather report back to Moriarty," Joanna predicted.

"To what end?"

"So that Moriarty will know we are reacting to his moves, just as he planned we would."

My father's brow went up in surprise. "Do you truly believe that Moriarty wanted us to track the German?"

"Of course, for he is performing like a chess master, making moves that entice us to follow," Joanna elucidated. "Again, my dear Watson, be good enough to consider all the pieces of this remarkable puzzle. He placed the German at the site of the abduction of Prince Harry, and left clues behind to show that the Hun was involved. He knew of the prince's impregnation of the barmaid Martha Ann Miller, who happened to work at the pub which the foreign agent frequented. Then he entangled us in the tragic and botched abortion which caused the barmaid's death, and once more displayed clues for us to find her flat. Do you think all of this occurred by chance?"

"It would certainly seem not," my father replied.

"And then he set the stage for us to come to The Rose and Lamb in our search for the German."

"But the Hun will lead us to his residence."

"From which he may well be gone by morning, long before the Irregulars report back to us."

"But why then send them back to track Moriarty's agent?"

"Because I, too, know how to play chess," said Joanna and, upon hearing a rap on the door, opened it for Miss Hudson carrying in a most sumptuous lunch.

CHAPTER TWENTY

The Rehearsal

At four o'clock that afternoon, 221b Baker Street had been turned into a temporary fortress by Scotland Yard, with constables guarding both the front and tradesman entrances and armed detectives seated in motor vehicles parked directly across from our rooms. The adjacent alleyway was closed off to all visitors, with yet another constable stationed nearby to move along any curious passersby. All of these precautions were part and parcel of a practice run, which had to be completed to the commissioner's satisfaction. Once done so, Scotland Yard would vacate the premises, only to return the following morning to deliver the Sovereign Orb, then stand down upon our departure for the National Gallery.

The rehearsal for the exchange was now underway, with me being positioned an arm's length next to Joanna, whilst my father was farther away, standing behind our workbench, his hand on his holstered Webley revolver.

The commissioner reached for a lidded white box that was bound by a bright red ribbon and passed it over to Joanna. Inside the box was a block of wood to give it the approximate weight of the jeweled orb.

"You should hold the package tightly by your side and not display it until you approach da Vinci's *The Virgin of the Rocks*," he instructed. "It is essential that you keep both hands on the box, in the event they foolishly attempt a grab and run."

"I have considered that move," said Joanna. "Accordingly, I plan to place my wrist between the box and the lower part of the ribbon. This placement will cause the thief to extend his arm as he takes hold of the prize, which will allow me to perform the lock-and-break maneuver. Should this occur, he will never use his elbow again."

"Show me," Sir Charles insisted.

My wife held the white box out and permitted the commissioner to grab for it. She drew the package back, which extended his arm, and quickly applied the lock-and-break move of jujitsu.

"Ow!" he cried out, hurriedly withdrawing his arm and rubbing his elbow. "That was most painful."

"But I doubt he will come at us in that manner," she informed. "You must remember that Moriarty is very clever and no doubt has read of my adventures, in which there are several descriptions of my talents in jujitsu."

"A black belt, no less," I added.

Joanna nodded at her qualification. "Of which he is aware, and thus will appear to avoid my reach. But this prize is irresistible, so he no doubt will devise countersteps to thwart the more common jujitsu moves."

"It sounds as if you expect him to engage you directly," Sir Charles surmised.

My wife waved away the notion. "The Moriartys do not perform in that fashion. They much prefer to use their brains, and employ the brawn of others to achieve their ends."

"Who will come after you, then?"

"The one we least expect."

"Surely, not a thug."

"Too easily recognized."

"You obviously believe that Moriarty will not live up to his side of the bargain."

"That lot never does."

There was a quick rap on the door, and Roger Mallsby was escorted in by a young detective.

"We have been looking for you," Joanna said tersely.

"I was sent to Windsor on royal business," Mallsby stated in an uneven voice as beads of perspiration appeared on his brow.

"Was it more important than the life of Prince Harry?"

The private secretary gestured with his hands, for he had no answer.

"I have two questions for you," Joanna went on. "First, I need to know the name of the prince's favorite pet."

"He has no pets, madam."

"None in the past?"

"None during my stay."

"He does seem to enjoy horses, nonetheless."

"Very much so."

"Did he attend the races at Ascot last year?"

"He did."

"Did he place a wager?"

Mallsby nodded. "On Magic Circle who came in third."

"Very good," said my wife. "Now for the second question, and allow me to remind you that a false statement will go harshly for you and could bring a charge of obstruction of justice by Scotland Yard. Are we clear on this point?"

"Yes, madam."

"The question can be answered with a simple yes or no," Joanna prompted, giving the private secretary a lengthy stare. "Did you arrange for the abortion on Martha Ann Miller?"

Mallsby hesitated before speaking, as if searching for a way to avoid the answer, but not finding one. His eyelids began to flutter, which was a sure sign, according to my wife, that a falsehood was forthcoming.

"You are wasting time," she said, the tone of her voice sharper now. "Lie to us and the commissioner will see to it that you are marched out of here in handcuffs, with Buckingham Palace being notified of your arrest."

"I was instructed to do so by the prince," he said finally.

"I must know the steps you went through, beginning with how you planned the prince's abduction."

The heads of the investigative team spun around at the revelation that the private secretary was intimately involved in the disappearance of Prince Harry. To say we were caught by complete surprise would be an understatement. I immediately wondered if my dear wife had known this fact from the very beginning. And if so, what was the clue that led to her conclusion?

Mallsby was fumbling for words, no doubt again searching for a way to extricate himself from this sullied matter.

"Come, come," Joanna snapped. "You continue to waste time which we have precious little of."

"I was directed by the prince to speak with the barmaid and inquire if she knew someone who could perform this service, and she told me she did."

"Were you given a name?"

Mallsby shook his head, now staring at the floor. "Only that it was someone experienced who she would trust."

"Did she tell you where the abortion would be performed?"

"She did not."

"But she herself knew the place."

"That is what I believed."

"And Prince Harry, with your help, concocted his disappearance so he could be by her side whilst she underwent the procedure," Joanna concluded the story. "He would thus appear to have vanished on one of his occasional dalliances, and would return to the palace later in the day, with no one being the wiser."

"That was the manner in which it was planned."

"Until the plan went awry and he was in fact abducted."

"Had I even an inkling this was to occur, I would have strongly advised the prince against it," the private secretary pleaded his case.

"I am certain you would have."

Mallsby's lower lip quivered with anxiety. "Will I be charged?"

"Only with stupidity," said Joanna, and gestured his dismissal. Once the door closed, Sir Charles roared, "That brainless idiot set us off on a wild-goose chase!"

"Perhaps it was intended," Joanna proposed.

A quizzical look came to the commissioner's face. "Why in the world would he choose to do so?"

"On orders from Moriarty."

Sir Charles's jaw dropped. "Do you believe him to be a turncoat?"

"The thought has crossed my mind," said she. "Is it not interesting that Mallsby has been placed at every step of this most unpleasant business, from the abduction to Ah Sing's opium den to the abortion itself? Once again the pieces of the puzzle fall into position too easily. If the private secretary is involved, it would be a masterful plot that could only be conjured up by the cleverest of criminals."

"But we have no proof of Mallsby's guilt," the commissioner argued.

"We have no proof of his innocence either."

"Do you believe it worthwhile to have him tailed?"

"That would bear no fruit, for his end of the bargain is now done," Joanna replied. "But it would be of interest to look into his bank account for any recent large deposit."

Sir Charles nodded and appeared to make a mental note to carry out the suggestion. "But I suspect you may have given away too much when you inquired about the prince's wagers at Ascot. A look-alike could use that information to pass himself off as being the prince."

"That, too, came to my mind, which is why I will ask you to contact the royal family and learn the name of the first horse the prince rode as a child. His older brother Albert may be the best source of this information."

"It will be done promptly, and the name passed on to you," said the commissioner. "Now let us return to the rehearsal for the exchange itself, for any lapse on our part could prove disastrous. To begin with, whom do you believe Moriarty will choose as his intermediary?"

"The German," Joanna answered at once. "He of course is a very sly devil and, with that in mind, we must watch every step he takes as he approaches. I will only remove the ribbon and lift the lid when I can clearly see both of his hands. If he makes a sudden, untoward move, I will drop the box and fall upon it."

My wife turned to me and continued, "If necessary, shoot him with intent to kill, but only at point-blank range. Please keep in mind that an errant shot in a crowded gallery could cause great harm."

"I shall aim for the mid-chest, from which a fired round is most unlikely to exit," I responded.

"Excellent," said she, now looking to my father. "You, dear Watson, will have the best overall view of the entire situation. If a second intruder hurries past you and approaches the German's side, be prepared to intervene with a shot to the upper leg which, even if it goes through, will be slowed enough so as not to seriously endanger others."

"A round to the knee would be best," my father recommended. "It not only causes extreme pain, but the joint itself has very dense bone which would stop the bullet in midflight."

"Very well, then," Joanna approved. "Now, to the finale. Once the exchange has occurred to everyone's satisfaction, we shall exit the gallery, with the prince at my side. My husband will lead, whilst Watson covers the rear. A motor vehicle from Scotland Yard will appear shortly to carry us away."

"Let us pray there are no mishaps," my father beseeched.

There was a soft rap on the door and we wondered, to a person, if Roger Mallsby had returned to correct a misstatement. But it was Miss Hudson who appeared and announced warmly, "I have the pleasure of welcoming home Master Johnny Blalock."

The lad stepped into the parlor with an expressionless face and a firm stride. He seemed a head taller than on his last visit, and now surpassed his mother in height. He was wearing a black Inverness cape which protected him from the weather that had suddenly turned wet and even colder.

"My God!" Sir Charles gasped at the sight. "He has returned from the dead!"

The commissioner was old enough to remember Sherlock Holmes, for Sir Charles was a young detective when the Great Detective made his frequent appearances at various crime scenes. And now before him stood the grandson who bore a striking resemblance to his famous grandfather, with a handsome, narrow face and drooping eyelids. Even their lips were the same, they being perfectly contoured and pasted together in a sphinxlike guise.

"I can assure you I am very much alive, and to the best of my knowledge never dead," said he, and hurried over to give his mother a tender embrace. Only then did he gaze upon the commissioner to study him briefly. "With the obvious presence of Scotland Yard, I fear I have come at an inopportune moment."

"You are always welcome, my good fellow," greeted my father who, along with me, rushed over to shake Johnny's hand.

"But pray tell what brings you back to Baker Street with Eton still in session?" Joanna inquired.

"A late spring break," he replied, and once again gazed for a moment at the commissioner who was easily recognizable from his frequent photograph in the newspapers. "I see you must be involved in a most difficult case."

"I am indeed," said Joanna. "Would you care to hear the details?"

"Most assuredly."

Both the commissioner and Inspector Lestrade nodded their approval, for they recalled young Johnny's quick mind from his brief involvement in several earlier cases.

"I am told you possess the brain of your esteemed grandfather," Sir Charles remarked.

"I have inherited in large measure my dear mother's brain matter which I believe to be every bit the equal of her father's," Johnny said without inflection. Upon removing his cape, he strode over to the fire and warmed his hands. "You may proceed, Mother, if you so wish."

"It is a three-pipe case," she noted, referring to Sherlock Holmes's description of a complex investigation which required three pipefuls of smoking to bring to resolution.

"Then allow me to light up the first pipeful," said he, reaching into a pocket of his jacket for a cherrywood pipe. "Do you have an adequate supply of your favorite Arcadia Mixture, Dr. Watson?"

"More than enough to share," my father replied, and handed the lad a nearly filled pouch of tobacco. "May I ask when you began enjoying a pipe?"

"Last year during my studies in advanced hieroglyphics," he replied. "For whatever reason, the nicotine seemed to accelerate the thought process."

"Not to overdo it, then."

"Only in case of real need," said Johnny as a brief smile came and went. "And now, Mother, the details, please."

Joanna described the investigation into the prince's disappearance point by point, paying particular attention to the individuals involved and the attempts on our lives. Even an account of the botched abortion, with its gruesome ending, was included.

"Someone with a very sharp mind is orchestrating every move you make," the lad concluded.

"I should tell you that I have good reason to believe we are up against the younger brother of the long-dead Professor Moriarty."

"The colonel, then, who I read about in one of grandfather's last adventures."

"It is he, and I fear he is seeking revenge for his brother's death."

"Is he as clever as the professor was reputed to be?"

"So it would appear."

"Then you must take extraordinary care, for revenge can be the strongest of motives."

"That is my plan."

Johnny bit down on his pipe and began pacing once more, his hands clasped behind him, his head down, as he concentrated on the danger his mother faced. He remained expressionless, for like his grandfather and mother before him, threats were simply a problem that needed to be solved. Of course the adversary had to be vanquished, but that was part of the solution.

The lad abruptly turned to us and asked, "Do you have any idea of his next move?"

"There will be an exchange for the prince tomorrow at the

National Gallery in front of da Vinci's *The Virgin of the Rocks*," Sir Charles answered.

"And what are you to give up?"

"The Sovereign Orb."

Johnny narrowed his heavily lidded eyes and gazed at length at the commissioner, whilst considering the royal ransom. "A tall order indeed."

"But one His Majesty readily agreed to."

"He no doubt had little choice," the lad remarked as he reached for a match to light his pipe. "At what hour will the exchange take place?"

"Noon."

"At which time Moriarty will attempt to deceive you."

"We are taking every precaution."

"I suspect it will not be good enough, for Moriarty will have every advantage," Johnny noted and, sending up a plume of smoke, resumed pacing. Back and forth he went, mumbling to himself much as his mother did whilst attempting to solve a difficult problem. Abruptly, he stopped and turned to her. "Why does Moriarty insist on a meeting at the National Gallery in front of *The Virgin of the Rocks*?"

"Because at noon the area surrounding the painting will be crowded with visitors, any of whom could be used as a shield or impediment," Joanna replied.

Johnny shook his head at the answer. "I am afraid there is more to it than that, Mother. I can recite a dozen displays in London around which visitors would flock at noon. For example, the Rosetta stone at the British Museum or equally famous items at the Victoria and Albert. Moreover, there is no guarantee that a mass of humanity will descend on *The Virgin of the Rocks* at noon."

"But there is a high degree of probability that will occur," Sir Charles challenged.

"With all due respect, sir, we are dealing with a criminal genius who will not rely on chance or probability, for too much is at stake," Johnny countered. "Moriarty has demanded the exchange take place precisely at noon in front of *The Virgin of the Rocks,* and not before a Raphael or Rembrandt. Which is essential to this mastermind's plan."

"Do you have any idea what it might be?"

"My best guess is that a player will be stationed close to the painting, someone who is unassuming and even expected to be present."

"But to what end?"

"To cause a distraction or disturbance."

Joanna chimed in quickly, "By lunging at the da Vinci with a knife or splashing it with dark ink, which would create utter chaos."

"And at that moment, the Sovereign Orb will be snatched from your grasp, with the thief disappearing into the chaos."

"Will the perpetrator be heavily disguised?" Sir Charles asked at once.

"That will not be required, sir," the lad said, pausing to relight his pipe. "It could be an art student studying the painting whilst taking notes or a woman pretending to be a tour guide. With that in mind, my mother and Dr. Watson will have to closely watch the movement of anyone close enough to do damage."

"We shall keep a careful eye," Joanna asserted.

"And you have undoubtedly considered the very real possibility they will try to deceive you with a false prince."

"We shall have a question available that only the prince can answer."

"Do not make it difficult, for Prince Harry is not the brightest of the royals."

Joanna's brow went up. "Are you familiar with him?"

"He is an Etonian, currently finishing postgraduate studies, but with little success, for he is not the best of students," Johnny replied. "He spends far more time away than at the college."

"On royal duties, I would think."

"To the contrary, Mother, he is a playboy and takes great pride in being so," the lad went on. "He has the looks of a matinee idol, with loads of money at his disposal, which makes him quite the lady's man."

"I trust he has demonstrated some degree of discretion in these activities," Joanna probed, obviously wondering if the prince ever spoke of his meetings with the barmaid.

"Again, to the contrary, he seemed to delight in boasting of his romantic conquests, one of which nearly cost him dearly."

"In what regard, might I ask?"

"It was his escape from one of his latest liaisons which he described so graphically," Johnny recounted. "Whilst bedding an unfaithful wife, her seagoing husband returned home unexpectedly. On hearing the front door open, our good prince—the third in line to the throne, mind you—flew out the bedroom window. He was last seen by a gardener scampering over the back fence, with his trousers at half-mast."

My wife and I exchanged knowing glances, for the escapade Johnny was describing to us no doubt involved Prince Harry and Lady Charlotte Spenser. But why take the risk of meeting in her home rather than a secret rendezvous?

"It sounds as if he was somewhat of a daredevil," Joanna said, breaking the silence.

"Quite so, particularly in sports such as football, where he continually took unwarranted chances."

"Did he excel at football?"

"To a remarkable degree."

"Was he quite powerful, then?"

The lad waved away the notion. "It was his agility rather than his strength which saw him through. But misfortune struck last month when he suffered a badly sprained ankle during a rugged match, and so went his agility."

Joanna interrupted immediately. "Did he have a noticeable limp?"

"It was both obvious and painful."

"Was it the left or right ankle which he favored?"

Johnny thought for a moment before answering, "The right."

"And tell me again, when was the last time you saw the prince with his limp?"

"Nearly five weeks ago."

Joanna turned to my father. "Watson, how long is required for a moderate sprain to heal?"

"Three weeks or so, and a bit longer for a more severe sprain," my father estimated.

"Not long enough," Joanna said unhappily. "A persistent limp would be helpful in making a positive identification of the prince."

"Perhaps the painful ankle has not healed as of yet," Sir Charles wondered aloud.

"The evidence states otherwise," my father contended. "You will recall that the prince went riding on the day of his abduction. Placing a sprained foot in a stirrup would surely aggravate the pain."

"Well thought out, Watson," my wife praised the important deduction. "Let us hope that the prince's answer to a hidden fact will suffice in securing his identification."

"It should," said Sir Charles, reaching for his derby on the coatrack.

"But, sir, even with a positive identification, do you have a plan to rescue the prince in the event the exchange fails?" Johnny asked.

"Unfortunately, we do not," Sir Charles admitted as he adjusted the brim on his derby. "But then again, we have a prince who is agile and prefers to take chances, which might work in our favor."

"Perhaps," Joanna agreed mildly. "But in all likelihood, Sir Charles, it will be our wits and not his qualities which will win the day."

"We shall see," said the commissioner, and departed with Inspector Lestrade by his side.

Once the door closed, Johnny gathered the three of us nearer and said, "Mother, there are several additional features that the prince possesses which concerns you and the Watsons, and not Scotland Yard."

"And those are?"

"He can be quite brave when you least expect it."

"How so?"

"I once saw him stand up against a rugby player of considerable size who was taunting a rather frail, stuttering student. When the bully persisted, the prince delivered a swift kick to an area which made it most uncomfortable for the offender to sit. Harry has a history of coming to the defense of others, particularly those who cannot defend themselves."

"Good show," my father approved.

Returning to his mother, Johnny said, "Nevertheless, there is another, less desirable habit which the prince also possesses."

"And that is?"

"Prince Harry tends to act on a whim, and such a move could place the three of you in real danger."

"Would he be so foolish as to do so?"

"As I stated earlier, he is not the brightest of the royals."

Chapter Twenty-One

The Track of the German

It had been a long and tiring day, but it was not yet about to end. After seeing a fatigued Johnny off to bed, we were seated in our overstuffed chairs before glowing coals which gave comfort against the wind howling outside. The windowpanes that had been shattered by the explosion days earlier had yet to be repaired and allowed gusts of the wind in, which caused the curtains to billow. Because of the necessary blackout, all lamps and the chandelier were switched off so that no light might escape from the edges of the curtains. The dimness in the parlor seemed to increase the heaviness of our eyelids and, on finishing our brandies, we prepared to retire. At that moment, as Big Ben was striking the eleven o'clock hour, there was a rap on our door and Miss Hudson entered with sleep still in her eyes. She was attired in a dressing gown and obviously ruffled at having been awakened.

"I am so sorry to bother you at this late hour, but the leader of the Irregulars demands to see you," said she. "I tried to convince him to return at a more civilized hour, but he stated his visit was most urgent."

"Please see him up, Miss Hudson," my father requested in a

gentle voice. "And do accept our apologies for this intrusion into your otherwise pleasant evening."

"I do indeed, Dr. Watson, but you really should set limits for the hours in which visits will be allowed."

The moment the door closed, we hurriedly arose from our overstuffed chairs in a state of excitement and anticipation.

"They have tracked down the Hun!" my father gushed.

"And just in the nick of time!" I added, and looked at my wife whose face remained expressionless. "Are you not enthused at this most welcome development?"

"Why is Wiggins here by himself?" Joanna thought aloud. "When the Irregulars complete their task, they always return en masse to collect their fee."

"Perhaps they are continuing to track him," my father suggested.

"If they are in the process, why the urgent, late visit?" she asked.

"Something must have gone amiss."

"Obviously."

"Do you believe Little Alfie and Sarah The Gypsy may have been discovered?"

"Unlikely."

"Then what?"

"I suspect they have been stymied."

The door opened and Wiggins was shown in. He nodded his appreciation to Miss Hudson, who closed the door with a bit of force to show her displeasure.

"Pray tell, Wiggins, what brings you back at this ungodly hour?" asked Joanna.

"A dilemma, ma'am, in which you must decide the course we are to take next," he replied.

"And what is this dilemma?"

"I shall start at the beginning, so you can see the difficulty we faced."

"I trust the opening act is the end of the dart match at The Rose and Lamb."

"It is, ma'am, for at that point all was moving along as planned," Wiggins recounted. "He was a bloody good thrower and easily won the local championship. Like you instructed, I remained concealed in the crowd until he received his award and reached for his topcoat. On his departure, I lighted a cigarette in the side window which signaled Little Alfie and Sarah The Gypsy that the target was about to exit. I then moved back to the bar and waited whilst Little Alfie and Sarah picked up the track. He did not go to the underground station, ma'am, but continued down Durward sly as can be, with multiple changes in direction."

"Had he detected the trackers?"

"Not according to Sarah The Gypsy who did not develop an itch, which is a certain tell she is being watched."

My father sighed loudly and said, "Not the most reliable of indicators."

"It works well for us, sir, and has never failed her or Little Alfie on countless occasions," Wiggins responded. "Moreover, his movements were not those of a man aware that he was being shadowed. In any event, the track continued until the bloke circled the same block twice, then entered a seedy hotel which we were familiar with. Little Alfie remembered your instructions that the target would choose a second-class hotel, not one that was only a notch above a doss-house. And his instincts were dead-on. Little Alfie dashed to the rear of the hotel just in time to see the foreigner exit and board a taxi which drove away into a thick fog."

"Where does this dilemma you speak of begin?" my father asked impatiently. "The taxi has disappeared, and the chase is over."

"Not quite yet, sir," Wiggins continued on. "For Little Alfie has keen eyesight in addition to his keen brain, and was able to see and remember the license plate on the taxi. He hurried back to The Lamb and Rose and we quickly made our way to the garage where the taxis were housed. Once there, we bribed the security guard to allow us to remain until the taxi driver returned his motor vehicle to the garage for the evening. He recalled that he had had two late-night passengers before retiring. One he dropped off at the Metropole Hotel, the other at the Aldgate."

"Did he recall if either of the final passengers had a facial scar?" Joanna asked at once.

"He did not, ma'am, for his taxi is not well lighted," Wiggins replied. "Our next move was to station Sarah at the Metropole and Little Alfie at the Aldgate in an effort to determine which hotel the foreigner is currently residing."

"Have you considered bribing the doorman or night porter for this information?" I queried.

"This type of hotel does not have a doorman, sir, and questioning a porter carries a real risk," he answered. "And that brings us to the dilemma we are facing."

Joanna lighted a cigarette and began pacing the floor as she placed the final pieces of the puzzle together. "You are worried that if you were to seek such information from a night porter with a bribe, he will estimate its value and attempt to sell your inquiry to the foreigner who would pay him an additional fee."

The leader of the Irregulars nodded firmly. "That is how the game is played in Whitechapel, ma'am, and it is commonly known as double dipping."

"And as a result the target would disappear in a flash."

"Most certainly, ma'am."

Joanna drew deeply on her cigarette, and did so once again before speaking. "You are correct in your assessment that making inquiries to the hotel staff carries too great a risk. Rather then, you are to keep Little Alfie and Sarah The Gypsy stationed at their current posts with a keen eye out, and report back to us as soon as you discover which hotel the foreigner is staying at. I am afraid you will have to depend on a visual sighting."

"Very good, ma'am."

"And there is an extra fiver if you can learn which room he occupies at that hotel."

"We shall do our best, ma'am."

"Be off, then."

Once Wiggins had departed, my father asked the very same question which was on my mind. "Do you think it unwise to alert Scotland Yard of these new findings?"

"I fear that they would bumble it, for their first impulse would be to surround the hotel, and locate the Hun's room number via the registration desk," Joanna responded. "They would then devise a plan to suddenly invade that room and capture the foreign agent before he could swallow his concealed cyanide capsule."

"Not an altogether bad plan," I suggested.

"But one which would defeat our purpose," said she. "The German would in all likelihood offer no worthwhile information."

"Perhaps a trip to the gallows would persuade him otherwise."

Joanna shook her head at the idea. "His type would rather die than incur the displeasure of the Kaiser."

"So we just wait whilst the prince's life may well hang in the balance."

"That is the smart move, for a dead or captured Hun would be of little use to us," she elucidated. "We need him alive and unaware he is being followed, for only then will he lead us to Prince Harry."

"Is it not a gamble?" my father warned. "And a daring one at that."

"But we must take it if we are to return the prince to Buckingham Palace alive and well."

"You do realize that the commissioner will be most upset that you chose not to share this information with Scotland Yard."

"At the moment, I am not concerned with the commissioner's mood, but rather with rescuing Prince Harry from the grip of the evilest man in all London."

"Have you considered the very real possibility that Moriarty knows we will track the Hun, which again is part of his overall plan?"

"Of course," Joanna acknowledged. "We must take that into account, for he is a master schemer who has managed to stay one step ahead of us, and no doubt will continue to do so."

"How, then, do you hope to outwit him?"

"With a sleight of hand," said she and, lighting another cigarette from the end of the one she was currently smoking, began to again pace the floor, which she would do for the entire night through, all the while searching for a flaw in the devilish scheme being orchestrated by the new Napoleon of crime.

CHAPTER TWENTY-TWO

The Final Rehearsal

I was in the process of repairing the shattered window in our parlor when Joanna returned from her reconnaissance mission to the National Gallery. She was carrying an armful of the day's newspapers, indicating her journey to the gallery was quickly done and in all likelihood unproductive.

"No luck, then?" I queried.

"None whatsoever, for everything seems to be in Moriarty's favor," said she and, after depositing the newspapers on a chair, strolled over to inspect my workmanship. "What so occupies my dear husband?"

"He is replacing our badly damaged windows."

"Do you fancy yourself a glazier?"

"Hardly, but with all the handymen in London working night and day on London's badly damaged homes, Miss Hudson believes it will be weeks before one is freed up. Thus I thought it worthwhile to give it a try."

"If only for its entertainment value," she jested with a smile and leaned in to peck my cheek.

"Have you no confidence in your talented husband?" I retorted, and attempted to place a new pane in the vacant space. It was a poor fit and did not hold long enough for me to apply the melted putty. I attempted it once again but with the same result, which brought forth a good-natured chuckle from my wife.

"I fear my husband is a far better pathologist than glazier," said Joanna, and reached for the cardboard cutout which had previously occupied the vacant window space. "We should glue the patch back in place and keep out the cold night air."

"Ah, my dear wife to the rescue," I praised with a loving wink, and watched her perform the replacement with ease. "I wish the rescue of Prince Harry was so simple."

"That is not to be," said she. "For it is even more complex than I anticipated."

"How so?"

Just as she was about to respond, the door to our parlor opened and my father hurried in, his attire damp with the day's constant drizzle. He shook the wetness from his derby before sauntering over to view my failed workmanship.

"What have you two been conjuring up in my absence?" asked he.

"Your son has been demonstrating the art of glazing," Joanna said, with a playful nudge to my side.

"From the look of things, I would say his efforts have been less than impressive," my father commented. "I am afraid that, like most forms of manual labor, those of a glazier appear to be easily done, whilst it is the opposite which is true."

"Which I have learned the hard way," I admitted. "Nevertheless, I shall save my unused materials for the glazier Miss Hudson summons."

"And that, my son, will be far in the future, for half the windows in West London have been either cracked or shattered," said my father as he reached inside his vest for a program from the National Gallery. "I bought this on my way out, for it shows the most famous paintings and their positions in the gallery. We should give it close attention in that it will orient us to the various sections and to the nearest exits."

"Excellent, Watson," Joanna commended, and rapidly thumbed through the pages which included masterful paintings by Leonardo da Vinci, van Gogh, Titian, and Caravaggio. She paused briefly to admire the *Mond Crucifixion* by Raphael before returning to my father. "Now, I take it you watched my every move in the gallery at a suitable distance."

"I did and can assure you that none of Moriarty's men were in attendance," he replied. "But, as you surmised, Moriarty's plan is exceptionally well thought out. At noon, the gallery will be crowded with visitors, with the largest concentration gathered around the more famous of the works, such as da Vinci's *The Virgin of the Rocks*. Your adversary will for the most part be strolling by, with his motion blending in with the ebb and flow of the human tide, which provides excellent cover. And there are various exits to this particular section, which makes for a rapid escape."

"He knows how to set a plan," said Joanna, with a nod of admiration. "And I suspect there is a trap hidden within it."

"What sort of trap?" my father asked at once. "I hope not one which endangers you."

Before Joanna could answer, our attention went to the sudden activity on the street below. Motor vehicles came to screeching halts as uniformed officers rapidly cleared the footpaths.

"Here they are!" I called out, watching Scotland Yard arrive en masse. A dozen or more constables disembarked from a large van and hurried to their stations to secure all entrances, including the alleyway itself. A moment later several motor vehicles carrying armed detectives came to grinding stops directly across the street. Finally, a limousine appeared near our doorstep, and the commissioner and Inspector Lestrade emerged under the protection of two additional detectives. The inspector was holding a simple package under his arm.

"They are taking no chances," said Johnny, glancing over my shoulder.

"Nor will they, for they wish to avoid any blame should the Sovereign Orb go missing," my father opined.

"If it does vanish prior to the exchange, I can assure you that they, too, will be held responsible," Joanna remarked, and glanced at my father who was checking the rounds in two identical Webley revolvers. "Is all in order, Watson?"

"Quite so," he replied, and walked over to hand me one of the weapons. "Now remember, my son, if the need arises to fire, do not hesitate to do so, for your adversary will take advantage of your hesitancy."

"I am prepared to fire on demand," said I resolutely.

"And I suggest you aim at the mid-chest area where the target will be largest," he advised. "The bullet will certainly pierce the sternum and do immense damage within the thorax itself. Moreover, the spine will prevent its posterior exit and thus prevent the wounding of any innocent bystander."

"Understood, Father."

"But you, Watson, will not have the advantage of a close-range shot," Joanna noted. "In all likelihood there will be some distance between you and the suddenly appearing assailant."

"I shall move for a clear shot as soon as the individual makes himself known."

"And how will you identify him?"

"You, my dear Joanna, will send me a signal, for you have very keen eyes when it comes to unexpected intruders."

"I shall feign a cough, with my little finger pointing."

"We are at the ready, then."

With a nod, I firmly clutched the grip of my Webley, which

felt quite comfortable as it always did when I visited the practice range with my father. My marksmanship did not begin to
approach his, but it was certainly good enough to fire a round
through an assailant's sternum at point-blank range.

After a brief rap on the door, the commissioner and Inspector
Lestrade entered, with a young detective closing the door and
standing guard in the hallway.

"Good morning to all," said Sir Charles and, without waiting
for a reply, took the plain package from the inspector and placed
it on our workbench. With care he opened it and then signaled
for us to gather around. Our collective eyes focused on a black
velvet wrapping which Sir Charles untied to reveal the most precious of the Crown's jewels. He held it up to the light and solemnly uttered, "Behold!"

"Magnificent!" Johnny declared, transfixed as we all were by
its stunning beauty and elegance.

The Sovereign Orb was a hollow gold sphere, the size of a
small melon, which was encircled with two intersecting bands of
emeralds, rubies, and sapphires, all surrounded by rose-cut diamonds. Atop it was a cross encrusted with sparkling diamonds
and perfectly placed pearls.

"This very special orb has been held in the left hand of every
monarch at their coronation since the reign of Charles the Second," the commissioner informed us. "And now we have the
dishonor of passing it on to the worst of scoundrels."

"We have no choice," said Joanna.

"That does not make it less distasteful," Sir Charles stated
unhappily. "But now let us review the exchange itself, for there
must be no blunders. Thus, every step has to be carried out exactly as rehearsed. If there are any interruptions or intrusions,
the exchange has to be terminated immediately. Is that clearly
understood?"

We all nodded simultaneously.

"Good," the commissioner said, returning the Sovereign Orb to its black velvet covering. "Once the orb is encased in its velvet wrapping and placed in the white box, only its jeweled cross should be visible, for that will be its identifying marker."

"The intermediary will demand to see the entire orb," Joanna predicted.

"Which you will not allow until after Prince Harry is shown to be present and proven to be so by providing the name of the first horse he rode. It was a mare called Bluebonnet."

"Let us hope he remembers from such a long time ago," said she.

"He will, for as a young lad he actually composed a song that included the horse's name," Sir Charles assured, then continued on with the procedure for the exchange. "Once you are convinced our requirements have been met, you may permit their intermediary to view the orb in its entirety, but he must not touch or hold it in any way or fashion until Prince Harry is firmly in your grasp. Only when both sides are satisfied can the exchange take place. Now let us again review your exit, which I believe is the most vulnerable part of the plan and may well offer Moriarty the best opportunity to make his play. The Watsons should have their hands on their holstered revolvers at all times. As the departure begins, the younger Dr. Watson will position himself in front of his wife and the prince, whilst the senior Dr. Watson moves in to cover the rear. The group will then slowly exit via the front entrance of the gallery where a limousine will shortly be at your disposal."

The commissioner gazed around the parlor at length before asking, "Do you have the white box and red ribbon ready to receive the Sovereign Orb?"

"It remains tucked away in my bedroom, for we do have occasional visitors to our parlor, who might inquire as to its presence," Joanna replied.

"Very good," said Sir Charles. "From this moment on, you are to keep the Sovereign Orb within your sight at all times. It is not to be seen or spoken of except amongst the four of you."

"Of course."

The commissioner sighed haplessly. "And so begins this most unpleasant journey."

There was a loud rap on the door and a young detective looked in. "Sorry to interrupt, sir, but there is a chap named Wiggins downstairs who states he has urgent business with Mrs. Watson."

"He does indeed," Joanna said, quickly closing the package which held the Sovereign Orb. "Please allow him up, but keep him in the hallway well away from the door until instructed otherwise by the commissioner."

"Yes, ma'am," the young detective replied and passed on the directions.

The arrival of the leader of the Irregulars occurred at a most inopportune moment, for it placed us in the uncomfortable position of explaining to the commissioner why we had not informed him that we had located and were in the process of tracking the single most important lead to the whereabouts of Prince Harry.

Joanna decided to deal with the matter in a straightforward manner and thus avoid any confrontation with Scotland Yard whose assistance was vitally needed at the moment.

"Wiggins is the leader of the Baker Street Irregulars who I have mentioned to you in the past, Commissioner," said she, then requested that Lestrade delay Wiggins's entrance into the parlor, which he promptly did. "We were informed of the German's whereabouts late last evening and instructed the Irregulars to track him to his abode. We considered notifying Scotland Yard of this development, but thought it best to wait until we had a definite location for the Hun."

"We could have assisted," Sir Charles responded, with a bite to his tone. "Scotland Yard has detectives who are quite good at tracking foreign agents."

"But not good enough," Joanna said candidly. "For if your detectives were to suddenly appear in Whitechapel, even in disguise, they would be noticed by the locals who can spot unwelcome intruders a block away. Word would have spread and the German would have vanished into thin air. The Irregulars, by contrast, are street urchins who would draw little attention. And when it comes to tracking, I can assure you they are far more skilled than your detectives could ever hope to be. With all this in mind, we set loose the Irregulars at the latest hour, and they were shortly able to narrow down the Hun's destination to two hotels in Whitechapel. We were awaiting Wiggins's return to notify us in which hotel the foreign agent is staying before informing you. Let us hope Wiggins carries this information with him."

"Show him in," Sir Charles called out in a loud voice.

The door opened and Wiggins entered, taking slow, measured steps, whilst his eyes danced around at the unexpected visitors. He quickly removed his woolen cap as a sign of respect.

"Scotland Yard is here to share the information you bring with you," Joanna explained. "They have been told you were tracking the foreigner under our instructions, so you can rest assured that no laws have been broken. With this in mind, pray tell at which hotel the target is residing."

"The Aldgate, ma'am."

"No doubts?"

"None whatsoever."

"Do you have his room number?"

"Three twenty-seven, ma'am."

"And how did you come by this information?"

"It was Little Alfie's doing."

"The cleverest of the lot," Joanna said to inform the commissioner of the lad's talents.

"By far, ma'am."

"Proceed, then, providing us with every detail."

Wiggins cleared his throat, as if he were about to give a formal presentation. "As we discussed earlier, ma'am, we could not make inquiries of the porter or other hotel employees, for fear they might pass on the word to the foreigner in hopes of collecting an additional fee. Little Alfie, then, decided that the lower-level workers, particularly those who are employed part time, would be the best source to approach. So he came upon the lad who shined the guest's shoes."

"A good choice," Joanna said, nodding her approval. "The guests place their boots to be shined outside their doors before retiring for the night."

Wiggins nodded in return. "The foreigner was displeased with the quality of the shine and demanded the lad come back and apply more wax to the shoes. Once the job was done to the foreigner's satisfaction, he rewarded the shine-boy with a shilling. And that is when the lad noticed the scar across the man's cheek."

"Can we be certain the boot polisher did not pass on the inquiry to the foreigner for an additional fee?" Joanna asked.

"He will not, ma'am, for it is in his best interest to remain on the quiet," Wiggins replied.

"A rather stern threat, then, eh?" Lestrade surmised.

"No, sir," the leader of the Irregulars responded promptly. "The street lads are not bothered by threats which come their way on a daily basis. It was best to use money to seal his lips."

"With an explanation, I would hope," said Joanna.

"Of course, ma'am," Wiggins went on. "He was told the foreigner was suspected of being unfaithful to his wife, and was being tailed by Little Alfie who was receiving a fee from a private investigator. If the tail was completed without the foreigner being aware, the boot polisher would be rewarded with a half crown. He will surely stay silent as a rock, for in Whitechapel money speaks far louder than threats."

"I take it the foreigner has remained in his hotel thus far today?" Joanna inquired.

"He has, with Little Alfie stationed at the front of the Aldgate, and Sarah The Gypsy covering the rear and tradesman entrances," Wiggins answered. "Is it your wish they stay put?"

"It is," Joanna replied, and turned to the commissioner. "The next move is yours, Sir Charles."

"We must be very careful here, for if the Hun has even a hint he is about to be taken prisoner, he will swallow a cyanide capsule, and we will lose the best lead we have," said he.

"Precisely so, Commissioner," Joanna agreed and quickly glanced at her timepiece. "It is half eleven and he may yet leave his hotel to meet up with Moriarty's lot."

"Then he should be followed."

Joanna nodded at the directive. "By both the Irregulars and Scotland Yard, each of whom are to remain in deep cover. Here is what I propose, with your approval, Sir Charles. The Irregulars are to stay in place, with Wiggins disguised as a street sweeper just across the way from the hotel. On receiving a signal from Little Alfie or Sarah that the foreigner is departing, Wiggins will accidentally drop his sweeper which is a sign to the detectives in a taxi nearby that the target is on the move. The Irregulars will follow him if he travels on foot; the detectives will do so if he goes by taxi."

The commissioner considered the proposal at length before speaking. "It will be a gift if the Hun leads us to Moriarty."

"Which is most unlikely, for time is passing and the German must go directly to a meeting where he will set up all the pieces for the exchange."

"What pieces are you referring to, may I ask?"

"Those which will allow Moriarty to gain possession of the orb without releasing the captive."

"Is he truly that clever?"

"And some."

"Do you have any idea how this will occur?"

"Only that it will incur violence, for Moriarty knows that both Watsons will be armed and he will take that into account."

Sir Charles exhaled uneasily. "There are risks all around which makes this venture most chancy, with our adversaries obviously having the advantage."

"But we must proceed, for it may well represent our best and only opportunity to free the prisoner."

"I have a bad feeling here."

"As do I, but we have little choice."

"Then let us pray the exchange takes place without incident."

"And without harm to the captive."

"That foremost," said Sir Charles and departed with Lestrade at his side.

Once the door closed, Joanna quickly turned to Wiggins. "You are to follow my directions to the letter, with one exception. When the foreigner exits the hotel and enters a taxi, have Little Alfie and Sarah wait thirty seconds before signaling you. Only then are you to drop your sweeper."

"But, ma'am, that will allow him too much of a head start," Wiggins protested. "The coppers will never catch up with him."

"So it would seem," Joanna said without inflection. "Simply do as instructed, then be on your way."

"Thirty seconds, eh?"

"Thirty seconds," my wife repeated and walked over to her purse, from which she extracted a ten-pound note that she handed to the leader of the Irregulars. "This should cover all of your expenses, including the fiver for discovering the foreigner's room."

"Indeed it will, ma'am."

"Then, be off."

Upon Wiggins's departure, my father quickly turned to Joanna. "Why not allow Scotland Yard to follow the Hun if they are instructed to keep their distance? The trackers could switch positions intermittently, much as the Irregulars do."

"Too risky," she replied. "The clever Hun in all likelihood will become aware that he is being followed, and so inform Moriarty."

"Will he then shy away from the exchange?"

"Of course he would, for now the German is compromised and the entire plan falls apart," said Joanna. "Which makes for a very dangerous situation."

"And we could end up with a dead prince," my father noted grimly.

"Which serves neither Moriarty's nor our cause."

"So it would seem best we continue on as planned, knowing full well we are walking into a trap."

"Thus it would seem."

"Perhaps the violence you have been speaking of will not occur," I said, hoping against hope.

"Oh, it will occur, my dear John, and be applied just prior to the exchange taking place, for that is the opportune time to act," Joanna responded. "That is when you must be ready to quickly draw your revolver."

"Pray tell, how are you able to predict this sequence of events with such certainty?" said I.

"Simply put, these are the moves I would make were I in Moriarty's stead."

"Perhaps we should reschedule the exchange to a less dangerous setting," I suggested worriedly.

"Why delay the inevitable, knowing that the danger will not subside?" asked she, reaching for the velvet-covered orb. "I shall now retire to my bedroom and place the Sovereign Orb in its ribboned white box so that Moriarty's man can clearly identify it."

Johnny waited for the bedroom door to close before hurrying over to my father. "You must keep the sharpest of lookouts on every step my dear mother takes," he implored.

"We shall, laddie," my father vowed. "We will remain quite close to your mother, and not a fly will come near without our noticing it."

"And do not allow yourselves to be distracted," he beseeched.

"By what, pray tell?"

"The unexpected."

"I assure you we will be on the highest alert, dear boy."

Joanna heard my father's words as she returned, carrying a white box with a red ribbon neatly tied around it. "We shall all be on the highest alert," she promised her son. "And at the first sign of danger, I will drop to the floor and give the Watsons a clear shot at he who brings the danger."

As Joanna was reaching for her topcoat, Johnny dashed over and embraced her a final time. He held her close for a long moment before stepping back and speaking in a most serious voice. "Mother, I should like to give you some advice, which may serve you well in a face-to-face confrontation."

"I shall be more than happy to receive it."

"Please watch my right shoulder," he requested, and drew his right arm back. "Pray tell what did you observe?"

"Your shoulder moved."

"Which preceded the movement of my hand," Johnny explained. "Thus the shoulder's motion heralds the blow to be struck by the hand, be it a fist or a held weapon."

"It is a warning, then."

"Precisely, Mother. It is an observation I made whilst facing opponents in jiujitsu class, and one I later noticed in boxing matches at Eton. For unknown reasons, opponents tend to stare at each other's heads and eyes, which offer little advantage, for they move with the hands. You must watch the German's shoulder, Mother. If it moves, then strike the first blow."

A brief smile crossed Joanna's face. "Have you shared this observation with your classmates?"

"Not to my recollection," Johnny replied and returned her smile, which lasted ever so briefly, for he seemed to suddenly lose his composure before tightly embracing his mother once more, now with a tearful expression on his face. It was the look of a son who believed he might never see his mother again.

CHAPTER TWENTY-THREE

The Exchange

We entered the National Gallery at ten before noon and found it crowded with visitors, most of whom appeared to be speaking English. One could not help but be impressed with the gallery's magnificent vaulted ceilings and highly polished wooden floors. The walls themselves were painted in various shades of blue, gray, and red, which accentuated the breathtaking beauty of the paintings they held. My father led the way to the Impressionist section, then stepped aside to a position which gave him a clear view of the entire area. My wife and I continued to stroll past the eye-catching works of Manet, Monet, and Cezanne, measuring each of the onlookers, some standing in rows two deep. As we approached the paintings by van Gogh, our line of vision was obstructed by a group of Americans who were studying the famous *Sunflowers* and gushing at its brilliance.

"Look at the way he used the various shades of yellow," one admired.

"And see how the flowers seem to glow, as if there is a light behind them," another noted.

But there was no such light, I thought to myself, having viewed the painting on a number of occasions. It was simply the touch of a master craftsman who was so talented he could even bring life to dead flowers. We stopped near a painting of ballerinas by Degas and waited patiently for another group of Americans to vacate the large space reserved for *The Virgin on the Rocks*. The delay allowed us the opportunity to surveil the entire section in an attempt to detect agents sent by Moriarty, who would be dispersed amongst the throng of visitors. None were apparent.

"How many agents will be employed for the exchange?" I asked in a whisper.

"Three," Joanna whispered back. "Two will hold Prince Harry with their revolvers pointed at his ribs, and the third will be the German who makes the actual exchange."

"Will he be armed?"

"No doubt."

At that moment an elderly man in a wheelchair was being pushed forward by a tall, well-groomed manservant. I reached for my Webley as the old man raised a hand to point with tremulous fingers at a nearby painting.

"No worries there," Joanna said, gently touching my wrist to bring my arm down.

"Too obvious, eh?" said I.

Joanna nodded. "And the fact that we can clearly see every move they make. You will also note the elderly man's uncontrollable tremor, which would render him useless in a struggle."

"He has Parkinson's disease, I suspect."

"The rather blank expression on his face would indicate that diagnosis as well."

The group of nearby Americans moved on and we quickly occupied the space before da Vinci's *The Virgin of the Rocks*. My wife and I continued to intermittently survey the throng of tourists, some of whom were moving from painting to painting, whilst others remained fixed in place as they gazed at wonderous works of art. With a subtle glance at my father, I caught his attention and gestured with my head that there was an absence of any apparent mischief. He returned the gesture.

Joanna interrupted our exchange of silent messages, saying, "They will not come at us in full view."

"Even with a surprise?" I queried.

"The surprise will be a distraction."

"Of what sort?"

"That is to be determined."

Out of the mass of visitors, a heavyset man, with Teutonic features and a scar on his left cheek, appeared. I again reached for my revolver as he strolled toward us with slow, even steps.

"*Guten tag, Frau Watson,*" he greeted in a low, barely audible voice, obviously aware my wife was fluent in German.

"*Guten tag,*" Joanna replied in a neutral tone. "From this point on, you are to speak English so that my husband understands every word."

"Very well," said he in perfect English. "Do you have the Sovereign Orb?"

"I do."

"I must see it."

Joanna untied the red ribbon surrounding the white box and, on lifting the lid, exposed the velvet-wrapped orb, with only its bejeweled cross showing.

"I have been ordered to see the entire orb," the German demanded.

"That will only occur after we have identified the prince and can be assured he is safe and sound," said Joanna. "To this end, you are to ask him the name of the very first horse he rode."

The Hun responded with a stiff, Teutonic nod. "I shall return shortly with the answer."

"You should know that there are two revolvers which can instantly be aimed at your head."

"I am aware," said he, unconcerned.

"Then be off, so we can conclude this business."

The German seemed to disappear into the crowd, and even my father standing on his tiptoes had difficulty tracking the foreign agent's route out of the Impressionist section.

"He is quite skilled at vanishing before one's very eyes," I noted.

"They are trained to do so, for the first rule of being a spy is never to be caught."

"Where do you believe they are hiding Prince Harry?"

"In a distant area of the gallery, near a side exit which leads to a well-traveled street."

"He of course will be disguised."

"Only to a partial extent, with perhaps a scarf around his neck and a derby which covers most of his forehead."

I glanced at my timepiece which read half past the noon hour. "The Hun will no doubt make us wait to increase our level of anxiety."

"He is no longer concerned with our anxiety, but will take his time and circle about to make certain he is not being followed."

Joanna surveyed the mass of visitors once again, searching for the unexpected or for an individual who appeared to be out of place. I saw nothing of interest, but Joanna did. Abruptly, she craned her neck and leaned forward for a better view. "It's him! It's Moriarty!" she whispered.

"Where?"

"Standing next to the Monet."

I caught a glimpse of Moriarty who, with his tall frame and domed forehead, so resembled his dead brother. The hairs on the back of my neck stood briefly, for even at a distance one could perceive the presence of evil. He stared at us without expression before melding into the crowd. "Why is he here?"

"To watch every move and make certain his plan is carried out to perfection."

"Does he not trust his German cohorts?"

"Oh, he trusts them to carry out his orders, but it is their timing he wishes to control."

"To what end?"

"The answer to your question will come shortly," said Joanna. "Now, be on your toes, with your Webley at the ready."

Our senses heightened as a middle-aged, dark-complected couple, with Mediterranean features, approached us hesitantly. The goateed, taller of the companions spoke in a voice which told of an Italian background. "*Scusa*, may we have a look at *The Virgin of the Rocks* if you have completed your viewing?"

"We require another minute or two, for my grandfather will be here shortly to once again enjoy his favorite work of art," Joanna lied easily. "Could you give us a bit more time?"

"Of course, signora," said the visitor. "We shall return later."

"You are very kind," Joanna said gratefully, and waited for the couple to move on before craning her neck to once again survey the throng of visitors.

"Do you see anything of interest?"

"Nothing," she reported. "But I remain wary that Moriarty may have a few of his associates hidden and ready to pounce."

I reached inside my jacket to make certain my Webley was loose in its holster.

The German reappeared, with a step that was more hurried than that on his initial approach. In a low voice which had an edge to it, he said, "Your prince rode several horses as a youngster. You must be more specific."

"Inform him that he wrote a song about this particular horse," Joanna responded.

"We have a time schedule, and if it is not met the exchange will be canceled."

"Then I advise you to move faster."

The Hun spun around and hurried off, once again disappearing into the crowd.

"Why the need to expedite the exchange?" I wondered.

"I suspect they have a plan which must be executed with precise timing."

"For a straightforward exchange?"

"They do not wish for an exchange, dear heart, for that is not how a chess master plays the game."

"What then?"

"It will be a move which allows him to capture our queen whilst retaining his."

We waited in silence as the throng of visitors before us seemed to ebb and flow in size, with no one paying particular attention to us. The elderly man in the wheelchair was now positioned in front of the Degas painting and was happily pointing to the lovely ballerinas. My gaze quickly went back to the multitude of people before us as the German made his way through them.

"His rapid return tells us the prince is nearby," Joanna whispered.

The Hun stopped and appeared to admire the da Vinci painting beside us. "The name of the horse was Bluebonnet," said he.

"Correct," Joanna replied. "Now you have to bring the prince forward, and have him briefly remove his derby so that we can clearly identify him. His handlers are to keep their hands in full view at all times. Do you understand?"

"Your wishes will be carried out."

"But if by chance harm comes to the prince, your body will be shipped back to Germany in a plain casket, upon which your Kaiser can lay an Iron Cross."

"I already have an Iron Cross, madam."

"Then let us hope another is not in the offing."

The Hun hurried away and again seemed to vanish into the crowd.

"Keep your eyes on the German when he returns," Joanna instructed. "I shall deal with the operatives by the prince's sides."

Our senses were heightened even higher when we were approached once more by the couple with Mediterranean features. Their hands were clearly visible.

Joanna reacted promptly to their reappearance. "Ah, signore, we have just learned my dear grandfather has arrived, so we require only a moment more of your time. After he has viewed *The Virgin of the Rocks,* we shall hold this space for you, then retire to the Rembrandts which are also a favorite of my grandfather's."

The visitor's brow went up. "The National Gallery possesses Rembrandts as well?"

"There is a section dedicated to his paintings on the second level."

"Then we shall pay it a visit and return shortly."

"You are most kind."

The couple departed for the stairs which allowed us to refocus on the mass of tourists before us, most of whom were in motion and chatting quietly with one another. Then they seemed to part as the German appeared and strode toward us. Behind him was Prince Harry, with an operative on each side grasping his arms. We had no difficulty seeing their hands. The prince briefly doffed his derby to reveal a handsome, but somewhat haggard face. His steps were slow and measured, like those of a man walking to the gallows.

A wisp of smoke suddenly appeared and rose in the air.

"Fire!" a voice cried out.

"It is the distraction!" Joanna shouted, clutching the white box to her bosom.

The smoke became thick and fog-like, which obscured the throng of visitors now fleeing in panic. But I could still see the

outline of the Hun charging toward us, head down, arms outstretched. I fired a shot, but could not tell if my aim was accurate,
for the cloud of smoke had grown even thicker. Yet even in the
dimness I could see a large, ill-defined object speeding toward us.
I leaped in front of Joanna just as the missile struck and threw us
to the floor. My quick action prevented a direct hit, but the force
remained great enough to momentarily stun us. Its wheels were
still spinning when I regained my senses and pushed it away.

The smoke slowly began to rise and the air cleared enough
for us to see our surroundings. Beside us was a wheelchair turned
on its side, with the frail, elderly man still strapped in his seat.
His manservant was gone and so was Prince Harry as well as the
white box holding the Sovereign Orb. A few feet away lay the
German, semiconscious and bleeding profusely from a shoulder
wound. As we got to our feet, the chaos around us became obvious. Dazed individuals were strewn about the floor, some injured
by falls, others from being trampled upon. Most were upright and
staggering toward the main entrance.

"It was a smoke bomb which I had not considered," Joanna
admonished herself. "Moriarty used a smoke device for his distraction, and it worked perfectly."

"But who detonated it?" asked I. "I clearly saw the hands of
the German and both of his operatives, and they made no such
move."

"It must have been the manservant pushing the wheelchair,"
Joanna surmised. "He not only detonated the smoke bomb but
shoved the wheelchair into us with enough force to bowl us over.
You will note that he is no longer present."

My father dashed over to inquire, "Are you injured?"

"Only our egos," she responded, and described Moriarty's
perfectly executed plan to him.

"I would say not so perfect, for he has lost his top lieutenant,"
my father countered, and pointed to the semiconscious German

who was making a feeble attempt to stop the massive bleeding from his shoulder wound.

Joanna shrugged. "The loss is of little matter to Moriarty, for the Hun was nothing more than a disposable pawn."

"I guess I should tend to him," my father said unhappily.

I watched him address the wound, which was caused by my shot being off-center. The round had not pierced the sternum and entered the thoracic cavity, but rather had inflicted a through-and-through wound to the Hun's right shoulder, which had torn apart the subclavian artery that was spurting blood as if it were a fountain. My father was now applying deep pressure in an effort to stem the hemorrhage.

The commissioner, with Lestrade at his side, rushed in and quickly assessed the damage. "Do not tell me the very worst has happened."

"So it would appear, Sir Charles," said Joanna.

"Did you actually see the prince?"

"I did."

"But now he is obviously gone."

"I am afraid so."

"And the white box?"

"Gone with him."

Sir Charles growled to himself, clearly showing his displeasure. "What am I to tell His Majesty?"

"Inform him that the Sovereign Orb will be returned to him."

"And how do you propose performing this feat of magic?"

"With a sleight of hand," said she, and gazed down at my father who was using a handkerchief to patch the Hun's wound. "Will you be accompanying him to St. Bart's?"

"I shall, in the event the wound starts spouting blood again," he replied.

"When he is disrobed preoperatively, you should inspect his

clothing carefully, searching for a hidden cyanide capsule," Joanna instructed. "And remove all jewelry as well, for at times toxins are contained in rings which possess a needle-like injecting mechanism."

"I will give it my closest attention."

"Well and good," said she. "And do try to keep the Hun alive, for we no doubt will have further use of him."

"We shall do our best."

"Then let us be off."

"But what of the proposed return of the Sovereign Orb?" the commissioner inquired hurriedly as we began to depart.

"We shall discuss it over tea," Joanna said and, taking my arm, led the way out of the National Gallery.

CHAPTER TWENTY-FOUR

The Deception

"Look who has returned fit as can be!" Johnny called out as he dashed over to greet her home with a warm embrace. "I am delighted you are unharmed."

"I am delighted as well," she quipped. "And I am sorry to have caused you so much worry."

Johnny waved off the concern and studied his mother more closely, now noticing a small bruise on her chin. "I see there was a struggle."

"Of no great consequence."

"But the prince was rescued, was he not?"

"Unfortunately not."

The disappointment showed on the lad's face. "And I do not observe the ribboned white box."

"That, too, is missing."

"All done in by a smoke bomb," the commissioner grumbled, entering the parlor behind us.

"It was a smoke grenade," Joanna corrected. "As I think back on the event, it was most likely a grenade, for they are more compact and thus easier to conceal. Moreover, grenades give off a far larger amount of smoke."

"Is it silent?"

My wife shook her head. "Once detonated, it makes a low hissing sound which would not be detected against the background noise in the gallery."

"Thus it was the old snatch-and-run maneuver which we were totally unprepared for."

"To the contrary, Sir Charles, it was the move I believed would occur."

"But the Sovereign Orb is gone and in all likelihood will never be recovered."

"It is closer than you think," said she, with a mischievous smile, and retreated into our bedroom. Moments later she returned, holding high the bejeweled orb. "They snatched an imitation orb, for the true one rests firmly in my hand."

"How did you manage this?" asked Sir Charles, obviously elated with the turn of events.

"I went to a play entitled *The Last Coronation*."

Joanna explained in detail how she devised a plan to outwit Moriarty. "The idea came to mind at the end of the play when I watched the young queen hold aloft the Sovereign Orb, which of course was an imitation, as she ascended to the throne. After the performance, we visited backstage with the fine actress Pretty Penny, who you will recall we rescued from Jack the Ripper. I took aside the director and convinced him to loan us the orb for a most important mission. Substituting it for the genuine orb was easily done when I excused myself to fetch the white box from my bedroom."

"And you felt it wise not to share this secret with us?"

"With all respect, Commissioner, the only hard and fast secret is one that is held by a single individual."

"Which I learned from a sad experience a long time ago," said Sir Charles, nodding firmly.

"Well done indeed," I congratulated my wife. "But we must remember to reimburse the good director."

"We shall present the commissioner with a bill that he will forward to the Crown."

"I am afraid the Crown will be most disappointed with the result," Sir Charles remarked. "They were expecting a happy reunion with Prince Harry."

"Which may yet occur, for the game remains in play."

"Might Moriarty still be interested in an exchange?"

"That would be most unlikely, for master chess players never repeat an unsuccessful move."

"Are you suggesting he might attempt to transport Prince Harry into Germany without further delay?"

"That, too, is unlikely, for Moriarty wishes to inflict vengeance for his brother's death, and thus the game will go on."

My father and Inspector Lestrade entered the parlor and, upon viewing the Sovereign Orb on the workbench, stared at it with stunned expressions.

Joanna quickly repeated the plan which outwitted Moriarty, much to my father's delight. He rubbed his hands together gleefully, with his eyes sparkling at the daughter of the Great Detective.

"Moriarty will be furious," said he.

"Let us say that this was not one of his better days," Joanna noted. "Now be good enough to tell us of the Hun's condition."

"He is currently in surgery under the skillful knife of Mr. Harry Askins," my father reported. "A major branch of the right subclavian artery had been severed, requiring the ends of which to be tied off. According to Askins, the shoulder joint itself has suffered a fair amount of damage and will be of limited use to the Hun in the future."

"But he is expected to live, is he not?"

"All signs say that he will, although he had an unstable start whilst anesthesia was being administered. His blood pressure dropped precipitously, but rose back to acceptable levels when he was transfused with whole blood."

"Askins is quite skilled at thoracic surgery, every bit the equal, if not superior to Thaddeus Rudd," I commented.

"Interestingly, Rudd was in the operating room, gowned and gloved, and ready to commence elective surgery on another patient when the Hun arrived," my father went on. "He should have been the one to perform the surgery, but refused and Askins stepped in."

"Did he give a reason for his refusal?"

"With a most bitter response, which I believe you will all understand." My father shook his head sadly. "Rudd is still mourning the loss of his son who was killed in the Second Battle of the Somme."

We held a moment of silence, all remembering the disastrous losses the British army suffered at the battle which took place along the Somme River on the Western Front. On the first day alone over 19,000 British soldiers were killed.

"In any event, the surgery was proceeding smoothly when I departed from St. Bart's," my father continued on, breaking the silence.

"I take it that it was not possible to question the Hun prior to surgery?" said Joanna.

"It was impossible to do so, for the spy was in a semicomatose state from blood loss, and was babbling incoherently. "But there were one or maybe two words that he muttered repeatedly. It sounded like *rolstu nachvo*."

"He was speaking of the wheelchair," Joanna translated. "His words were *rollstuhl nach vorne*—meaning wheelchair forward—which were his instructions to push the wheelchair forward once the smoke grenade was detonated."

"Do you believe the elderly man in the wheelchair was in fact part of the plot?" asked I.

"Definitely not," Lestrade replied, and took out his notepad to refer to. "I questioned the old gentleman and learned the following. His name is Arthur Alan Davis, and he is a retired architect who currently lives with his son's family in Kensington. He is a lover of the arts and, despite his infirmities, visits museums several times a week. His favorite is the National Gallery where he demands to see da Vinci's *The Virgin of the Rocks,* which he believes is the world's greatest painting."

"And his manservant only worked part time," Joanna surmised.

"Exactly right, madam."

"And came to his current employment by what mechanism?"

"A newspaper advertisement."

"Which was the perfect arrangement for Moriarty," she concluded as all the pieces of information fell into place. "He learned of the advertisement and sent one of his well-groomed operatives to apply for the position. Once he was informed the retired architect visited the National Gallery repeatedly to view *The Virgin of the Rocks,* the consummate plan came to mind. The supposed exchange would occur at the gallery in front of the famous da Vinci painting, where a smoke grenade would be detonated, and the wheelchair, with the elderly gentleman strapped in, would be used as a missile to bowl us over. In the melee that followed, the Sovereign Orb would be snatched and the prince hurried out a side door."

"What an ingenious plan," Sir Charles was forced to admit. "Who would have ever thought that an elderly man strapped in a wheelchair would be employed as a weapon?"

"And the icing on the cake was that the old man had a noticeable tremor and a blank expression, which informed us that he had Parkinson's disease," Joanna added. "Thus he and his wheel-chair would be considered totally harmless."

Sir Charles grumbled under his breath. "Are there any more surprises to be had?"

"One, which may have disastrous consequences," my father responded.

"Which is?"

"When the Hun was disrobed prior to surgery, I noticed a penile lesion called a chancre, which is diagnostic of syphilis."

"Why should that concern us?"

"Because, Sir Charles, the Hun had a relationship with the barmaid who became a favorite of Prince Harry," my father answered frankly.

The commissioner's brow went up. "Are you suggesting the prince may be infected?"

"That possibility exists."

"Dr. Watson, please be good enough to take us through the various stages of this disorder, so we can understand how you reached this conclusion."

"The earliest stage is the appearance of a chancre which makes itself known three to four weeks after exposure. It is a wet, painless ulcer on the penis which may go unnoticed. Untreated, the disease progresses to the second stage, with the patient experiencing fever and rash. Eventually, these subside and a year or more later the final stage, with heart problems and dementia, sets it."

Sir Charles gave the matter lengthy consideration before speaking. "I am having problems with the time sequence here. If the Hun contracted the disease three weeks ago, was not the barmaid strongly involved with the prince during that period?"

"She was."

"Then the Hun could not have infected her, and she could not have passed it on to Prince Harry."

"The problem here, Commissioner, is that barmaids such as this one are known to be quite promiscuous, and she may have continued to see the Hun whilst appearing to favor the prince."

"But she may not have done so, and thus would not be infected."

"That, too, is a possibility, but we cannot close our eyes to this situation, for we are dealing with Britain's royal family."

"What do you suggest, then?"

My father turned to me. "As I recall, John, blood specimens from patients hospitalized at St. Bart's are kept in storage for seven to ten days after discharge."

"That is correct, Father."

"At your earliest convenience, obtain a sample of her blood and have a Wassermann test performed which will tell us whether the barmaid was infected. If negative, all well and good. If positive, the prince will have to be tested, assuming we can bring about a rescue."

"Even with a positive test, there is treatment, is there not?"

"With salvarsan, which has an arsenic derivative," my father replied. "It can be effective, but not always so."

"Let us pray for a negative test, but whilst we wait, not a word of this discussion is to leave this room. Am I understood?" Sir Charles demanded, and waited for all to nod, including young Johnny. "Then we shall talk no more of it."

Lestrade's notepad was still open. "Are there other matters to be settled?"

"We need to keep the Hun safe and secure for obvious reasons," Joanna responded. "To this end, I suggest Scotland Yard station a detective outside the room where the postoperative recovery will take place."

"Done," Lestrade said. "I shall post another at the sister's desk to carefully watch for unexpected visitors."

"Be certain to instruct the detective to pay close attention to all, including those wearing a hospital uniform, for those are easily obtained."

"And make for an excellent disguise, which would go unnoticed by most."

"Exactly, Inspector. In addition, please instruct your man to question and search any suspicious visitor for concealed weapons."

"Such as loaded syringes," Lestrade appended.

"Particularly those," said Joanna, turning to my father. "And finally, Watson, did you have the opportunity to carefully examine the Hun's clothing?"

"I did indeed and could not discover any concealed cyanide capsules," he replied. "In addition, I ripped open the shoulders of his jacket and uncovered the usual items carried by foreign agents, which included stashes of English and American currency, along with a number of passports that are probably false."

"Do you recall the countries of the passports?"

"Belgium and France and a third whose origin slips my mind."

"That presents no problem, for it will be easy enough to restudy them on our immediate return to St. Bart's, where hopefully the surgery has been completed and we can question the Hun."

"But, my dear, you must remember that he will be in a heavily sedated state from the anesthesia, and thus will not be nearly alert enough to answer your questions, even if he wished to do so."

"That may be the most opportune time to interrogate him," Joanna said, searching for her scarf and jacket. "For in his confused state, he might blurt out information which he would otherwise hold secret, such as *push the wheelchair*."

"In all likelihood be spoken in German."

"Better yet, for those responses will be closer to the truth."

Chapter Twenty-Five

The Postoperative Patient

As we approached the door to the surgery amphitheater, it opened with a bang and Mr. Harry Askins hurried out, with the front of his gown heavily stained with blood.

On seeing our presence, the skilled thoracic surgeon came over to us, wiping the perspiration from his brow. "Ah, the Watsons," said he. "I was told to expect you, what with the Hun business and all."

"Who told you of the Hun?" Joanna asked at once.

"The detective who accompanied the patient in the ambulance described the situation to me and the nearby sisters."

"Thus I assume the word of his admission has spread throughout the hospital."

"I am afraid it has, for everyone is speaking of it."

"Well then, we shall have to take added precautions, for he is a valuable asset to both us and Scotland Yard."

"Tell me what is required."

"First, he must be isolated in a postoperative care room, with a sister continuously at his bedside."

"Easily done."

"Do you have a sister who is fluent in German?"

"Not that I am aware of."

"That is unfortunate, but do ask around."

"I shall."

"Secondly, I take it that the Hun's condition is now stable?"

"For the moment, and it should remain so unless an unexpected hemorrhage occurs."

My father interrupted, "But the severed artery was tied off, so there should be no further bleeding."

"That should be the case, but there was considerable damage to the entire shoulder, and thus we must be on the watch for hidden bleeders waiting to erupt," Askins cautioned.

"An experienced sister at bedside should detect that event," said Joanna.

The surgeon nodded in agreement. "Even if it is a hidden bleeder, a sudden change in the patient's vital signs will alert us."

"Finally," my wife went on. "You no doubt thoroughly examined the patient prior to surgery."

"I did."

"And noted the chancre."

"Of course."

"And the well-healed scar on his left cheek?"

"It was quite evident."

"Now, think back and tell me if you observed any other scars," Joanna queried. "I am particularly interested in a fresh scar, one that still has some redness to it."

After a moment's reflection, he replied, "Nothing of that nature was seen."

"Please examine the patient's skin once more before he leaves the operating room."

"Why, may I ask, is such a scar important?"

"Because it might be concealing an encasement of cyanide, which upon squeezing will release its deadly contents."

I watched Askins dash back into the surgery amphitheater before asking my wife, "Have you ever seen such an instrument for instant suicide?"

"No, but I have read of it," said she.

"In fiction?"

"In reality, for to a spy sudden death from cyanide is much preferred to a hangman's noose."

"Do British spies carry hidden cyanide as well?"

"You will have to ask Carter-Smith, the director of MI5, that question."

Askins hurried back to us. "All clear," said he. "There are no such scars."

"Good," Joanna approved, turning to depart. "Please inform us if there is any change in the Hun's condition."

We quickly moved out of the surgical section at St. Bart's and took the stairs two flights down to the department of pathology, speaking in hushed voices as we went along our way.

"Do you remain convinced the spy has concealed cyanide on his person?" my father asked.

"They never leave the Fatherland without it," Joanna replied.

"But I literally tore apart his apparel from the jacket lining to the cuffs on his trousers, and found naught."

"It is there," she insisted.

"But which item should we examine next?"

"Everything which has been examined before."

We continued down the corridor, moving aside for a gurney carrying a covered corpse whose charred arms protruded from beneath the sheet. Many of its fingers were curled and burned down to bare bones. Even to our experienced eyes, the sight was horrific enough to make one wince.

"Surely, a complete autopsy cannot be performed on those remains," said my father.

"Only a partial one," I informed. "On occasion we are presented with bomb victims who are so disfigured by flame that identification is impossible. They are referred to a special unit at St. Bart's, with the hope that dental and X-ray studies might identify the victim and allow for a proper funeral."

"Is there any part of England unaffected by this dreadful war?" my father asked, shaking his head. "Is there any family left untouched?"

"Sadly not, Father," I replied.

Onward we went to the room where personal items are kept, and found Detective Sergeant Harry Stone waiting for us at the entrance.

"Good afternoon, all," said he, known to us from encounters in several of our previous cases.

"And to you, Detective Sergeant," Joanna replied. "We are delighted to have you on board once again."

"It is my honor, ma'am."

"Were you given instructions by the commissioner?"

"He told me you would do so, ma'am."

"Very well, then," said she. "You have no doubt been informed about the Hun, who requires our closest attention."

"I have, ma'am."

"He will shortly be taken to a postoperative care room, which he alone will occupy. I believe you are familiar with this room."

"I am indeed, for it was there I stood guard whilst Lieutenant Smits was recovering," Stone recalled, referring to a member of a South African security team, who, whilst guarding the Governor-General, was wounded in an assassination attempt.

"And a fine job of it you did," Joanna went on. "You are to perform the exact same tasks whilst keeping watch on the Hun. No one is to be allowed entrance into that room other than medical personnel and your fellow officers from Scotland Yard. It is the medical personnel, such as the orderlies and cleaning crews, that you must pay particular attention to. Before any hospital employees are permitted to enter, they must be recognized by the sister who will be stationed at the Hun's bedside. Are we absolutely clear on this?"

"Quite so, ma'am."

"You are appropriately armed?"

"I am."

"If necessary, you must shoot to kill, for your intruder will be prepared to do so."

"Understood, ma'am."

"And lastly, do you speak German?" asked Joanna.

"A little, ma'am, but I am certainly not fluent."

"How little, and be precise."

"Mainly common expressions, which I learned whilst playing against German football teams as a lad."

"Such as?"

"*Macht schnell,* which means *go faster.*"

"Excellent," said she, pleased with his Germanic pronunciation. "Then you have an additional duty whilst standing guard. If the Hun begins to babble in his semiconscious state, you are to write down the exact words, whether you understand them or not."

"I shall keep my ears tuned, ma'am."

"Then be on your way," said Joanna, and waited for the detective to disappear into the staircase before speaking. "The Hun will be expected to kill himself, and if he doesn't, Moriarty will do it for him."

I nodded at my wife's assessment. "The Hun knows too much."

"He knows everything," Joanna said, and led the way into the room containing the personal items of patients.

On the table before us were the Hun's torn clothing and articles of jewelry, which included a timepiece, ring, and cuff links. Beside them were stacks of freshly minted British and American currency and three opened passports.

Joanna began her search with the passports, carefully examining each and looking for secret compartments, but finding
none. "He has passports which will allow entry into Belgium and
France, and a third for Switzerland." She tapped a finger against
the latter, lost in thought for a moment. "Why Switzerland?"

"Perhaps because it is neutral and gives the Hun an easy route
back to Germany," I surmised.

My wife shook her head at the notion. "It is too far away, and
he would have to travel through France, which can be risky. A
better, safer route would go through Sweden, which is not only
neutral, but continues to have trade ties with Germany. That,
plus the fact that the Swiss do not tolerate international intrigue.
If it is discovered, the offending country receives a sharp rebuke,
with public exposure of the incident and those involved. The
Swiss will happily accept your money, but not your spies."

"Would he travel to Switzerland to replenish his funds?" my
father wondered.

"He has more than enough on hand," Joanna replied, and
quickly flipped through the stacks of currency on the workbench. "And if more were needed, Moriarty would supply it on
demand."

"Then, why?"

"That is to be determined," said she, and started probing
through the individual pieces of clothing, beginning with the
undergarments, then continuing on to the trousers and shirt, and
finally to the ripped-apart jacket. She paid close attention to its
lapels and buttons, and finding nothing of interest, moved on to
a pair of shoes and searched them for secret compartments which
did not exist. The timepiece and cuff links were likewise nonre-
vealing. But something about the Hun's large, gold ring caught
her attention. She quickly reached for her magnifying glass and
studied the ring at length before saying, "Most interesting."

"What?" asked I.

"Its surface, which is quite smooth except for a center stone that appears to be a black opal," Joanna described. "But on each side of the gem is a small protuberance, resembling a knob. Let's see what happens when we press on them." She turned to us with a request. "I require a sheet of white paper."

My father reached over to a nearby shelf for a sheet which was plain except for a title which read *Department of Pathology*. "This should do nicely."

Joanna aimed the gemstone on the ring at the white paper and pressed on one of the tiny knobs, with no results, then on the other to no avail. But when she pressed on both simultaneously, a tiny needle projected into view. Joanna then pushed the needle into the paper, much as one might when giving an injection. A small drop of liquid soaked into the white sheet. "In all likelihood it is cyanide," said she, and placed the paper and ring safely aside. "John, please have the hospital chemist test both for known deadly toxins."

After thoroughly washing her hands at the basin, Joanna returned to the workbench and examined the buckle and every inch of the Hun's belt, but could uncover nothing of interest. The socks were also unremarkable except for a hole in one where the little toe would be located. The final item was a small vial, with a prescription label on it.

Joanna held the vial up to the light and read from its label. "Mercury pills," said she. "Which were prescribed by Dr. Arthur Fleming. Do you know him, Watson?"

"Indeed I do," my father replied. "He was a well-respected colleague of mine at St. Bartholomew's, and last I heard had a very busy practice in St. John's Wood."

"Why would he be prescribing mercury pills?"

"That is most strange," said my father. "You will recall that the Hun had a chancre which is characteristic of syphilis. The disease was treated with mercury for hundreds of years until salvarsan was introduced at the turn of the century. The latter was far more effective and was by far the preferred treatment of this dread disease. Virtually no one now uses mercury, which is so odd here, for Fleming is a fine physician and would surely be up to date on the treatment of syphilis."

"But he must have had a bona fide reason to prescribe mercury."

"Which I must admit is beyond me unless the patient could not tolerate salvarsan, or refused to take the drug because of its side effects."

"Whatever the case, the Hun must have been seen by Dr. Fleming for a prescription to have been written."

"Beyond any doubt."

"Be good enough, Watson, to call Dr. Fleming and ask that he see us later this afternoon on a most urgent matter."

My father quickly reached for a nearby telephone. "I shall have to go through the hospital registry for his number."

"Do so, but under no circumstances are you to mention the purpose of our visit."

"He will surely insist on knowing the urgency of our visit."

"Simply say that one of his patients has run afoul of the law," said she, with a smile that came and went.

"I see a most pleased expression on my wife's face," I noted.

"That is because she is about to learn where Prince Harry is being held."

CHAPTER TWENTY-SIX

Dr. Arthur Fleming

Dr. Fleming remained occupied with his last patient of the day when we arrived at his office just past the five o'clock hour. The waiting room itself was vacant except for a prim, gray-haired secretary who sat behind an uncluttered desk and greeted us with a warm smile.

"The doctor will be with you shortly," said she, reaching out to answer a ringing phone and speaking in a low voice so as not to reveal the nature of the call.

My father watched her every move, then glanced around the small, but neat office, with its polished furniture and paintings of the English countryside hanging from the walls. A look of nostalgia crossed his face, for the office no doubt reminded him of his own, from which he practiced his beloved medicine for over thirty years. I could not help but wonder if he was recalling the time when his dear colleague Sherlock Holmes would hurry into the practice and request that Watson find someone to cover his patients, for the game was afoot.

The door to the consulting room opened, and the elderly doctor escorted a coughing woman into the reception area. Behind them was a small dog that was dutifully following his mistress.

"The medicine should relieve your cough, but if a fever occurs you must notify me," said he.

"I shall, and thank you again for seeing me on such short notice."

"It was a pleasure to do so," replied her physician, then gestured to his secretary. "Please see Mrs. Turner out, Alice, and you may be on your way as well, for it has already been a long day."

Once the patient and secretary had departed, Dr. Fleming quickly turned to my father. "Watson, how good to see you again," he said, shaking hands with genuine delight. "And I must say you are holding up well."

"My joints tell otherwise, but I do my best to ignore them," my father disclosed. "You, too, are looking fit."

"But showing the years," Fleming admitted, without regret.

"Aren't we all?" my father said jovially, and motioned toward my wife and me. "Allow me to introduce my son, John, and his lovely wife, Joanna."

"Ah, the famous daughter and her noteworthy companion whom I so enjoy reading about," he remarked. "When Watson called and told me of a most important matter to be discussed with you, I immediately conjured up a scene of some criminal activity. Am I correct in that assumption?"

"You are indeed, Dr. Fleming," Joanna answered. "For one of your patients may be so involved, and we require information on the individual. Now we are of course aware of doctor-patient confidentiality, but we are dealing with a crime of great moment and will have no difficulty obtaining a court order to open the patient's chart, if you so wish."

"Can you describe the crime?"

"I cannot, for I am bound by the Official Secrets Act not to do so," she replied. "That alone should give you some idea of the gravity of the matter."

Fleming nodded affirmatively. "Tell me the information you require."

"It involves one of your patients who carries the diagnosis of syphilis in its initial stage."

"A chancre, then?"

"Correct, which you treated with mercury."

"There are more than a few of those," Fleming said. "Although the arsenic derivative, salvarsan, is the much preferred treatment, it can also induce the most unpleasant side effects, including severe nausea and vomiting which can persist for the entire day."

"Thus, in these patients, you have no choice but to switch to oral mercury, which is less toxic, but considerably less effective," Joanna concluded.

"You are correct and, as I mentioned earlier, I have treated a goodly number of such patients."

"There is one in particular we are interested in."

"Do you have a name?"

"I suspect he would use an alias, but he has a distinctive feature which you are certain to remember."

"A disfiguration?"

"In a manner of speaking," she replied. "For he has a dueling scar running across his left cheek."

"I do recall him," Fleming said at once. "He was a foreigner, with a bit of an accent and a clearly visible chancre. I initially treated him with salvarsan, to which he reacted violently. Some hours following the infusion he developed such severe nausea and vomiting he could not leave the bathroom, for fear of soiling the floor elsewhere."

Joanna interrupted, "So this must have required you to make a home visit."

"Such was the continuous retching that he could not have possibly made his way to my office," Fleming replied. "When I arrived at his home, he was lying upon the bathroom floor on his side, and worn out by the terrible vomiting. I gave him an injection of scopolamine which quieted things down."

"Do you recall the house you visited?"

Fleming gave the matter thought before answering with a shrug. "There was nothing unusual about it to the best of my recollection."

"By chance, do you remember the address?"

"Not offhand, but it should be noted in his chart."

"Very good," said Joanna, obviously pleased she was about to uncover a most important clue. "Please obtain it for us."

"Without a name, it would take some time, for I must review the charts of all the patients I have seen in the past month."

"How will you be certain to include all such patients?"

"By referring to my appointment ledger and matching the names against their charts."

"Very good," she said again, "and be assured your effort could provide the key to a most difficult case."

Fleming hurried back into the consulting area, with the expression of a man determined to complete his mission.

"The Hun may have also used a fake address," I whispered.

"Impossible," she whispered back.

"Why so?"

"Because the good doctor had to make a house call, and thus the address must be correct."

"Well thought out," my father commended. "And with this in mind, we should inform the commissioner at our earliest moment."

"Who may wish to call in the Secret Intelligence Service who are particularly talented at snatching up spies," Joanna added. "There can be no slipups here, for we are dealing with a prince of England, and were we to lose him, all involved would carry the blame for the rest of their lives."

"Can you begin to imagine the newspaper headlines?" my father said unhappily. "They would read *Prince Harry Dead,* with a subtitle *Rescue Attempt Fails.* All England would go into mourning, whilst the Huns danced in the streets of Berlin."

The door to the consulting area opened and the elder doctor dashed out, holding up a thin chart. "I have it!"

"Excellent work, Fleming!" my father praised. "There is nothing which compares to the experienced hand."

"It was more luck than experience, Watson," said he. "I began my search with the patients who had appointments to see me a month ago. When I came to the third week in my office ledger, the foreigner with the chancre was near the top of the list."

"His name?" Joanna asked quickly.

"Frederick Hartman," Fleming replied.

"And his address?"

"Eighteen twenty-eight Hazelmere Road."

"Do you recall the house?"

Fleming thought back for a moment. "It was late afternoon when I arrived, and my only recollection was there was a sizeable garden in the front of the home."

"How many stories to the house?"

"Two," he responded promptly. "For I remember walking up a flight of stairs to the loo where the patient was situated. He was quite ill and continued to retch in my presence. The odor of vomit was indeed overwhelming. After treating him, I requested a cold washcloth be placed over his forehead."

Joanna's eyes narrowed. "To whom did you make this request?"

"The gentleman who answered the door and accompanied me up to the bathroom."

"How many men were in the house other than the patient?"

"Two that I recall."

"Please be good enough to describe them in as much detail as possible."

Fleming slowly shook his head. "I do not remember the features of the man standing outside the loo. But he was positioned at the door, like a guard who had been stationed there."

"What of the second man?"

"The one who led me up the stairs, then?"

"Yes."

"He was no foreigner, of that I am certain."

"Why so?"

"His speech was that of an English gentleman."

"Would you describe him as having an aristocratic bearing?"

"I would."

"Thus I think we can say you had a very good look at him."

Fleming nodded. "Particularly when we were upstairs near the loo where the light was brightest. Although I was called to see the man's employer, I could not help but be impressed by his striking paleness."

"Oh?" Joanna probed subtly. "Rather obvious, eh?"

"Obvious would be an understatement, madam," he went on. "His complexion was white as a sheet, which was made even more marked by his slick black hair."

Roger Mallsby! we all thought immediately.

Fleming must have noticed the stunned expression on my father's face, for he promptly amended his description. "I can assure you, Watson, the man was so pale I wondered if he was suffering from a severe anemia."

"Like the end stage of pernicious anemia," my father suggested, covering his surprise nicely.

"Indeed, but I did not consider it my place to question the man at that moment."

"Perhaps later."

"My thoughts exactly."

"Well, then," my wife said, arising from her chair, "I know you have already had a very long day, so we shall not intrude on you further. Before leaving, however, I must thank you for your detailed information which has been most helpful."

"I am delighted to have been of assistance," Fleming said and, turning to my father, added, "And, Watson, I expect a phone call from you in the not-too-distant future so we can get together for a nice chat down memory lane."

"It would be my pleasure," he responded, with a warm hand-shake.

Outside, the weather had become chilly and dark, as black clouds gathered to warn of a storm approaching from the North Sea. A strong gust of wind nearly dislodged our derbies whilst we watched one motor vehicle after another pass by, with no sign of a taxi. As a rule, we did not discuss surprising and important revelations on a footpath, but the disclosure which just came to light would not wait for the privacy of our rooms.

"Mallsby! A traitor!" I spat out. "A bloody traitor!"

"Not only to his country, but to the Crown itself," my father agreed disgustedly. "He deserves to have a hangman's noose strung around his treasonous neck."

"Come, come, gentlemen, you had to have suspected him, as I did earlier," Joanna said in a neutral tone. "Mallsby was there every step of the way, from the abduction to Ah Sing's to the barmaid and her tragic abortion. His fingerprints were on every move. You see, Moriarty needed an insider and he chose the private secretary, who was a perfect fit."

"We should have him promptly arrested and imprisoned in the Tower of London where the other traitors are housed," my father snapped, raising his voice.

"Not as yet."

"And why not?"

"Because I have a further use for him," Joanna said, and waved down a passing taxi.

CHAPTER TWENTY-SEVEN

The Storm

We waited impatiently for the call from Scotland Yard to inform us of its plan to rescue Prince Harry, which we knew would be delayed, for the predicted storm was now arriving in full force. A torrential rain pounded down on all London, accompanied by hail and swirling winds which markedly reduced visibility. Of great concern to all of us was the immeasurable harm the storm would do to the already badly damaged city of London. Bombed-out homes and cratered streets were certain to be flooded and further ruined by the heavy downpour. And the underground tube stations, where people sought shelter from the German bombs, would be inundated with water and become uninhabitable. In addition, the inclement weather was certain to slow the gathering of critical information required for a successful rescue.

"The only good part of this storm is that it provides excellent cover," said Joanna as she placed an additional log on the fire. "But not nearly enough for a doable attempt. Scotland Yard has to garner intelligence from a number of sources before they can put together a workable plan."

"Such as?" I asked.

"To begin with, they have to obtain records and documents to ascertain if the house is owned by the occupants or leased. Next, the neighbors have to be questioned about the occupants of the house. It would be of vital importance to know how many individuals live there, along with their descriptions and habits. And of course the nearby neighbors would have to be evacuated in the event guns are fired."

"Which is likely to occur," my father noted. "Particularly when dealing with this murderous lot."

"And that brings us to the attack itself," Joanna went on. "They cannot simply burst in, for, as Dr. Fleming described, it is a two-story house and the prince would no doubt be kept on the second floor. There he would be used as a shield or bargaining device, or killed in the battle which ensued. With this in mind, the detectives would seek out prior occupants to learn of the layout and possible hidden entrances or exits, particularly those on the rooftop."

"An attic entrance would be most helpful," my father added.

"Indeed, for it would not only serve as a secret way in but as a listening post as well," I chimed in. "With a sound magnifier, a detective could determine how many individuals were present and their precise location. They might even be overheard chatting about what each was to do in the case of an attack."

"But of greatest value, we would surely learn where the prince was being held prisoner," said Joanna. "If it were a bedroom with a window, a detective might use a ladder in the darkness to smash his way in, and—voilà!—you have a rescued prince."

"With a force of detectives bursting in through the front entrance at the same moment," my father envisioned.

"All well and good," said Joanna. "But I suspect Moriarty is too clever to place the prince in a room with a window, from which he might signal a neighbor or passerby."

"Wishful thinking, then."

"Unfortunately."

"Mother," Johnny joined in the discussion, whilst pacing the floor and listening to every word, "speaking of signals, there might be a means to alert the prince of an impending rescue."

"What comes to your mind?" she asked. "And be precise."

Johnny gave the matter considerable thought before offering a method of alert. "Prince Harry, being a lady's man, might have a singular song which he and his current love enjoy sharing."

"His private secretary might be aware of it and the secretary, being a traitor, may well be at the prince's side when the rescue attempt begins. The song would be a tip-off."

"Then, the signal would have to come from the prince's distant past, prior to the secretary being hired."

Joanna's eyes suddenly lighted up. "As a youngster, he was so fond of a horse named Bluebonnet he composed a song dedicated to it. And only the prince's older brother Albert knew of it. We shall have the commissioner make the necessary inquiry to learn if the brother recalls the words."

"But how will it be delivered to Prince Harry's ears?"

"You give me the song, and I will come up with a device," said she, and smiled at the mental quickness of her son. "Very good, Johnny, very good indeed."

The lad seemed to ignore his mother's praise as he went back to pacing, no doubt trying to come up with a means to bring the song to the prince's ears.

The phone rang loudly and Joanna rushed over to answer it. It was the commissioner. "Yes, Sir Charles, I can hear you clearly. Please continue."

There was a pause before she began repeating the commissioner's words. "You say the house was purchased by a French businessman some months ago? . . . In cash, eh? . . . Reclusive to what extent? . . . No pets, then. . . . Very well. Please keep us informed." She ended the call and placed the receiver back in its cradle.

"The house was purchased by a Mr. Dupree, a French businessman, who paid for it in cash. He apparently conducts his business from the house, with only occasional visitors. The owner himself is reclusive and rarely seen, and when viewed it is always from a distance. He has no pets. Deliveries are never made by truck or lorry, with all goods being carried in by what are believed to be manservants. Scotland Yard is in the process of contacting previous owners for detailed information on the layout of the house."

"Not much there," my father remarked. "Let us hope for more to come."

"But why own the house?" Joanna queried. "That is not the modus operandi for spies. They let the residence rather than buy it, for purchasing requires paperwork and legal documents, often with the stamp of notary publics and other officials. Those are the very things most spies wish to avoid."

"Perhaps Moriarty is being double clever to confuse us," my father surmised.

"A possibility."

There was a single rap on the door and Miss Hudson looked in. "Mrs. Watson, the leader of the ruffians has appeared in this dreadful weather and wishes to see you on a most important matter."

"Please show him in," my wife replied. "And allow me to assure you this will be the last visitor of the night."

"I would hope so, for the storm is predicted to grow even worse before midnight."

As the door closed, Joanna turned quickly to us. "Something untoward has happened in the absence of the Hun."

"But what at this late hour?" asked I.

"It is either Moriarty or someone doing his bidding."

"To what end?"

"I believe we shall shortly have the answer to that question."

We heard another rap on the door and Wiggins entered, soaking wet head to toe. His short mac was dripping into puddles of water at his feet.

"I thought our work was done, ma'am," said he. "But there is now new information which I am certain will be of great interest to you."

"Let us hear every word," said Joanna. "You may stand by the fire if you wish."

"I am fine, ma'am," Wiggins refused, with a nod of gratitude before he muffled a cough. "I shall start at the very beginning and give you the details as they were given to me by Little Alfie. The lad was hurrying past the Aldgate Hotel when he was approached by the boot polisher who I believe you remember from our earlier watch on the foreigner. The polisher was doing his work a bit sooner than usual because of the storm and wanted to return to his dwelling as soon as possible. Whilst on the floor where the foreigner resides, he saw two men pick the lock of his room and enter, looking over their shoulders as they did."

"Up to no good, were they?" asked Joanna.

"Oh, yes, ma'am, the street lads of Whitechapel know a professional thief when they spot one. Now, the polisher recalled Little Alfie from their prior encounter, and rushed over to tell him of the break-in in hopes of receiving yet another reward. They stood there in the bloody rain and waited for the two men to dash out of the front entrance, one of whom was carrying a suitcase. They were driven off in a motor vehicle disguised as a taxi, which it most definitely was not, according to Little Alfie. And that is the story, ma'am."

"Well told," my wife said. "Was the boot polisher rewarded?"

"With a sixpence, ma'am."

"Your work is now done, and I would think an extra guinea would more than cover your expenses."

"That is most generous, ma'am."

Joanna went to her purse and handed Wiggins the agreed-upon fee. "And give the boot polisher an additional sixpence for his continued silence."

"I shall, ma'am."

"Then be off with you."

Once the door closed, Joanna turned to us and asked, "What do you make of that, my dear Watsons?"

"Obviously they wished to clear out the Hun's room," I replied.

"Of what?"

"Of evidence that shows he is a German spy."

"We already know that, and Moriarty is aware we know that."

"Then what?"

"I suspect that hotel room contained the single most important item which Moriarty wishes to keep secret."

"Which is?"

"His final move in the game we are playing."

Chapter Twenty-Eight

A Strange Coincidence

By definition, a coincidence is a situation in which events happen at the same time in a way that is neither planned nor expected. Joanna was of the firm opinion that when coincidences occurred during a criminal investigation, they had far more relevance than those which were obvious to the casual observer. Such was the case when I stepped into my office the following morning and was told that Mr. Harold Markham, the director of pharmacology at St. Bart's, requested my immediate presence.

As I turned to leave, my secretary handed me two reports which she believed to merit my attention. The first was a laboratory slip stating that the Wassermann test on the barmaid's blood was negative, which indicated she did not have syphilis and thus could not have transmitted the dreaded disease to the prince. The second report was a note from Adam Sharpe stating that there had been no further cases of *Pseudomonas* infection, and it was now certain that an outbreak had been averted. Two potential problems had been avoided, I thought clinically, but neither aided our cause to locate and rescue Prince Harry. Perhaps my visit to the pharmacology section might be of help in that regard.

I hurried up the stairs, now recalling how Joanna had injected a probable toxin onto a sheet of paper, using a needle that was hidden within the Hun's ring. I had submitted the paper to Markham's research laboratory for analysis to ascertain which toxin was involved. There were a number of poisons that could be quite deadly in this instance, but cyanide topped the list because its lethal dose was so small and its action so rapid there was no hope of counteracting its effect. The presence of cyanide in an innocuous ring was so ingenious and perfect for spies. It could be used to kill one's self or an adversary, with the death being rapid and certain.

I entered Markham's laboratory and found the senior pharmacologist, with his curly gray hair and horn-rimmed spectacles, removing a set of test tubes from a water bath. Although jovial by nature, he was a well-known authority on deadly poisons and had written a treatise on the subject which was considered by many to be a gold standard.

"Ah, Watson," he greeted me. "Always a pleasure to see you."

"And you as well," said I. "Your message indicated you have uncovered something of keen interest. Are we dealing with a toxin?"

"Indeed, but first allow me to inform you that the textbook on *Poisons and Toxins* has gone into yet another printing."

"Congratulations, Harold!" said I.

"And to you for your excellent chapter on *Response to Poisonous Gases*, which was so well received."

I shrugged modestly. "It consisted of mainly suggestions."

"Which was of considerable help to our soldiers on the front who had been exposed to mustard gas," he went on. "It was surely a worthwhile contribution."

"If you insist."

"I do indeed," said he. "Now let us turn to the sheet of paper you sent to me for toxin analysis."

"Have you discovered a new poison?" I asked.

"I am afraid not," Markham replied. "It is common cyanide, but it was its dose which was quite remarkable."

"How so?"

He paused a moment to shake the test tubes before returning them to a heated water bath. "Its dose was far greater than we usually come across. Of course the cyanide solution on the paper had dried out, and thus I had to reconstitute it with a measured amount of saline. In any event, should a single cc have been injected into a human subject, it would have been enough to kill him and three of his average-sized colleagues."

"Exactly how much is needed to dispatch a single individual?"

"One milligram per kilogram will suffice in that regard."

I nodded at the calculation. "Which could easily be concealed within a ring."

"Say again?" Markham asked, with a puzzled expression.

I described in detail the Hun's ring, with its semiprecious gem and small protruding knobs beside it. "One simultaneous application of pressure to the knobs and out comes a needle projecting from the outer surface, which when pressed down injects a lethal dose of cyanide."

The pharmacologist gave considerable thought to the intricate mechanism before inquiring, "How large was the opal in the center of the ring?"

"It was rather oversized, perhaps a half inch across," I responded. "Why do you ask?"

"Because in all likelihood it had to be hollowed out to contain the toxin," said he. "I wonder if the space would be great enough to hold multiple doses."

"A very good question, and one we shall ask when the ring is turned over to one of our intelligence services."

Markham's brow went up. "The SIS?"

"I am not at liberty to say, but you may draw your own conclusion."

"I love good secrets," said he as a smile crossed his face.

"As do I," I replied and, thanking him for his helpful expertise, departed as he turned his attention back to the test tubes in the water bath.

Down the stairs I went, wondering if indeed the ring could be refilled with cyanide and, if it could, how many individuals had been killed by injection. Joanna's discovery of the poisonous ring was of far greater significance than simply prohibiting the Hun from killing himself. The SIS, which spent a fair amount of time chasing down spies, would now know to remove rings from any Hun agent to prevent them from doing themselves in, thus saving the spies for questioning. And of utmost importance, SIS operatives would be aware of the ring, and how to avoid the lethal jab in the event of a close struggle.

On entering my office, Rose quickly arose from the secretary's desk and pointed to the phone. "Sergeant Stone called from the postoperative care room. He needs your presence immediately."

I rushed out the door, hoping the worst had not happened. Had Moriarty somehow gotten past the usually alert detective and permanently silenced what might have been an important source of information? That was the most likely possibility, but there were others as well. Perhaps the Hun was now babbling half sentences in German regarding Prince Harry and his whereabouts. Or perhaps he was garbling about the location of Moriarty himself. Either of the latter two could be of immense importance in bringing this most difficult case to a successful conclusion. And both would require fluency in German, which I lacked.

I dashed through the surgery ward and into the area which housed the postoperative care room. Standing outside its door was Sergeant Stone, the surgeon Harry Askins, and the sister who should have been at the patient's bedside. It was a picture of death.

"I am afraid the Hun has expired," Askins said without inflection.

"Was there any evidence of foul play?" I asked at once.

"None whatsoever," he replied. "The patient was recovering nicely, with no signs of infection or further blood loss."

"Was his hemoglobin level checked this morning?"

"It was, and remained stable at ten grams percent," Askins replied. "And had there been any substantial blood loss later in the morning, it would have been reflected in his vital signs."

The sister handed me the handwritten recording of the patient's blood pressure, pulse, and respiratory rate over the past two hours. All were normal and steady. "So it had to have been a sudden death," I concluded.

"Most sudden," the surgeon agreed. "On my visit this morning, he was sitting up in bed with minimal discomfort, wishing for breakfast. I prescribed a soft diet which seemed to suit him."

"Particularly soup," the sister noted. "He had an appetite for soup and requested a large bowl of chicken broth, which Mr. Askins thought would be good for starters."

"So he sipped the soup in good spirits, did he?" I queried.

"Quite so," the sister replied. "He literally slurped down large spoonsful."

"Did he finish the entire bowl?"

"No, Doctor, only half and then he laid back, telling me he was a bit fatigued," she reported. "I checked his vital signs immediately and they had not changed."

I turned back to Askins and asked, "With all this in mind, what do you consider the most likely cause of death?"

"Either a massive myocardial infarction or large pulmonary embolus, for they are far and away the most common cause of sudden, unexpected death in a postoperative patient."

I glanced at the postoperative care room and briefly studied the Hun's uncovered corpse. "Is there a reason for all to be standing outside the room?"

Sergeant Stone stepped forward to answer. "I contacted the commissioner and Mrs. Watson. It was she who instructed me to allow no one in the room until she arrived. Furthermore, none of the items within were to be removed or in any way altered."

"Ever the detective, eh?" Askins remarked.

"She sees things which others do not," I reminded the surgeon.

"I fear there is not a great deal to be seen, other than a dead Hun and an unfinished breakfast," Askins said, and glanced at his timepiece, implying that he was on a tight schedule. "When is she due to arrive?"

"Shortly, for Scotland Yard has sent a motor vehicle for her," Stone responded. "The commissioner wishes for all of you to remain in place until Mrs. Watson completes her investigation."

As if on cue, Joanna hurried up to the group and, without entering, studied the postoperative care room at length. Her line of vision appeared to go back and forth between the corpse and the cold bowl of soup. She then reached for her magnifying glass and said, "I need to know the entire train of events prior to the untoward moment."

I gave my wife a complete summary, with several small details being added by Askins and the sister. Joanna asked only a few questions, which for the most part were related to the time sequence between breakfast and death. After assimilating the information, she stepped into the room and carefully examined the corpse's exterior, no doubt searching for signs of trauma or a struggle, but finding none. Next, using her magnifying glass, she examined every inch of the Hun's arms, chest, and abdomen, then shook her head at the results.

"There are no injection sites other than those on his arms where intravenous infusions were administered," Joanna noted.

"And none under his bandaged right shoulder," Askins added.

"An assassin would not inject there, for a quite long needle would be required to pierce through the thick dressing," said she.

The surgeon shrugged at the objection. "But in any event, no intruders entered the room."

"I was thinking in terms of the Hun injecting himself."

"Are you speaking of a deadly toxin?"

"I am."

"But where would he conceal it?"

"You would be most surprised, Mr. Askins," said Joanna, now reviewing the sheet of vital signs which had been recorded throughout the evening. "So, on the surface, it appears we are dealing with an unexplained, sudden death."

"So it would seem, with myocardial infarction or pulmonary embolism being the most likely causes."

"Based on what?"

"My experience and those of my colleagues."

"Not good enough without proof."

Askins shrugged once again, not overly concerned. "We shall know for certain at autopsy which your husband undoubtedly will perform."

Joanna returned the vital signs sheet to the sister, then looked over to me. "John, please use all of your skills to uncover a method or device which induced sudden death. We should keep in mind that when a death occurs which benefits an adversary, you must wonder if it was indeed caused by that adversary."

"But there is no evidence to point to such an event," Askins argued mildly.

"Which doesn't exclude its presence."

Joanna walked over to the cold bowl of soup and examined

it closely with her magnifying glass. I suspected she was searching for cracks or spaces in the bowl itself which might have held
a hidden toxin. Then she went to the soup itself and sniffed its
aroma. "Chicken broth," she announced.

"Yes, madam," the sister confirmed. "It is prepared in a large
pot by a cook in our kitchen, and ladled out in individual portions as ordered by the doctor."

"Are the portions always this size?"

"Most are much smaller, but the patient insisted on having
such a large bowl."

"Which is most unusual for a patient less than twenty-four
hours off an operating table," Joanna thought aloud. "Because of
the lingering effects of anesthesia and what have you, they often
have little appetite, if any at all."

The sister nodded. "That is my experience as well."

Joanna paused and tapped a finger against her chin, giving
the matter more thought, for she, too, had extensive experience
with postoperative patients whilst a surgical nurse at St. Bartholomew's. It was during that time that she met and married
John Blalock, distinguished surgeon, who tragically died of chol-
era shortly after the birth of their only child.

"Why are you so concerned with the soup?" Askins asked,
breaking the silence.

"Because he demanded it and shouldn't have," she replied,
then came back to the sister. "Who delivered the soup?"

"Jerome, an elderly Jamaican, who has been with us for years
and is totally trustworthy."

"Do you believe the soup may have been poisoned?" asked I.

"That would be most unlikely, for it went from a large pot to
a known and trusted server, and finally to the patient's bedside,"
Joanna reasoned. "Moreover, the large amount of soup would
dilute out most of the frequently used toxins."

Her gaze went back to the soup bowl and the large spoon

next to it. There was nothing remarkable about either, except that the spoon was encrusted with dried soup. She sniffed at the soup once again and, finding nothing of interest, moved on to the large spoon. With her magnifying glass in hand, she leaned over to examine the spoon's head, then its handle. Abruptly, Joanna jerked her head up and backed away.

"Cyanide!" she cried out.

"In the spoon?" I asked quickly.

"On its handle," she replied. "There is a definite smell of almonds."

"So there must be a cavity within the handle," I surmised.

"No, no, John, you must think it through," Joanna instructed. "The spoon came directly from the kitchen to the server to the bedside. That would make it impossible for a uniquely poisoned spoon to be delivered to the Hun. Who was to know to pick that one from the many?"

"How then?"

Joanna leaned over and sniffed at the corpse's partially opened mouth. "Almonds again," said she and turned to the thoracic surgeon. "Askins, please examine the corpse's entire mouth. You are searching for a broken tooth."

The surgeon moved to the bedside and, prying the dead Hun's jaws apart, inserted a tongue blade. He explored the oral cavity at length before requesting, "A small torch, Sister."

She switched on a pencil-sized torch and handed it to Askins. She backed away to avoid possible exposure to the poison.

"A gold filling on a molar is cracked wide open," he reported.

"And that is why he insisted on a large bowl of soup, for he knew it would be accompanied by a big, sturdy spoon which he could use to pry open a filling and release a deadly dose of cyanide," Joanna elucidated. "It was a perfect suicide."

"With yet another setback," said the commissioner, who was standing at the door and listening to every word.

"I am afraid so, Sir Charles," Joanna replied. "And it was done so cleverly that no one could have prevented it."

"Most clever indeed," he concurred, nodding, as he approached Askins and the sister. "I know both of you did your best and nobody could have done more. Scotland Yard commends you for your fine efforts."

"Thank you for the kind words, Commissioner," Askins said. "And now, with your permission, I shall have the corpse transported to pathology for autopsy."

"And again with your permission, sir, we will have the room thoroughly cleaned and scrubbed," added the sister.

"Very well," Sir Charles consented, and gave a subtle signal for Sergeant Stone to lead the pair away.

Once they were out of hearing distance, the commissioner turned to my wife and me, as a look of displeasure crossed his face. "And I bring even more bad news. The address the Hun gave Dr. Fleming was a false one. The house on Hazelmere Road was purchased by a Mr. Jean-Claude Dupree, who is a French industrialist with textile mills in France and England. The family moved here six months ago because their young son suffers from seizures and is being cared for by a specialist at the Hospital for Sick Children." He sighed unhappily to himself before noting, "I had a gnawing suspicion that the Hun had given the doctor a sham address."

"That possibility also crossed my mind," Joanna admitted. "Particularly when we were aware he was residing at Aldgate Hotel."

"I must tell you that the situation of the house would have been perfect for a rescue," he went on. "We had even learned the words of a song which would have alerted the prince that a rescue operation was in progress."

Joanna permitted herself a brief smile. "So our recollection that the prince had written a song to his horse proved to be important. And in all likelihood Roger Mallsby would not have been aware of the prince's favorite horse since His Royal Highness rode it as a lad."

"What does Mallsby's awareness have to do with a rescue?"

"A great deal, for Roger Mallsby is a turncoat," she said matter-of-factly.

"What!" The commissioner's voice was loud enough to carry into the adjoining surgery ward.

Joanna summarized in detail all the evidence to clearly show that Roger Mallsby was a traitor and had been from the very beginning. "Thus whatever conversations we had in his presence quickly reached the ears of the prince's abductors."

"You should have informed me," Sir Charles snapped.

"It was an oversight," Joanna lied.

"The daughter of Sherlock Holmes does not commit oversights in such an important case."

Joanna nodded at the accuracy of the statement. "I withheld the information for fear you would have been obliged to tell His Majesty who would have insisted the private secretary be arrested and summarily hanged for treason. Had that happened, we would have lost an asset that could lead us to the prince."

"He would have talked to save his traitorous neck," Sir Charles insisted.

"To no avail, for Moriarty would have learned of Mallsby's arrest and promptly moved the prince to another location."

The commissioner considered Joanna's line of reasoning at length before speaking. "You do realize that we are rapidly reaching the point where we will have no choice but to arrest and question Mallsby."

Detective Sergeant Stone hurried into the postoperative care room and, pausing to catch his breath, said, "Commissioner, I have just received a call from headquarters with information that is to be passed immediately to you."

"Which is?" Sir Charles asked.

"Dr. Fleming's office was broken into sometime during the night."

"Moriarty," Joanna said in a whisper.

CHAPTER TWENTY-NINE

The Break-In

Dr. Arthur Fleming appeared calm and collected as he described the break-in to his office which had occurred overnight. "There was evidence of forced entry," said he. "The lock on the door appeared to be pried apart, so it opened easily without the key being turned."

"So you were the first to arrive this morning," Joanna deduced.

"I was, which is usually the case, for I hurry over in the early hours after visiting my hospitalized patients," Fleming went on. "Alice follows me shortly and is always at her desk a quarter before eight sharp."

Joanna glanced at the secretary who was wiping tears from her eyes, obviously distraught over the turn of events. "Is there anything missing from your desk?"

"No, madam," she replied. "Even the cup containing my petty money was left untouched."

"Had the drawers been rummaged through?"

"No, madam."

Joanna came back to Fleming and said, "I take it there was nothing missing or amiss in the waiting room?"

"That is correct, for all the mischief was done in the consulting area," he replied. "My stethoscope and a number of surgical instruments, including scalpels and tweezers, had been removed, and a glass cabinet containing drugs had been broken into."

"Please list the drugs."

"There were bottles of iodine and alcohol to be used as antiseptics, and small amounts of cocaine and morphine for pain relief," Fleming itemized and, arising from his chair, pointed to the consulting area. "Come this way and I will show you."

The consulting room itself was quite small, with scarcely enough room for an examining table, a chair, a tiny desk, and a glass cabinet whose front had been smashed open. The desk drawers remained closed.

"Perhaps the damage to the cabinet was the work of a drug addict seeking drugs," Fleming suggested. "Or he may have intended to sell them on the street, for these are hard times."

"What was the quantity of these drugs?" Joanna asked.

"They were quite trivial, with enough morphine for only two or three injections, and a supply of cocaine for a half dozen topical applications."

"Not very valuable," Sir Charles commented.

"That depends on how desperate the thief was," Fleming retorted.

"Your point is well taken."

"A stethoscope and the surgical instruments might bring a bit more," I opined.

"Not very much, I am afraid," the elderly doctor responded. "For they were old and used, and would most likely end up at a pawnshop where the thief would be offered a pittance."

Joanna gazed around the small examining room, which had

two shelves on the wall, both bending under the weight of files and medical textbooks. "Are charts kept in this room as well?"

"No, Mrs. Watson," he replied. "Those are stored in an area just outside my personal office."

"May we see them?"

"Of course. This way, please."

Fleming led the way out to rows of shelves that went from ceiling to floor, each packed to the fullest with the charts of patients. They attested to the length of time he had been in practice and to the great number of patients he had seen over the years.

The doctor reached down to pick up ten or so charts which were scattered on the floor in front of the shelves. He carefully reinserted them into their appropriate slots, using the alphabetic markings on the shelves.

"Whilst you are at it, could you please fetch the chart of Mr. Frederick Hartman?" Joanna requested.

Fleming stood on his tiptoes and quickly thumbed the charts which had the label *H* attached to it. He then repeated the search a second time. "I am afraid it is missing."

"As expected," Joanna noted.

"Why would someone remove Mr. Hartman's chart?" he queried.

"Because they would like him to disappear," Joanna said, and left it at that.

The doctor's secretary peeked into the chart area and motioned to Fleming. "Sorry to interrupt, sir, but Mrs. Simpson is calling and wishes to speak with you. Her cough is worse, and she now has a fever."

"You will excuse me," he said to us as an expression of concern crossed his face. "I must answer her call."

"Of course," said the commissioner, then waited for Fleming

and the secretary to depart from the inner office. But still he spoke in a whisper. "What could be in the missing chart?"

"Something Moriarty does not wish to be disclosed," replied Joanna.

"But how could Moriarty know we would return for the Hun's chart?"

"Perhaps we were trailed to the doctor's office on our first visit?" I suggested.

Joanna shook her head at the notion. "On the off chance we would be visiting Fleming's office in St. John's Wood? I think not."

"Then how?" the commissioner persisted.

"A better question, Sir Charles, is how did the Hun end up at a cozy practice in such a posh area of London?"

"Perhaps he was referred by a friend."

"Spies do not make friends."

"Then an acquaintance, perhaps," I wondered.

"The Hun spent his time in Whitechapel, either at the pub or at the Aldgate Hotel," Joanna refuted. "Those are hardly the places where he would learn of a fine practice in St. John's Wood."

"A colleague might have told him of Dr. Fleming," I proposed.

"Very good, John, but which of his colleagues would be familiar with a practice in such a fine neighborhood?"

Fleming hurried back to the chart area and apologized, "I am sorry to have taken so much time, but the patient is quite ill," said he. "She has to be seen, and I must ask if your investigation will soon end, so we can schedule an appointment for her."

"We shan't be much longer, for only a few questions remain to be asked," Joanna informed him. "In particular, do any of your patients reside in Whitechapel?"

"None that I know of," he replied immediately, then hesitated, with his brow furrowing in thought. "Oh, I believe I see your line of reasoning. With Whitechapel being a high-crime area, you were wondering if a patient from that district might be responsible for the break-in."

"Your deduction is correct," my wife acknowledged. "But we did not place much credence in that connection, for we learned from a reliable source that your practice consists primarily of upper-end patients, including some from Buckingham Palace itself."

"Ah," Fleming said, permitting himself a brief smile. "I see you have been speaking with my old and dear colleague John Watson."

"We have indeed," Joanna lied. "He even mentioned a position of one patient from the palace, in a confidential manner of course. I believe he was a private secretary of some sort."

"Oh, yes, he was no doubt referring to Mr. Harold Carmichael, an elderly gentleman, who held that position," the doctor recalled. "Watson might have remembered him from years back when the fellow was admitted to St. Bartholomew's with the presumptive diagnosis of malaria, which turned out not to be true. If memory serves me correctly, he was a private secretary to Prince Harry."

Joanna's eyes narrowed at the disconnect, for it was Roger Mallsby, not an elderly gentleman, who was the prince's private secretary. "Was he an assistant of some sort?"

"Oh, no, he was quite high in ranking until he retired five years ago or so, and relinquished his position to a much younger chap who he was rather fond of. He referred to his replacement by his first name, which was Robert or Roger."

"I see," said Joanna as she connected the new pieces of information together. It was Mallsby who took over the position and had learned of the former secretary's physician. It seemed a safe and out-of-the-way practice to send the syphilitic Hun, to be seen, treated, and discharged.

"Well, that is of little matter in the current case," said she, waving away the association of the private secretary to the Hun. "It is Hartman who garners most of our interest. As you may recall, he has a criminal past, and now his chart is missing."

"Is he a suspect, then?"

"Of the first order."

"But why would he remove his chart?" the doctor inquired. "There is nothing in it which points to a criminal activity."

"Perhaps he wishes to conceal the fact that he has been diagnosed with a socially unacceptable disease," Joanna lied convincingly.

"But it is curable," Fleming argued.

"Not when one has dreadful side effects to salvarsan."

"So true, particularly with mercury being far less effective."

"With all the information at our disposal, we should like to question Mr. Hartman for the current crime as well as others he may have participated in."

"That should not present a problem, for you had acquired his address from your last visit to my office."

"But alas, that address turned out to be a false one."

"Oh, dear, that does present a quandary."

"But there may yet be a way to discover his true address, for which we must bank on your memory."

"I shall help in any manner I can."

"Excellent, for I believe you to be quite observant, no doubt as a consequence of your extensive experience in medicine," Joanna continued on. "Now, as I recall, you paid a house call to this patient who was suffering from terrible nausea. Correct?"

"Correct."

"And you described the patient's house as having two stories, with a leafy, green garden in its front. Is that an accurate statement regarding the dwelling?"

"To the best of my recollection," replied he. "And now that I think back, there was a small statue of some sort off to my right."

Joanna quickly turned to the commissioner. "Now tell us, Sir Charles, does that description match the house you surveilled on Hazelmere Road?"

"In no form or fashion," he responded. "The house we visited possessed three stories and had no front garden, for its door was only steps away from the footpath."

Joanna gave the contradiction in the two descriptions lengthy consideration before reaching for her purse for a Turkish cigarette, then decided against it, for we were in a physician's office. Instead, she began pacing around the chart area, going from one side to the other, deep in thought and muttering to herself. Abruptly, she stopped and came back to Fleming. "When you make a house call, how do you know which address to visit?"

"I am given a slip by my secretary which contains the address."

"Do you still have the slip?"

"No, I am afraid I discarded it."

"Would your secretary keep a copy?"

Fleming thought for a moment before slowly nodding. "I believe she does, in the event the patient has to be sent a bill later on."

"Please check with your secretary now," Joanna requested, then waited for the doctor to leave the chart room and be out of hearing distance. "It is our last and best chance," said she. "For without a true address, we are in total and complete darkness."

"If the bill has already been mailed out, she, too, may have discarded it," I thought aloud.

Joanna shook her head. "She wouldn't have thrown it away until the account was satisfied."

"And how do you know it wasn't?"

"Because the slip of paper would only show the street and its number. For the complete address, which not only contained the street but the London postal code as well, she would have referred to the patient's chart. Thus the Hun could not have paid for the house call because the bill was sent to a false address."

"But this would hold only if the secretary conducted herself in the manner you proposed."

"Let us pray she did so."

Fleming hurried back into the chart area, holding up a small slip of paper. "The house I visited was located at 550 Gloucester Avenue which is only a few miles away."

"We have him," Joanna said as a Mona Lisa–like smile crossed her face.

CHAPTER THIRTY

The Secret Intelligence Service

With the rescue of Prince Harry now in the hands of the SIS, all information necessary for a successful execution was being rapidly acquired. Capt. Vernon Carter-Smith, the director of the specialized unit, had established a command center on the second floor of an evacuated house which was located directly across the street from 550 Gloucester Avenue. The latter, only now under close surveillance, was a two-story, redbrick building that was fronted by a green garden, with a manicured lawn and blooming trees. Near its thick, oak door was a small statue, just as Fleming had described.

The target house was Victorian in style, with multiple windows and a roof that was surrounded by a parapet three feet or so in height. There were narrow alleyways on each side which separated the dwelling from the adjacent homes. A trash bin was of particular interest to Carter-Smith, as he focused his binoculars on the object which seemed ordinary in every regard. A lorry suddenly appeared, and a dustman hurried over to the bin to empty its contents. Joanna, my father, and I viewed the unfolding events with Zeiss monoculars which had been issued to us earlier.

"The dustman is one of our operatives," Carter-Smith commented.

"Exactly what do you expect to find in the rubbish?" I asked.

"Clues."

"Such as?"

"Food wrappings and similar used items might indicate the number of people in the house," the director replied. "If there are pieces of cut rope it would tell us the prince was bound, and emptied vials of medicine would inform us that Prince Harry was sedated."

Sir Charles nodded at the significance of the emptied medicine vials. "If the prince was heavily sedated, it could be to our advantage, for he would not be awake and running about whilst gunshots were being fired."

"Or to our disadvantage, for he would not hear the song to his favorite horse which will be sung prior to his rescue. Such a warning could save his life."

"I take it you have a plan to suddenly enter the house, which will catch the captors by surprise," Joanna queried.

"We have several in mind," Carter-Smith replied. "But each depends on a detailed knowledge of the dwelling's interior, which we are unfortunately lacking. None of the neighbors have ever been inside the house, you see, and our only source thus far has been Dr. Fleming whose information is scant at best."

"In all likelihood, Director, the property was leased," said Joanna. "If so, you should contact the leasing agent who will know every foot of that house."

"Very good, Mrs. Watson, for the house was indeed leased by the Knight Frampton Agency," he responded. "The agent in charge, however, is currently in Bath on real estate business. We have dispatched an operative to find him and bring back detailed drawings."

"Some Victorian houses have secret entrances and exits," she remarked.

"We are aware, madam."

Joanna pondered the problem at length, nodding at one solution and shaking her head at another, before she spoke. "Assuming the house was leased, please ascertain if the locks were changed which is often done when a new tenant moves in, and of course determine who possesses the keys."

"We shall make inquiries."

"In addition, it might be helpful to learn if the house uses natural gas for cooking. That being the case, a leak in the gas line would induce a hurried evacuation by the residents."

"We considered that possibility, but unfortunately it would require entrance into the house itself," the director replied. "But do let me know if other thoughts on the matter come to mind."

It was obvious that my wife was seeking an entrance which would be quick and totally unexpected. But so was the SIS, with no apparent success.

A black motor vehicle drew up to the footpath outside the dwelling across the street, and a large, heavyset man carrying an armful of packages exited from the rear door. We quickly backed away from the window, so as not to be noticed, but the director kept his binoculars focused on the arriver who was hurrying up the path to the front door which he opened without knocking.

"We have seen him before, and believe he is one of the spies sent out for food," Carter-Smith said. "The very same vehicle he arrived in had circled the block twice in an effort to spot any individuals who might be surveilling the house."

"Careful devils, aren't they?" my father noted.

"That is a requirement for one to stay alive in the spying business, Dr. Watson."

As the director continued to view the surroundings with his

binoculars, I could not help but think how unremarkable his appearance was for that of a master spy. He was a man of average height and frame, with thinning gray hair and pale blue eyes that were partially obscured by horn-rimmed spectacles. His features were such that he would go unnoticed by most, which of course was ideal for an individual who worked in the world of shadows.

The door suddenly opened and an SIS agent rushed in carrying a boxful of items that gave off the odor of spoiled refuse. He placed the box down on a nearby desk and stepped back. "Here are some of the items from the dustbin which I believe you will find of interest, sir. The number of articles related to food consumption would indicate there are three or four occupants in the house."

"Is the number closer to three or four?"

"Four, sir, assuming average-sized servings."

Carter-Smith donned rubber gloves and began rummaging through the collection of rubbish which seemed to consist mainly of discarded food wrappings and the receipts for the same. There were several handkerchiefs with bloodstains that were encased in a glue-like substance. "Someone was bleeding."

My father moved in for a close examination and said, "It appears to be bloody sputum or phlegm."

"Which indicates?"

"The individual has either pneumonia or consumption," my father diagnosed.

"Was either present in the prince prior to his abduction?"

"Not to our knowledge."

"Which signifies one of the captors was ill, and that could work to our advantage," said the director, and went back to rummaging. At the very bottom of the box were two emptied bottles of medicines. "One of these is for codeine syrup which was dispensed three weeks ago."

"It is prescribed to suppress coughing," my father explained.

"Which informs us it belonged to the ill spy, for at the time the prescription was filled, the prince had not yet been abducted."

"And the second vial was for paraldehyde."

"Which is a sedative known to induce sleep."

"And what if given throughout the day?"

"Then you have a heavily sedated prince who spends most of his time asleep."

"Thank you, Dr. Watson," said Carter-Smith. "Your knowledge is of great help to us."

"I am delighted to be of assistance."

I nodded to myself, now realizing yet another reason why the director had insisted on my father's presence. The first and foremost purpose for having him on site during the rescue operation was his vast experience in the treatment of gunshot wounds. Prior to him setting up his practice in London, my father had been a British army surgeon who served valiantly in the Second Afghan War. In that dreadful conflict, he had treated the most severe of injuries caused by enemy gunfire, and was aware of every available technique to save the lives of those suffering from such wounds. I think it fair to say that very few had the practical skills my father had learned on the battlefields of Afghanistan. It was obvious that Carter-Smith expected a fierce gunfight to erupt during the rescue mission, and the prince himself as well as SIS operatives might sustain terrible wounds, with their very survival depending on my dear father's surgical skills. Yet, for most rescue undertakings by the SIS, I doubted that a surgeon would be present during the attack itself, but this mission was different in that it involved a prince of England. He would be the first treated, regardless of the severity of his wound.

Carter-Smith had also requested the presence of my wife, for not only was she fluent in German but knew every detail of Prince Harry's abduction. Thus she could decipher all of the words and any hidden messages uttered by a captured spy. Such information might be of great importance in hunting down other, secluded foreign agents. In addition, Joanna's skill as a former surgery nurse would be of immense help to my father in the treatment of serious gunshot wounds.

Another SIS agent burst into the command center and held up a gas mask for all to see. It consisted of heavy cloth, with large goggles to peer through and a tube which was connected to a small tank of a decontaminating substance. "The masks have arrived, sir, and will be dispensed to those in the attack force."

"Very good," said Carter-Smith. "And make certain one is available for the prince, as well as gloves for all."

"The men refuse to wear gloves, sir, for fear it will interfere with the firing of their weapons."

"Understood," the director said, and waited for the operative to disappear before turning to me. "Will the lack of gloves present a problem?"

"It shouldn't," I replied. "The vapor of mustard gas will settle on the skin, but can be effectively washed off, for the burns do not occur until an hour or two have passed."

"But the masks will protect the eyes and lungs, will they not?"

"As long as they remain in place and are well fitted against the face."

"My men have been instructed on how to do so," Carter-Smith said and, raising his binoculars, returned to surveilling the house against the street.

How strange, I thought once again, that a professor of pathology would be an integral part of an SIS team preparing a frontal attack to rescue an abducted prince. It was all based on my experience performing autopsies on British soldiers exposed to mustard gas on the Western Front, and my later questioning of those who had survived. I had been enlisted by His Majesty's government to participate in studies on human volunteers, which were designed to protect our soldiers and to treat those exposed to the terrifying gas. I could still recall the autopsies on corpses from the front, which showed widespread blistering of the skin and eyes, and massive inflammation of the lungs which had surely resulted in suffocating shortness of breath. But there were other gases as well, such as chlorine and phosgene, which were even more deadly.

I cleared my throat audibly and asked, "Are we certain that the agent to be used by the captors will be mustard gas?"

"The messages we have intercepted over the past week repeatedly mentioned the use of mustard gas on special targets," Carter-Smith replied. "The messages came from a U-boat in the Channel to an enemy agent located in East London. The term *special target* had previously been employed by the Huns to indicate the locale where their bombs would be dropped. That locale was London. So, putting all these pieces of information together, we believe this lot have mustard gas at their disposal."

"It is beyond barbaric," my father commented.

"War brings out the worst."

A grandfather clock in the hallway began striking the hour of half six. The director rapidly glanced at his own timepiece before calling out in a raised voice, "Where is the operative we sent to Bath?"

"Just arriving, sir," an agent outside the door called back.

"With the floor plans?"

"In hand, sir."

A young operative dashed into the command center and, using drawing pins, attached a large sheet of paper to the wall above the desk. On it were carefully diagrammed sketches of the interior of the house.

"Here we are, sir," the operative said, and pointed to the uppermost sketch. "The ground floor consists of a wide entryway which leads to a flight of stairs. Off to the right is a large dining room, kitchen, and storage area. The tradesman entrance is located between the latter two. On the opposite side of the staircase is an expansive study, behind which is a small loo and spare room."

"Do the rooms have windows?" asked Carter-Smith.

"All except for the storage room," he replied, then continued on. "Upstairs, there are four bedrooms, two a side, with loos tucked in between each pair of bedrooms."

"Did you inquire as to the size of the bedrooms?"

"The larger ones face the street, with the smaller ones behind quite small. All have windows."

"I need the size of the windows."

"Average, with a width of at least three feet."

"And the loos?"

"Much smaller windows, as one might expect."

"Are there any hidden exits or entrances?"

"None, sir."

"Did you inquire if the locks on the doors had been changed for the new occupants?"

"I did, sir, and they weren't."

"Well done," the director praised. "Now, with all this information in mind, give us your best reckoning on which room holds the prince."

"It would be one of the back bedrooms on the second floor, sir," the young operative responded without hesitation. "They are away from the street and further back from the adjacent homes, so the captive would not have the opportunity to signal passersby or curious neighbors."

"And finally, were you able to determine the number of individuals currently occupying the house?"

"We had a bit of luck there, sir, for early last week a drain in one of the loos became blocked, and a plumber had to be called in. I interviewed him on my journey back to London. He had a good memory, sir, and recalled seeing three, but heard a fourth snoring loudly in an adjacent bedroom."

"Excellent," Carter-Smith said, obviously pleased with the information. "Signal the lieutenant to have the men prepare to attack on my command.".

He watched the operative hurriedly depart, then returned to the window and focused his binoculars on the street below as twilight descended. Traffic was scant at this time of evening, with only an occasional motor vehicle and lorry passing by. The footpaths were vacant. No pets could be seen or heard.

"Those vehicles are being driven by my men," Carter-Smith noted.

"You certainly do not wish an innocent neighbor to drive by at a most inopportune moment," said my father.

"That will not happen, for I have had Gloucester Avenue blocked off at both ends."

"Are your vehicles on the lookout for additional Huns?"

The director shook his head in response. "They have a specific act to perform."

"Will it not draw the attention of the Huns?"

"Not if properly done," Carter-Smith replied as a large lorry approached. With the quickest of motions, he reached for the curtains and closed and opened them twice.

The large lorry slowed and came to a stop in front of the house next to 550 Gloucester Avenue. Three men attired in workman's clothes alighted from the vehicle and began unloading a huge, sturdy bench, with thick iron legs and a metal backing. One of the men was Inspector Lestrade.

"Can you envision what is to happen next?" Carter-Smith asked Joanna.

"The bench will be delivered shortly, whilst the men sing a song to a horse named Bluebonnet," said she, raising her monocular to watch the action about to occur. "The song, which

Prince Harry should be familiar with, will alert him that a rescue is about to proceed."

"But what if he is sedated and unaware?"

"Then we shall escort a dead prince back to Buckingham Palace."

CHAPTER THIRTY-ONE

The Rescue Mission

As if on command, the men carrying the sturdy bench veered off course and, singing at the top of their lungs, rushed full speed for the oak door at 550 Gloucester Avenue. Lestrade was a step behind, his revolver at the ready. Simultaneously, operatives on both adjacent roofs swung large metal hooks attached to thick ropes round and round before tossing them outward and onto the roof of the Hun's house. They then pulled forcefully on the lines which caused the hooks to dig deeply into the inner side of the parapet. Once the cables were secured, operatives wearing black attire flew into midair and, with the skill of trapeze artists, crashed through the rear windows on the second floor of the adjacent home. At the very same moment, Lestrade and his men rammed the metal-reinforced bench into the front door, which smashed it open and allowed for immediate access.

We stood motionless and spellbound whilst a dozen or more gunshots rang out in rapid sequence. Then several isolated rounds were fired before all went quiet. Four additional operatives dressed in black sprinted across the lawn, weapons drawn, and darted into the house. There was shouting, but no further gunfire. A full minute passed until an operative appeared at the door and gave the all-clear signal.

We hurried down the stairs, with a young agent carrying a box of medical supplies a step ahead of us. The main thought on all our minds was whether Prince Harry had been severely wounded, or had he in fact been killed in the fierce firefight which was unavoidable. Had the latter occurred, it would deliver a most demoralizing blow to the British people.

Across the lawn and into the Hun's house we dashed, hoping for the best, but expecting the worst. At the door we were met with a grim-faced operative and the odor of gun smoke.

"The prince?" Carter-Smith asked at once.

"Not here, sir," the operative reported. "All we have is a cluster of dead Huns."

Our disappointment was palpable, for we had so hoped to rescue the prince and bring him back safe and sound to the royal family. But our best efforts and plans had failed, and we had returned once again to square one, with Prince Harry's life still in jeopardy.

"Has every room been carefully searched?" Carter-Smith asked, breaking the momentary silence.

"And every closet, sir. I am afraid he is gone."

"Take us through the house, then."

The operative led the way in and pointed to a body at the bottom of the stairs. The Hun's white shirt was soaked with blood which was beginning to gel. He was coatless. "This one was the work of Inspector Lestrade."

"And his coat?" Joanna asked.

"Downstairs in the large study," the operative replied. "We believe he was resting or asleep when the gunfire erupted."

"Have you searched the coat?"

"No, madam."

"Then allow me."

We walked into the study whose polished shelves and desk were bare. Folded over a couch by the fireplace was the jacket to the Hun's suit. In its inner pocket was a Swedish passport and a train ticket from Cherbourg, France, to Meiringen, Switzerland, which Joanna studied at length before discarding. She ripped apart the shoulders of the inexpensive suit and removed stacks of British and American currency. There was also a Portuguese passport tucked under a shoulder pad.

"The usual spy fare," noted Carter-Smith.

"It would so appear," Joanna said.

After a careful, unproductive inspection of the desk drawers, we stepped into the dining room where the corpse of a second Hun remained seated. He, too, was coatless, and showed multiple gunshot wounds to his chest. His blood continued to drip onto the carpeted floor.

"Another piece of work by Scotland Yard," the operative informed us. "His discharged weapon is on the carpet by his side."

"Is he wearing a ring?" Joanna asked.

"He is indeed."

"Gold, with a large opal in its center?"

"Quite so."

"Then be very careful when removing it," she cautioned. "For if the small protuberances next to the gem are pressed simultaneously, a needle will appear that is capable of injecting a lethal dose of cyanide."

"And so instruct the others," Carter-Smith directed at once.

"I shall, sir," said the operative, and motioned for us to follow him.

We ascended the stairs where the odor of gun smoke was far more intense. At the top was a third Hun, with the frontal portion of his head blown off. There was only exposed brain and no skull above his eyebrows. His trousers were down at half-mast.

"He was in the loo when we arrived, which was fortunate, for he had left his revolver in the bedroom," said the operative. "Yet, like a madman, he decided to charge at us. We had no choice but to take him down."

"Is he, too, wearing a ring?" asked the director.

The operative nodded his response. "It is identical to that worn by his colleague downstairs."

"Again, Stanton, be very careful in its removal, and do not attempt to pry it free."

"If necessary, we shall sever off his finger and discard it."

No one objected.

"Are there more bodies?"

"No, sir, but we did manage to capture a final Hun in the bedroom which contained the window I plunged through," Stanton replied.

"Has he been wounded?"

"Only with a blow to the head which I delivered," the operative reported without inflection. "This way, sir."

We entered a rear bedroom and found Roger Mallsby seated on the floor beneath a smashed window. There was a deep red bruise on his forehead which was made even more obvious by the paleness of his skin. He stared at us, wide-eyed, as he attempted to gather his senses.

"He charged for the door and had the misfortune of running into the barrel of my weapon," said Stanton, and signaled to another operative to apply handcuffs to the captive. "He briefly lost consciousness, but appears to be quite alert now."

We glanced down at the private secretary in silence, each of us filled with utter disgust. But my father could not contain his anger further. "You bloody traitor!" he roared.

Mallsby's eyelids began to flutter, which, according to Joanna, was a sure sign the individual was composing a lie. "I demand to be set free, for you are making a terrible mistake," he said in a rush. "I, too, was taken prisoner, and forced to carry out their orders under threat of death."

"To the contrary, Mr. Mallsby, you did so willingly," Joanna rebuffed. "And for this treasonous act, you will shortly find your-self dangling at the end of a very long rope."

"You have no proof," he said, regaining his composure.

"Oh, but I do, for you were part and parcel of every step in the kidnapping of Prince Harry, and will be tried and convicted before a hard-nosed British jury."

Mallsby stood his ground. "Not when they learn that all of your evidence is circumstantial."

"Was it circumstantial when you set up Martha Ann Miller's abortion and informed Moriarty of it in advance?"

"Again, there is no proof to back up that absurd accusation," Mallsby insisted. "You have nothing to document my association with the Germans."

"Then how do we explain your presence, unguarded and unrestrained, in a bedroom with a window, which could have been smashed open and items tossed out to alert the neighbors?"

Whilst the private secretary struggled to come up with a plau-sible answer, my wife closely examined the bedroom, including the closet which contained a heavy leather suitcase. She placed it on the bed and, without bothering to open its lid, moved over to a topcoat that was draped across a bedroom bench. The lapel of the cashmere coat was partially torn off, but its lining appeared intact. "Prince Harry was wearing this when a struggle ensued. I suspect he put up a good fight."

"Are you certain the topcoat belonged to the prince?" asked Carter-Smith.

"Beyond doubt, for its label carries the name Gieves and Hawkes, which is one of Savile Row's most distinguished and expensive tailors. A Hun spy would never step foot into that fine store."

"Perhaps it belongs to Mallsby," I suggested.

"I think not, for its size is far too large for the private secretary's slight frame."

Joanna next searched through the inner pockets of the coat and extracted a passport which was obviously not British. "It is Portuguese and well made, with a photograph bearing a resemblance to Prince Harry."

"Which is further evidence they planned to move him out of England," Sir Charles joined in the conversation. "But where is his train ticket?"

"Elsewhere," she replied. "For the Huns were intent on presenting this prize to the kaiser. Of course another possibility is they plan to ship him across the Channel in a crate, which would require a different type of ticket."

"But such a passage could result in death."

Joanna shrugged indifferently. "A corpse would also serve their purpose. They might even return the body to England as a sign of respect, but only after displaying it to the world."

"Have they no sense of decency?" my father growled.

"Very little, when you consider the horrifying effects of mustard gas which the Huns released on our troops," said she, and leaned over to examine the pockets of Roger Mallsby, from which she removed a suitcase key and a train ticket from Cherbourg to Meiringen. "So it appears he intended to travel with his German comrades."

"All the way to Berlin, I suspect," said Sir Charles.

"Not if my assumption about the suitcase is correct," Joanna replied, inserting the key.

"The suitcase was too heavy to simply be carrying clothes alone," said she and, opening the lid, exposed a small fortune in British currency. There were stacks upon stacks of hundred-pound notes, which were literally packed into the confined space. Most were newly minted and tightly bound. My wife quickly counted the top row, then examined those beneath to assure they were genuine. "Gentlemen, you are gazing down on at least one hundred pounds."

"The money of a Judas," my father spat out. "The price of a traitor to Crown and country."

"The suitcase does not belong to me," Mallsby asserted.

"But I see the initials *RM* engraved upon it," Joanna noted.

Mallsby hesitated for a brief moment before stating, "Those are the initials of one of the Huns whose first name I recall was Reinhardt."

Undeterred, Joanna pushed the stacks of currency aside and reached into the side pockets of the suitcase where she discovered a passport which she held up to us to see. "How curious that this passport carries your name and a photograph which bears a close resemblance to you."

Mallsby did not flinch. "They planned for me to be by the prince's side on his journey to Germany."

My wife continued her search and uncovered a folded letter which she quickly read. "Oh, yes, another, even more curious finding. Here we have a cordial letter addressed to you from the Bank of Zurich, in which they express their delight that you opened a private account, and look forward to future deposits." She glanced over to Mallsby with a humorless smile. "I'd wager the initial deposit was a down payment for your services to Moriarty."

The private secretary's face lost color. His eyelids were fluttering again, but no words were forthcoming.

"You are going to hang, Mr. Mallsby, and no one will shed a tear watching you being marched up the steps to the gallows," Carter-Smith said. "That being the case, there is one way to save your treasonous neck and instead be confined to one of His Majesty's most uncomfortable prisons for the rest of your miserable life."

"What must I do?" Mallsby asked, desperately searching for any process by which he could remain alive.

"Give us the whereabouts of Prince Harry."

"I am unaware," Mallsby said without hesitation. "He is being moved from place to place on a daily basis, and never in my presence. I would answer your question if I could."

"Well, then, perhaps a stay in a cold, damp cell at the Tower of London will refresh your memory." Carter-Smith signaled to his two operatives, and the traitorous secretary was roughly marched out of the bedroom. We waited for their footsteps to disappear.

"I am afraid he does not know where the prince is being held," said Joanna. "Moriarty would never share this information with the likes of Roger Mallsby who can be bought and sold so easily."

"Can we hope that Mallsby will offer a valuable clue as his execution nears?" my father asked.

"That is most unlikely, Watson, for the Huns have no doubt kept the traitor in the dark should his role in the abduction be uncovered," Joanna replied. "At this juncture, Moriarty will be glad to be rid of Mallsby, for he has served his purpose and is now considered to be excess baggage which needs to be discarded."

"As the German agents continue on to Berlin with their prized possession," I thought aloud.

"Not necessarily," Carter-Smith interjected. "Those train tickets to Switzerland may be a ruse to divert our attention to their intended destination which would be Sweden. That country is neutral and far closer to Germany. Moreover, Sweden and Germany remain trading partners, and thus shipment of a crate across the Baltic Sea would be easily done, with of course the prince concealed within it."

"So we are back to a guessing game," my father said unhappily.

"I am afraid so," Carter-Smith concurred. "And now the

commissioner and I have the most unpleasant task of traveling to Buckingham Palace to inform His Majesty of the disappointing news."

On that depressing note, we departed and waited outside for a Scotland Yard vehicle to return us to Baker Street. A cold wind was blowing as black clouds gathered overhead and turned twilight into darkness. The gloomy weather seemed to match our mood.

"And now we find ourselves facing yet another dead end," said my father. "I do not see any clues to dictate our next move."

"Oh, but I do, Watson."

"Based on what, may I ask?"

"The calling card Moriarty left for me," said she as our limousine drew up to the footpath.

CHAPTER THIRTY-TWO

The Calling Card

We decided to soothe our disappointment by having dinner at Simpson's-in-the-Strand, my father's favorite restaurant. The maître d', on recognizing my father, seated us at the very same table he and the Great Detective had frequented so many years ago. It was well situated near the distant wall, thus making our conversation difficult for others to overhear, particularly if we kept our voices low. Nevertheless, we rarely spoke of cases in public, for suspicious ears can at times invade one's privacy. Accordingly, we limited our table talk to the fine fare we were enjoying, which included Joanna having the lamb, I the beef Wellington, and my father roast beef carved off the trolley. All were accompanied by Yorkshire pudding and washed down with a superb Médoc. As we finished our Turkish coffee, however, my father could no longer contain his curiosity.

"Are you intent on keeping us in suspense the entire evening?" he asked in a whisper.

"Regarding what?" Joanna teased quietly.

"The supposed calling card."

"I am surprised the clue slipped by your keen eye, Watson."

"Which clue?"

"The one which presented itself twice."

My father groaned good-naturedly. "Are we to be at least given a hint?"

"Think back to the word *move* which you inquired about as we departed the Gloucester Avenue residence."

"I asked about *his* next move," my father replied, emphasizing *his* request to Moriarty.

"Correct," she went on. "Now connect the word to a physical movement."

My father considered the clue briefly, then replied, "I can only come up with the train tickets to Switzerland, which Carter-Smith believed to be false leads meant to throw us off track."

"Tsk! Tsk!" Joanna dismissed the erroneous conclusion with a flick of her wrist. "That is because he saw, but did not observe. Furthermore, he is only supplying us with a guess which serves no purpose."

"I am afraid you have me in a quandary."

"That is the result of you overlooking a most important observation, which you yourself made earlier."

"Which is?"

"The rather obvious fact that our adversary is leading us along by leaving clues behind," she elucidated. "Mind you, these were not false clues, but accurate ones in every instance. With this understanding, please reconsider the meaning of the train tickets which were left behind."

My father slowly nodded. "You are being led to Switzerland."

"But where in Switzerland?"

My father thought back before answering. "I believe it was a town whose name began with the letter *M*."

"Does that not ring a bell?"

"Not offhand."

"Think back to the deadly struggle between my father and"—

Joanna paused to lower her voice to the barest of whispers—
"between my father and Moriarty."

My father's eyes suddenly widened. "It occurred near the
Swiss village of Meiringen!" he breathed.

"And what marvelous work of nature lies within walking
distance?"

"The Reichenbach Falls," he uttered in a hushed voice.

"Yes."

"Where he now means to kill you."

"That is surely his plan, for it will be the best form of vengeance," Joanna said in a monotone. "He will delight in my death
at the same site my father disposed of his brother. In his evil
mind, it is a perfect ending."

"He will have every advantage."

"True."

"Then you must not go."

"I have no choice."

The subject was too delicate to continue our conversation in
public, even with whispered voices. So we promptly paid our bill
and hailed a taxi for our silent ride back to Baker Street. But no
words were needed, for our collective minds were on the mor-
tal struggle between Sherlock Holmes and Professor Moriarty. It
had transpired on a ledge overlooking the Falls of Reichenbach,
a cascading waterfall that has a precipitous drop of hundreds of
feet. Holmes, no stranger to hand-to-hand combat, had won the
battle, with Moriarty being tossed down the steep incline to his
death. Yet his body was never recovered, and some believe he
had miraculously survived, but, broken in bone and spirit, he
was never able to regain his title of the Napoleon of crime. But
according to my father, this ending was nonsense, for Holmes
himself had seen Moriarty fall a long way before he struck a large
rock, bounced off, and disappeared into the dark waters.

Upon our arrival to Baker Street, we hurried up the stairs

into our parlor and lighted a three-log fire to ward off the chilly night air. My father quickly retrieved his old notes on *The Return of Sherlock Holmes* which contained every detail on the final struggle between Holmes and Professor Moriarty at the Falls of Reichenbach.

He thumbed through the notes to their very beginning, then asked, "We were aware that Holmes had a lengthy conversation with Moriarty prior to our journey to the Continent?"

"Face-to-face?" Joanna queried at once.

"In this very room," my father replied. "He appeared unannounced and demanded that your father cease all attempts to interfere with the professor's criminal activities. When Holmes refused, Moriarty threatened him with extreme measures. This then was the beginning of the end, for it would be a fight to the death."

"What was Holmes's impression of his archenemy on that visit?" I inquired.

"Much to my surprise, Holmes found the manner of Moriarty somewhat unsettling, for here was a man with a soft, precise fashion of speech that left a conviction of sincerity, which a mere bully could not produce. Moreover, Moriarty's physical features were not what Holmes had expected. He was extremely tall, with a prominent, dome-shaped forehead and two eyes that were deeply sunken into his skull. He presented himself as being a quite formidable opponent."

"Who was most clever," I added.

"Not only clever, but a man of good birth and excellent education, with a brain that carried such phenomenal mathematical faculty that he held a chair at one of our smaller universities. But obviously a criminal strain ran in his blood, making him capable of the most diabolical deeds. His brother was to follow in his footsteps and has proved to be every bit as evil as the professor."

"And equally as clever," Joanna noted.

"Indeed, for he is luring you to the same village which was the site of the deadly struggle between his brother and your father."

"Was the earlier lure also a train ticket?"

My father shook his head in response. "It was a letter from an Englishwoman who learned of our presence in Meiringen. She was staying in a nearby village and suffering from end-stage consumption. Swiss doctors had little to offer, and she begged for my attendance at her bedside, which I supplied. It was whilst I was away that Holmes fell into Moriarty's trap."

"Of course the letter was written by Moriarty," Joanna deduced.

"Of course, for I was to learn that there was no such Englishwoman staying in the nearby village," my father went on. "Upon my return to Meiringen, I visited the Falls of Reichenbach and found evidence of the great struggle between Holmes and Moriarty, and believed both had perished in the violent waters below."

"I take it you have a detailed description of the Falls of Reichenbach in your notes."

"Quite detailed," said my father, and thumbed through several sheets of his notes. "It was a most fearsome place in which a torrent swollen by melting snow plunged down into a tremendous abyss. The shaft into which the river hurls itself is lined by coal-black rock top to bottom. The long sweep of green water roaring down sent up a curtain of spray which produced a humanlike shout. The last I saw of Holmes was a tall figure hurrying along a pathway, with a walking stick, that led to a ledge overlooking the falls. I was later to believe that it was the last I was to see of him in this world."

I envisioned the awesome scene my father had described, and for a brief moment a picture of my wife being thrown into the violent waters crossed my mind. "In all likelihood, Moriarty's brother has carefully surveyed all the pathways and ledges surrounding the Falls of Reichenbach, which will give him the advantage."

"And no doubt selected the exact ledge upon which the struggle will take place," said my father.

"That by itself offers him no advantage," Joanna remarked.

"But it will give one of Moriarty's men, who is stationed above, a clear view which will allow him to toss a large rock at your head," my father warned. "A similar event occurred after Holmes had disposed of Professor Moriarty, with the rock barely missing him. With this happening in mind, you should not expect the evilest of men to act alone."

"I am afraid this is not a battle you can win, Joanna," said I.

"We shall see," she responded, undeterred.

"My dear, I know you are experienced in jujitsu, but that alone will not suffice," my father counseled. "He will be aware of your martial art talent and be prepared to defend against it. Like my son, I am afraid you cannot prevail, for all goes against you."

"You must ignore the lure he has set up for you, dear heart," I pleaded. "Please reconsider."

"I cannot," said she.

"Why not, may I ask?"

"Because he has given me no choice, for I will not spend the rest of my days staring at the shadows whilst waiting for Moriarty to pounce."

On that note, we retired for the night, with Joanna falling asleep in my arms. I twisted and turned, dozing fitfully, as I worried for my wife's safety. She slept soundly.

CHAPTER THIRTY-THREE

The Instructions

In the midst of our late breakfast, Miss Hudson rapped on the door and entered with an envelope in hand.

"This was just delivered by messenger for Mrs. Watson," she announced. "He stated it came from the Continent."

"It's from him!" Joanna said, and hurried over for the envelope. "Thank you, Miss Hudson."

"Shall I clear the table?" she asked.

"Later, for there remain a few scraps of your delicious breakfast waiting to be consumed."

Our housekeeper blushed at the compliment and departed, quietly closing the door behind her.

"Perhaps it is another enticement to follow the lure," my father suggested.

"More likely it will instruct us on how to find the lure," said Joanna, unsealing the envelope. "Which will lead me directly into the trap."

She removed a single sheet of paper, with clear handwriting upon it, and began to read aloud.

My dear Mrs. Watson,
Here are the steps you must take for us to conclude our business
and bring this matter to an end.

You and the Drs. Watson are to depart from London at
the earliest morning hour and board a ship for Cherbourg. Once
there, you will travel by train on a five-hour journey to Swit-
zerland, which will allow you to disembark at Meiringen just
prior to sunset. Rooms have been reserved for you at the Hotel
Edelweiss. Needless to say, the Drs. Watson should remain
unarmed, for the discharge of weapons could cause irreparable
harm to Prince Harry.

At noon sharp the following day, the senior Dr. Watson
will assume a position on the hotel's rooftop to keep a close eye
on the surrounding area, which will permit him to warn you
in the event of any untoward happenings. The younger Dr.
Watson will find a message at the registration desk that informs
him of the suite in which the prince is comfortably housed. The
doctor is to report promptly to that suite and introduce himself
to my associate who is standing guard. The latter will also be
unarmed.

Once all is in place, you are to depart from the hotel
and follow the main path to the Falls of Reichenbach. Upon
reaching a fork, choose the narrow one and continue on until
you come to the ledge overlooking the falls. I shall be there
waiting. In the event I do not prevail, you will be allowed to
return to the hotel, from which you and the Watsons can depart
for home, with Prince Harry at your side. I should warn you
that any deviation on your behalf will result in the most dire of
consequences.

Yours,
Col. James Moriarty

Joanna placed the letter down and said, "Nicely set up."

"But surely you do not trust the scoundrel's words," my father refuted.

"His directions are correct," she replied. "The statement that his associate will be unarmed is nonsense, of course."

"And if you prevail, I think it most unlikely Moriarty will allow us to return home to England, with Prince Harry at our side."

"That will never occur," Joanna agreed. "If Moriarty dies, he will undoubtedly have plans for my demise as well."

"Such as a companion situated high above the ledge who is prepared to drop a sizeable rock upon your head," my father cautioned.

"That would be history repeating itself."

"Which would be his cup of tea."

"Perhaps," Joanna said, unconvinced. "And please keep in mind he has no intention of ever allowing Prince Harry to return to England. In the event of Moriarty's death, the German spies will see to it that the prince is presented to the Kaiser, with great fanfare for all the world to see."

"Do you believe he has plans to do away with me and John as well?" asked my father.

"I think not, for your deaths would serve no purpose," she replied. "If Moriarty succeeds, he would wish John to remain alive, so he could write the final adventure of *The Daughter of Sherlock Holmes*."

I gave my wife a long and worried look, concerned even more for her safety. The trap had been set for her, with all advantages favoring her nemesis, yet she appeared so calm despite the impending struggle with such a formidable foe. "Do you not find the letter unsettling?" I asked at length.

"The unsettling will come when I am face-to-face with

Moriarty on that narrow ledge overlooking the turbulent falls below," said she, and reached for a final piece of bacon which she nibbled on. "And now let us proceed to Selfridges department store for some last-minute shopping."

"For what purpose?" I inquired.

"To purchase winter garments, for Switzerland can be quite cold, even in spring."

Our taxi ride to Oxford Street took far longer than expected, for several streets were blocked off, whilst a hazard team dealt with a Hun bomb that had found its target but remained un-detonated. So we were diverted westward, then southward on Edgware Road, where the traffic was moving slowly due to large craters from an earlier bombing. Fortunately, none of the bombs were close enough to damage Marble Arch, one of London's treasured monuments, which we were now passing as we approached Selfridges.

Despite the early hour, the elegant department store was quite busy, with eager shoppers filling every aisle. Joanna led us by an extensive perfume section, then past a fine selection of topcoats before we came upon a handsome display of scarves and gloves. She quickly found a smart pair of black gloves which were fur-lined and provided a good fit. But her choice of scarves required far more time, for it was not only the color but its texture that caught her interest. Finally, she chose a Harris Tweed scarf which measured a good five feet in length and wrapped nicely around the neck and shoulders. It had a light gray color, which was not at all eye-catching, but matched well with her dark topcoat.

"Done," said she, and headed for a counter to pay for her stylish garments. The cost was five pounds one shilling, which was quite expensive, but then stylish goods always were. My wife handed the clerk six pounds, which of course would require a sizeable amount of coinage in return.

"Do you happen to have a shilling, madam?" the clerk asked.

"I do not," Joanna replied. "And besides, I should like the extra coinage to be used for gratuities as we begin our travels."

"Of course, madam," said she, and counted out a handful of shillings and half crowns.

"Home then, so we can begin our packing for the journey ahead," Joanna proposed.

On our return ride to Baker Street, we stopped at a tobacconist to replenish Joanna's supply of Turkish cigarettes for our travel abroad. It required a visit to a second tobacconist which my father favored for his Arcadia Mixture. We next paid a call to a large shop which carried the name Piccadilly Outdoors. Joanna entered alone and returned shortly with a wrapped package the size of a shoebox. "More winter gear," she explained, and left it at that. Finally, at my suggestion, we looked in to our poulterer and purchased a fine goose for our dear landlady who continued to put up with our eccentricities. But the real purpose of the purchase was to inject a note of cheer at our dinner for our last night in London, for tomorrow could bring us the greatest of sorrows.

On entering 221b Baker Street, we found Miss Hudson laboring over our lunch of haddock and crusty baked potato spuds. Wiping her hands on her apron, she sniffed the air and detected the aroma of fresh fowl. She was delighted with the goose we had purchased, and promised to baste it to perfection with her secret, yet delicious, recipe.

"Now, up to your rooms whilst I put the finishing touches on a tasty lunch," Miss Hudson commanded.

"Which we shall look forward to," said Joanna. "But I wonder if I might ask a favor on your way up."

"Most assuredly, Mrs. Watson."

"A label has been loose in one of my coats, and I would very much like to borrow a sewing needle and thread from you to reattach it."

"Oh, please allow me to attend to that task."

"I know of your expertise in stitching, Miss Hudson, but I have recently taken up sewing as a hobby," said Joanna. "It truly relaxes me and takes my mind off more challenging matters. Thus, on this occasion, I should like to do the simple stitching myself, and later show it to you for your approval and additional repairs if necessary."

"I would be happy to do so," Miss Hudson obliged. "And it just so happens I can fetch the sewing materials for you now, for they reside in a nearby drawer."

On reaching our parlor, Joanna immediately retired to her bedroom where she planned to relax whilst stitching on a detached label. I was unaware of my wife's newfound hobby, but grateful for her absence, for it allowed my father and me to have a most serious discussion on the extreme danger which lay ahead for Joanna.

"We must somehow dissuade her, for her very life is at stake here," I beseeched in a low voice.

"We will not be able to do so, for she has in fact no choice and neither did her father, who knew that Moriarty would desist only when removed from the face of the earth," my father responded quietly.

I groaned inwardly, for I had hoped my father would join me and demand that Joanna not participate in this deadly match. "It is madness to go up against such a formidable foe who has all the advantages."

"There is yet another reason why she must meet Moriarty's challenge," said he.

"Which is?"

"Moriarty will in all likelihood plan to kill her dear son, Johnny, next."

My brow went up at the unexpected answer. "But he is only a lad who poses no threat to this evil man, particularly now that he has returned to his studies at Eton."

"But you have written of his remarkable talents in your adventures of Holmes's daughter," my father went on. "Johnny has his mother's brain and tenacity, and will undoubtedly become a private detective, at which he will excel, much as she has. Should Moriarty dispose of his mother, I can assure you that Johnny will pursue Moriarty with a vengeance that neither Heaven nor Hell could fend off."

"Like a Sicilian vendetta?"

"The very same."

"Do you believe Joanna has considered this possibility?"

"Beyond any doubt," my father replied. "That may be the primary reason she intends to confront Moriarty and do away with him once and for all."

Later that evening we dined on Miss Hudson's splendidly roasted goose, and although Moriarty was on our minds, we spoke little of him. Because of our early start in the morning, my father and I retired as Big Ben struck the hour of eight, whilst Joanna remained in the parlor, pacing back and forth, lighting one Turkish cigarette after another.

I again slept fitfully as I continued to worry about my dear wife and the grave danger she faced ahead. Sometime later—hours perhaps—I was awakened by the sound of conversation taking place in the parlor. I peeked in and expected to find Joanna and my father planning and discussing defensive moves which might be available to her. But I saw only Joanna who was speaking on the telephone under a dense cloud of Turkish tobacco smoke.

Holding my curiosity in abeyance, I returned to bed for a fitful sleep.

CHAPTER THIRTY-FOUR

The Watchful Spy

Our journey was uneventful except for the man in the dark suit who seemed to be following our every step. Joanna first noticed him when we disembarked at Cherbourg, then again whilst we switched trains in Paris. It might of course have been coincidence, but he appeared once more in the rear of the dining car as our train neared the Swiss border. Our suspicion was confirmed when Joanna passed him on the way to the loo and observed a distinct bulge over the left side of his jacket.

"He is armed," she whispered on returning to her seat which did not face him. "His suit is nicely tailored but not well enough to conceal his weapon."

"Does he have Teutonic features?" my father asked in a low voice.

Joanna shrugged indifferently. "The ordinary ones, with blue eyes, blond hair, and a straight, narrow nose. Of course he could be Scandinavian, but gentlemen from those neutral countries are rarely armed."

"But why are we being followed?" I asked. "Is Moriarty concerned that we will not adhere to his instructions?"

"His major concern is to make certain we did not bring along reinforcements," Joanna replied.

"Which Moriarty no doubt already has at his disposal," my father growled under his breath.

"It is a devious, but smart move on his part," said she, and held up a polished soup spoon to catch the man's reflection. "You will note that he doesn't seem to care whether we discover him or not."

"Perhaps he has already determined that we are traveling alone," I wondered.

"That decision will not be reached until the last stop before Meiringen, where he will keep a sharp eye on those boarding."

"Clever fellow," my father remarked.

Joanna shook her head briefly. "He is simply following Moriarty's orders."

"Then his singular mission is near completion."

"I suspect his mission is not singular."

"What else, then?"

"To keep us in his sight whilst an associate searches our cabin."

"For what purpose?"

"To discover clues as to how I plan to defend myself."

"What makes you so confident they will do so?"

"Because it is what I would do were I in Moriarty's stead."

My father squinted an eye, unconvinced. "But it is impossible to prove such a move has taken place."

"Not so, Watson," said she. "Now that we have finished our rather tasteless salmon, let us arise from our table. At that very moment, our spy will leave his seat and dash away, so he can warn his associate that we are returning to our cabin."

"But a man hurrying away and a vacant cabin are hardly proof."

Joanna smiled humorlessly. "What if I showed you evidence that our suitcases had been tampered with?"

On arising from our table, the man in the dark suit abruptly stood and departed, just as Joanna had predicted. We strolled back to our cabin at a leisurely pace, stopping at openings to view the magnificent Swiss Alps which marked the border between France and Switzerland. The mountains were yet covered with glistening snow, but patches of green were visible at the lower elevations. Melting snow, I thought miserably, which produced the torrent that hurled down the Reichenbach Falls.

We entered our cabin and found all in order, with no evidence of a search or break-in. Joanna reached for her suitcase and, placing it on a small table, examined its lock and surrounding edges with her magnifying glass.

"So they have taken a look," she announced.

"Was the lock picked?" I asked.

"I suspect so, but it was done by an expert who left no scratch marks behind," she replied.

"Then what convinces you that the suitcase was searched?"

"Because it has been opened."

"How can you possibly know that?"

"Because the short strand of hair I pasted between the edges is gone."

"Could it not have fallen off?" my father inquired.

Joanna smiled at my father. "Saliva makes an excellent paste, Watson."

She opened the suitcase and found everything in order, including the heavy boots she had purchased the day before at Piccadilly Outdoors. On lifting the boots, she exposed a new set of crampons, nicely laid out.

Joanna removed and carefully inspected the crampons, which are metal plates with spikes that can be attached to boots for walking on ice or slippery rock. "They are as I left them," said she, and returned them to the suitcase which she shut and locked securely.

"Do you have any experience using those devices?" asked my father.

"None whatsoever," she replied and, leaning back in her seat, closed her eyes for a brief respite.

We arrived at Meiringen just before sunset and hired a carriage to take us to the Hotel Edelweiss where rooms had been reserved for us. The storied hotel was made of white stone, with each of its five floors supplied with large windows that faced the Swiss Alps. Atop it was a red, steepled roof, which had at its center a lookout platform that provided a panoramic view of the nearby mountain range. It was the space my father would occupy during the struggle between Joanna and Moriarty.

After depositing our luggage with the porter, we decided to stroll about until we found the path leading to the Falls of Reichenbach. The path itself was far more narrow than we had anticipated, but there was no question as to its authenticity, for at its entrance was a small plaque dedicated to Sherlock Holmes and his memorable struggle with Professor Moriarty. Joanna studied the plaque at length, and I could not help but wonder if she was contemplating the methods her father had used to overcome the most formidable of foes.

We continued down the path until we reached the fork which Moriarty had described, and veered off onto the narrowest of its components. Onward and upward we went, climbing to the very top of the falls before coming to a rather unstable bridge which we were obliged to cross. With Joanna leading the way, we followed the trail down the steep hill, at which point we came to a ledge that was so narrow it would not allow for the passage of two persons abreast. The path ended close to the falls, so close one could actually touch it.

The view below was mesmerizing, with a wide torrent of foaming water gushing down a shaft in the mountain which was quite jagged and coal-black in color. As the mass of the powerful flow descended into the valley below, it sent up an enormous spray and made a strange sound that resembled a human shout.

"Do you believe he will follow you down the path?" my father asked, breaking our silence.

"He will be on the ledge waiting for me," Joanna replied.

"Which reenacts the struggle between your father and his brother."

"That is his intent, with a different outcome, of course."

"Do you anticipate he will suddenly rush at you, much as Moriarty did to Holmes?"

"That is unlikely, for he no doubt believes that will be my expectation," said she. "I am of the opinion he will wait for the opportune moment to strike with a practiced Bartitsu move."

"You must avoid any form of wrestling or grappling, for I suspect that, like his brother before him, he is quite strong, which will allow him to overpower you."

"But he no doubt will employ the martial art of Bartitsu," Joanna contended. "And that, my dear Watson, demands close contact."

"Not if he applies French kick boxing or cane fighting, which are also tenets of Bartitsu," my father noted. "You must prepare for the unexpected from this clever devil."

"Who would do well to prepare for the same from me."

"What do you have in mind?"

"The totally unexpected," said she, and wrapped her Harris Tweed scarf around her neck, for night was falling and bringing a cold air with it.

We returned to the hotel and enjoyed a splendid dinner of veal and mushrooms in a cream sauce, washed down with a far too expensive Saint-Émilion. Over the rims of our wineglasses, we intermittently gazed around the dining room, searching for the spy wearing a dark suit who had followed us the entire journey.

He was not to be seen. With the clock striking nine, we decided to retire early, for a most challenging tomorrow awaited us. As I closed the door to our comfortable room, I watched my wife reach for her magnifying glass and carefully examine the locks and closed edges of our suitcases.

"Have the suitcases been tampered with?"

Joanna nodded her responses. "The pasted-on hairs have been dislodged."

"Moriarty again!" I said hoarsely. "Why does he bother with yet another search?"

"To discover any hidden clues on how I might go about defending myself."

"Did he uncover such clues?"

"Of course," Joanna said, firmly closing her suitcase. "That is why I left them only partially concealed."

CHAPTER THIRTY-FIVE

The Reichenbach Falls

The next morning brought with it a cold, dense fog, which presented the most adverse conditions for a struggle on a narrow mountain ledge. Despite my repeated pleas, Joanna would neither delay nor defer her encounter with Moriarty.

"You will be placed at an even greater disadvantage," I warned.

"Not so, for Moriarty's vision will also be dimmed, although he will see well enough to watch me remove my black leather gloves."

"For what purpose will you do so?"

"To allow my hands to have a better grasp, which of course will give the impression I am about to engage in hand-to-hand combat."

"How is that to be avoided?"

"With guile," she said simply.

There was a rap on the door, and my father entered, appropriately dressed in a derby, heavy topcoat, and a thick scarf around his neck. His hands were gloveless.

"Ready then, are we?" he asked.

"Ready," Joanna replied in a calm voice.

"You must of course be prepared to fend off a sudden rush, should Moriarty choose to do so," my father advised.

"If that is his first move, Watson, it will be his last."

"Good, for preparation is the best defense," my father went on, now reaching under the back of his topcoat for a Webley revolver. "I shall be observing all activities from my perch on the roof, and should I see anything untoward I will fire off a single shot."

"So you were armed after all," said Joanna. "I must admit I did not detect the presence of your weapon."

"That is because a holster attached to the back of one's belt produces little, if any, bulge in a topcoat."

"Well done, Watson."

"And well-practiced," said he, replacing the weapon to its hidden location. "Now do remember, on hearing my shot you must take immediate cover."

"Without a moment's hesitation," she promised.

"Head down at all times."

"Of course."

"Then let us be off."

As my father departed for the platform on the roof, I gave my wife a final, warm embrace and a kiss to her forehead. "Do be careful," I implored.

"I shall."

I hurried from our room and took the lift to the lobby, praying along the way that all would end well, but the terrible risks continued to weigh heavily on my mind. The lobby itself was crowded with guests who were mingling and chatting merrily whilst waiting for the weather to clear. Some would no doubt visit the famed Falls of Reichenbach where Holmes and Professor Moriarty had fought to the death. Little did they know the very same struggle was about to occur once again, with the same result I hoped. At the registration desk I was handed a message which simply read

> Room 528

I climbed the stairs to the fifth floor in order to ascertain whether I was being followed. That was not the case, for the staircase was cold and silent as a tomb. There was no activity on the top floor either, other than chambermaids who were quietly going about their duties. I noticed how they noiselessly approached the Hun's room and passed by without bothering to rap on its door. Of course no one would be allowed in, on the off chance they might see a man being held hostage.

I applied a single knock to the door numbered 528, which opened immediately. Before me stood a heavyset man with striking Teutonic features, the most prominent of which were his glacial blue eyes that were hard as stone. He was the very same man who had followed us from London to Meiringen.

"I am Dr. John—"

"I know who you are," he interrupted, and motioned me into the sitting room of a large suite which was in need of clearing. Off to the side were breakfast dishes which had served at least two individuals, and now filled the air with the aroma of burnt bacon. "You will be allowed to see the prince and speak briefly with him. You must limit your conversation to the state of his health and well-being. Should you attempt to send him a secret message, you will pay dearly for it. I have been instructed not to kill you, but I will if it becomes necessary."

"But if that occurs, who will write of the great struggle between Moriarty and the daughter of Sherlock Holmes?" I asked, gathering my courage and determined not to be intimidated by the Hun.

"Your father," he replied as if rehearsed for the question. "Come this way."

The Hun gave my back a forceful shove toward the door to an adjoining bedroom, which he opened with his fist. Seated before me was Prince Harry, the third in line of succession to the British throne. His once handsome face was now haggard and drawn, with swollen eyes and dark circles beneath them from lack of sleep.

"You have a visitor," the spy said to him.

The prince, who was seated on a wooden chair with his wrists bound to it, looked up and attempted to recognize me, but with little apparent success. "Who are you?" asked he, in a hoarse voice.

"I am Dr. John Watson who, along with my wife and father, have come to take you home."

Prince Harry's eyes suddenly widened. "Has the ransom been paid?"

"We are about to do so, Your Royal Highness."

"Excellent," said he, struggling for a moment against the ropes that limited the motion of his upper body. His legs were free, but small bells had been attached to his ankles, which would ring with any sudden movement. "When is my release to occur?"

"Soon," I replied as the Hun nudged my back with a sharp elbow, instructing me to end the conversation. "I must, however, report whether you have been harmed or injured."

"I have not, although my treatment has been rather harsh at times."

"Were actual blows delivered?"

"Only when I attempted to escape."

"Enough talk!" the spy ordered abruptly.

"Bugger off, you bloody Hun!" Prince Harry bellowed out.

A smile must have crossed my face, for never have I been more proud of a royal prince. Courage sometimes shows itself in the strangest of situations, thought I. The prince's sudden outburst must have upset the spy, for he grabbed my collar and force-fully marched me out of the bedroom and into an overstuffed chair by the window.

"Stay there, and only move when I tell you to do so," the Hun directed.

I nodded my acquiescence, all the while measuring the heavyset spy, with his broad shoulders and thick arms which were no doubt trained to deliver lethal blows. Any struggle with him would be in vain, for were I to begin to prevail, he would not hesitate to use his holstered weapon which would mark the end of my life. Moreover, an erratic shot could seriously wound or kill the prince as well. The final result would be a disaster, and of no benefit to Joanna.

The silence in the sitting room was broken by the distinct cry of a baby in the adjacent suite. The cry was of no concern to the spy, which suggested he had heard it earlier. But I found it most worrying, for it indicated that the wall between the rooms was thin and allowed the sound of voices to pass through. Was that the reason Moriarty had reserved rooms for us at the Edelweiss? Did he have an ear to the wall whilst Joanna and I were discuss-ing the clues she had purposefully left behind? Or even more damaging, had he overheard her methods of defense on being attacked? If so, my dear wife was doomed.

In my peripheral vision, I peeked out the window and watched Joanna walk into the clearing in front of the hotel, then pause briefly before continuing on to the path which led to the Reichenbach Falls. Her stride was steady and not at all awkward, unlike that of an individual who had fixed crampons onto their boots. With a final glance over her shoulder, she disappeared into the mist. The dreadful thought that I would never see my wife again came to mind once more.

A struggle with the Hun remained out of the question, I re-considered, because at this point in time it would be of no help to Joanna. Even if I were to prevail, she would reach the narrow ledge long before I caught up with her. For some strange reason, I suddenly recalled John Milton's famous line, "They also serve who stand and wait," and at that moment I had a much clearer understanding of the meaning.

"I must use the loo," the prince demanded.

"Not now," the Hun responded.

"I have an urgent need!"

"Then hold it."

"I cannot!"

"You have no choice."

"Then I shall relieve myself where I sit, after which you and your friends can deal with the cleanup and the stench."

The Hun hesitated as he attempted to solve the obvious dilemma. He was ordered to keep the prince restrained, but if the prince soiled himself, moving him outside would present a problem of some magnitude. The odor alone would draw considerable attention, and perhaps the offer of assistance from bystanders. Abruptly, the spy turned to me. "Dr. Watson, you will untie the prince and help him to the bathroom. You must then stand aside so that I can clearly see both of you. If there are any sudden moves, you will die where you stand. Now, do exactly as you are told, and do it slowly."

I arose from my chair and entered the bedroom, with the Hun at my back. Unhurriedly, I removed the ropes from the prince's wrists and assisted him to his feet. It was my belief that he would be weak from his captivity, but this was not the case. He stood strongly without wavering and proceeded to flex his legs, as if to bring the circulation back. His attire was unchanged from what he wore whilst riding in Hyde Park before his capture. His tan riding breeches and scarlet jacket were badly stained, his high ankle boots scuffed and in want of polish.

"You may lean on my arm, Your Highness," I offered.

"There is no need," said he.

Prince Harry walked into the loo, his step surprisingly steady, the bells around his ankles tinkling with each move. He relieved himself at length, with water splashing loudly in the toilet bowl. Upon finishing, he closed his trousers and returned to the bedroom. The Hun was motioning the prince back into his chair when a shot rang out from a roof near us. In an instant the spy raced for the window, his weapon at the ready, and stared out to determine the reason for the gunfire. Suddenly, Prince Harry sprinted past me and, on entering the sitting room, leaped into the air and delivered a vicious football-style kick to the Hun's back, which propelled the stunned spy through the closed window and sent shattered glass flying into the air. The Hun managed only the smallest of cries as he descended and collided with the frozen ground five floors below. The prince and I dashed over to the shattered window and saw the Hun sprawled out on the icy turf, faceup with his head bent at a most peculiar angle, no doubt the result of a severely broken neck.

"Nicely done, Your Highness," I praised.

"A holdover from my football days," he replied without bravado.

The door to the suite crashed open and, much to my surprise, Capt. Carter-Smith and one of his lieutenants rushed in, revolvers drawn. The director of the SIS quickly moved over to us and provided cover whilst his lieutenant searched the entire suite before giving the all-clear signal.

Carter-Smith leaned through the window and studied the corpse of the Hun below. "I take it there was a struggle," said he.

"Not in the true sense," I replied. "Whilst the prince was departing from the loo, a rifle shot rang out, which drew the Hun's attention to the window. His Highness used the opportunity to leap through the air and deliver a powerful kick to the Hun's back, which sent him flying out the window. I suspect the spy had no idea what had happened as he flew downward."

"Well, he found out soon enough," the director quipped, then turned to the prince. "I am Captain Carter-Smith, director of the SIS, Your Highness."

"It is my honor to meet you, sir, particularly under these circumstances," said Prince Harry.

"It appears you are unharmed."

"I am well."

"Excellent," the director said. "We shall do a bit of cleanup, then return you to the comforts of Buckingham Palace."

"Which I shall look forward to."

"But pray tell, Captain," I interrupted. "How did the SIS become involved?"

"That was your wife's doing," replied Carter-Smith, then added for the prince's benefit, "who happens to be the daughter of Sherlock Holmes. The clever woman contacted me in the middle of the night and told of the struggle which was to take place between her and Moriarty in Meiringen. Mrs. Watson of course realized that Moriarty had no intention of releasing the prince or allowing her to live, regardless of the outcome of their confrontation. To this end, should the famous daughter prevail, he would arrange for her to be killed at a most notable place as his final revenge."

"With a rifle shot as she emerged victorious from the path where the memorial plaque is located," I surmised.

"Precisely."

"But how could she determine the location of the shooter?"

"By the keenest of deductions," the director answered. "There was always the possibility that the senior Dr. Watson might see the concealed marksman from his perch, and thus be able to warn your wife of the imminent danger. Thus it would be necessary to take out both your wife and your father at the same time. With this in mind, where would the shooter position himself?"

"Atop an adjacent hotel," I replied at once.

"Which was the case," he went on. "Our own sharpshooter had the assassin in his sight at all times. When the shooter arose from his position, our marksman disposed of him."

"Did Joanna return, then?" I asked at once, my hopes suddenly soaring.

"I am afraid not," Carter-Smith replied. "At this moment she is no doubt engaged with Moriarty at the falls."

"Did you consider sending your man to assist her?"

"She gave specific instructions that such interference was not part of her plan," said he. "Her major concern was your father and the dangerous position he was being placed in."

"But I don't understand why Moriarty insisted that my father be situated on a platform as a lookout," I queried. "How did that serve his purpose?"

"Your wife believed that Moriarty knew the senior Dr. Watson would be armed, as was the case in most of the dangerous circumstances they had previously been involved in. Thus he wanted the good doctor at a distance and away from the prince, so he would not pose a problem."

"Was my father informed?"

"Of course, but only after he was stationed on his perch."

As if on cue, my father hurried into the suite, his Webley at the ready. He immediately recognized the prince and assessed the situation. "Ah," said he. "I see all is well."

"It is indeed, Dr. Watson," Carter-Smith reaffirmed.

My father came over to clap my shoulder hardily and said, "I feared it was you on the ground. But on closer inspection I could see his dark suit and knew it was not you, but rather the Hun."

"With an obviously snapped cervical spine," I added.

"May I ask how that was accomplished?" my father inquired.

"With a powerful football kick to the posterior thorax which propelled the Hun through the window," I replied. "It was applied by His Highness at a most opportune moment."

"Good show!" my father congratulated.

"It was well placed, I must say," Prince Harry noted matter-of-factly.

"But now we are faced with two dead Germans on Swiss soil, which will have to be explained," said I. "The Swiss authorities have a particular distaste for this sort of activity."

"They will simply say the evidence indicates both deaths were the result of a dispute over money," Carter-Smith explained in a monotone. "The bodies will then be unceremoniously shipped to Germany for burial."

My eyebrows went up. "Were the Swiss actually involved?"

"They owed us a favor," the director responded, without going into detail. "They are now looking the other way, but will only do so for a brief period of time, so we must make haste."

Hoping against hope, I asked, "Do you believe there is any chance Joanna decided it best not to encounter Moriarty when she heard the gunshot? Perhaps she thought it was a warning from my father."

"I doubt that would stand in her way," Carter-Smith replied. "She was determined to bring this matter to an end once and for all."

I walked over to the window and stared out at the mist which shrouded the mountain before us. "So we must wait."

"Surely, the SIS could have assisted her," my father said, with an edge to his voice, unaware of my earlier question on the subject.

The director shook his head briefly. "She would have none of it, sir."

"You should have demanded your participation."

"We did."

Prince Harry hobbled over to us with a painful limp and addressed my father. "Sir, I believe I heard you referred to as a doctor. Is that correct?"

"It is," said he.

"I wonder if you might examine my ankle which I twisted whilst landing awkwardly after the kick," the prince requested. "I am afraid I have aggravated an old football injury."

"Of course, Your Highness," my father responded. "Please have a seat to relieve the pressure of your injury."

The prince seated himself and, with considerable discomfort, removed his boot and sock which allowed for a thorough examination.

My father gently palpated the badly swollen ankle and, with care, moved it through a limited range of motion. "You have a severe sprain, Your Highness, but there is no evidence of a fracture. You would do best to keep your weight off the foot."

"For how long?"

"Three to four weeks."

"Too long," said the prince, and reached for his boot.

"A cane might help," my father suggested.

"It would give the impression of infirmity, which I would wish to avoid," said the prince, and placed his boot back on through the pain. He then strolled around the sitting room, limping noticeably and making every effort not to show his discomfort. At the window he glanced out and asked, "I say, why do we continue to wait? Should we not be on our way in the event the Huns bring reinforcements?"

Overwhelmed with fear of losing my dear Joanna, I burst for the door and raced down the stairs, hoping I would not be too late. I hurriedly weaved my way through the crowded lobby and past a startled hall porter who quickly stepped aside. Out the front entrance I went and sprinted for the plaque which commemorated the epic battle between Sherlock Holmes and Professor Moriarty, and which marked the start of the path to the Falls of Reichenbach. The air itself was misty and difficult to see through, but I threw all caution to the wind, and dashed up the slippery slope, now wondering what my approach to Moriarty should be. Should I call out to distract him or simply rush him which would serve the same purpose? At this moment, I sorely missed my Webley, for I would have no hesitation in putting a round through Moriarty's domed forehead. The mist began to lift as I crossed the unstable bridge leading to the thunderous falls. Now the narrow ledge came into view, and I saw two figures facing each other at a distance of no more than twenty feet. A chill ran down my spine at the appearance of Col. Moriarty, for he represented the utter personification of evil. Dressed entirely in black, he slowly advanced toward Joanna whilst swinging a thick cane back and forth in a most intimidating manner. For all the world, he appeared to be The Grim Reaper, with his deadly scythe, come to pay a visit.

I watched as Joanna removed her scarf, as if to use it as a defensive weapon. But instead, she seemed to lower the woolen scarf and mightily swing it at Moriarty's upper body, which caught him by total surprise and propelled him perilously close to the edge of the ledge. Before he could recover, Joanna delivered a second, powerful blow which lifted Moriarty off his feet and sent him toppling off the edge and into the roaring falls. I could hear his scream as he fell hundreds of feet down into his watery grave.

I rushed over to the ledge where Joanna met me with open arms and the warmest of smiles. We embraced tightly and exchanged numerous kisses as our pulses began to slow. But even in this tender moment, it was impossible for me to contain my admiration and curiosity.

"How in the world did you transform that scarf into a weapon?" I asked.

"Magic," she replied, with a mischievous smile. "And wasn't his scream on the way down delightful?"

"By far the best I have ever heard," I said as a light snow began to fall. "Now, let us leave this dreadful place and return to the comfort of our hotel, where my father sits deeply worried about you."

On our journey back to the Edelweiss, we paused at the marker which memorialized the Great Detective's victory and read it silently. My wife and I must have had the same thought, for in a soft voice she said, "If my father were here today, I do believe he would have approved."

"It would have been the finest day of his life."

"For the unemotional Sherlock Holmes?"

"He was not so unemotional, if you read between the lines of his last letter to my father."

We continued on and, as we approached the grounds of the hotel, the body of the dead Hun and the police examining it came into view. More than a few guests on the upper floors had their windows open, so they could watch the goings-on below.

"The Hun, who was guarding me, had a fall from our room on the fifth floor," said I.

"Was it your work?" Joanna asked.

"That of Prince Harry's," I replied, and recounted the prince's courageous act. "The move was delivered so perfectly the Hun did not have time to produce a scream on his way down."

"That happens when the frozen ground comes up to meet one suddenly."

The lobby of the hotel seemed even more crowded than before, with all seats taken and many of the standing guests engaged in conversation, whilst enjoying their late-morning beverages. We waved away a waiter who thought we were in need of service and hurried up the stairs, taking the steps two at a time. As we entered our hotel room, my father and Carter-Smith doffed their hats and cheered, "Hip! Hip! Hooray!" Then once again, "Hip! Hip! Hooray!"

My father rushed over and embraced Joanna warmly, with a

wide smile on his face. "We were so overjoyed to see you emerging from the mountain unharmed," he gushed. "What a splendid sight it was! And now, pray tell, give us every detail on how Moriarty was dispatched."

"With a magic scarf," said I.

A puzzled look crossed my father's face. "A magic scarf, you say?"

"Allow me to describe the actual struggle, so you can envision what transpired," I replied, and depicted the face-to-face confrontation on a most narrow ledge overlooking the Falls of Reichenbach. All eyes stayed fixed on me as I told of Joanna reaching for her scarf and delivering a powerful blow to Moriarty's upper body, which sent him screaming over the edge and into the deadly falls below.

"How could a simple, woolen scarf deliver such a powerful blow?" my father asked at once.

"Because it was loaded," Joanna explained. "You will recall that on purchasing the scarf, I insisted on the change from the clerk being a handful of shillings. On the return to our rooms, I combined those coins with others I had collected earlier, and sewed them into a pocket I had stitched into the end of the scarf. Permit me to show you its force." And with that statement, she gripped her scarf and, swinging it in a wide arc, pounded it against the thick door to our suite. The door shuddered violently. "And so went the evil colonel over the edge, with his arms flailing and his voice screaming."

We all stood in silence as we envisioned the vivid picture Joanna had just depicted. To every extent it appeared to be a re-enactment of the memorable struggle between Sherlock Holmes and Professor Moriarty, which had occurred so long ago. With an equally memorable outcome, thought I.

"Was the arming of the scarf your idea?" Carter-Smith asked, breaking the silence.

"Partly, for I had earlier read an article on Bartitsu in which a gentleman employed a topcoat folded over his arm in a similar fashion," Joanna replied.

"Still, your method was rather novel."

"I thought so as well, and I believe Moriarty would have been of the same opinion had he lived to tell of it."

"So it was thus a scarf in plain view that brought about the downfall of the clever Moriarty," Carter-Smith said with admiration.

"A scarf in plain view," Joanna repeated. "But one with a special purpose."

Carter-Smith gave the matter more thought before asking, "Are you convinced that it was Moriarty alone who orchestrated the entire sequence of events? Could the Huns have joined him as equal partners to the abduction of Prince Harry?"

"Masterminds such as Moriarty require pawns, not partners, for they must control every move to an exact degree," Joanna replied. "If you keep in mind that the colonel, like his brother before him, was the Napoleon of crime, with eyes and ears in every corner of London's underworld, all of the pieces of this puzzle will fall into place. Let us begin when he first learned of the barmaid's forthcoming abortion and Prince Harry's involvement. He promptly brought in the Huns, with the promise of turning over the abducted prince for transport to Germany, which no doubt would please the Kaiser greatly. Along the way, Moriarty led us down a murky trail, leaving tantalizing clues at the abduction site, then at Ah Sing's and at the barmaid's flat and at the house on Gloucester Avenue, knowing we would follow them and eventually be lured to the Falls of Reichenbach where he would seek his final revenge."

"But what of the demand for a ransom which seemed to have fallen by the wayside?" my father asked.

"A ransom was not the main item on Moriarty's menu,"

Joanna explained. "He planned to use the Sovereign Orb as a mechanism to demonstrate how clever he was to outwit the daughter of Sherlock Holmes. Had he fetched the orb without releasing the prince, the whole world would have known of it, for the disastrous news would have surely reached the newspapers."

"What remarkable ingenuity," the director commented.

"Quite so," my wife agreed.

"It is most fortunate indeed that we will not have to deal with this evil mastermind again," Carter-Smith said, and glanced quickly at his timepiece. "Now, we must be off before our Swiss colleagues become too impatient. Should one of my men assist you, Your Highness?"

"I shall walk out, head up, shoulders back," said he, and limped painfully to the door. Before departing, however, he turned to Joanna, my father, and me and, with an appreciative nod, said, "Well done, well done indeed. I owe you my life, which is a debt the royal family cannot hope to repay."

"His Majesty's faithful and never-ending service to all England is payment enough," Joanna replied graciously.

"I will tell him of your kind words."

And with that statement, Prince Harry, the third in line of succession to the British throne, disappeared, but on this occasion in the safest of hands.

CLOSURE

Three weeks were to pass before we were visited at 221b Baker Street by Sir Charles Bradberry who, over tea, was to provide us with the final pieces of the puzzle which brought the case of *The Wayward Prince* to its conclusion. But first, the commissioner delivered a handwritten invitation from Buckingham Palace to meet with His Majesty and receive his warmest gratitude for our role in rescuing his son.

"The Crown does have one request which they hope you will adhere to," Sir Charles said formally. "They would very much like you for the time being to withhold publication of this affair in *The Daughter of Sherlock Holmes* chronicles. It goes without saying that the details of how we nearly lost the prince will shine an unpleasant light on the royal family and give the Huns a cleverness that elevates their image, which is something we wish to avoid."

"It shall remain unpublished for the foreseeable future," I vowed.

"I will so inform His Majesty," said he. "Now, let us proceed to the matters which I know will be of interest to the Watsons. Allow me to begin by informing you that the body of Col. Moriarty was never recovered. Despite the use of professional divers and cadaver dogs sniffing along the banks, no human remains were discovered. The body is believed to have vanished in the deep water of the Reichenbach Falls and been consumed by the creatures that reside within. The colonel is now listed as officially dead by the Swiss authorities."

"Those listed as officially dead, without a body being discovered, have a bad habit of later turning up alive," Joanna reminded us.

"We should pray that is not the case, for the world is a far better place with the colonel's departure from it," said Sir Charles in a neutral tone. "We should now move on to more welcome news. A search warrant was issued for The Rose and Lamb, where Inspector Lestrade discovered hidden records which indicated the abortion on the barmaid had been performed at the pub by the sister-in-law of the owner, Nathaniel Day. The abortionist was quickly brought to trial, found guilty, and is currently serving a life sentence at Holloway Prison. Mr. Day was convicted as an accessory to the crime and was given a similar sentence. He was imprisoned at Pentonville where he was beaten to death by a fellow inmate over an earlier gambling debt. The Rose and Lamb was closed and no longer exists."

"Well-deserved justice for all," said my father.

"Indeed," the commissioner agreed, and furrowed his brow as if to recall a thought. "Ah, there is one question His Majesty requested that I ask you, for the King himself enjoys a jolly good adventure. He wishes to know if there was any warning that Moriarty was about to attack? Was there a subtle clue which alerted you?"

"His shoulder," Joanna replied.

A puzzled look came to Sir Charles's face. "I beg your pardon?"

"His right shoulder moved, which according to my son, is a tell that the hand connected to it will soon be coming your way."

"With a weapon, then?"

"It matters not, for it is the hand itself which delivers the blow."

Johnny, who had delayed his return to Eton, and had been listening to every word, chimed in, "I take it his right shoulder was the one closest to the edge of the ledge."

"It was," Joanna answered.

"Which gave you an added advantage, for he had no chance to regain his balance, once struck."

"I took that into account."

"Well done, Mother."

"Which brings us to the final chapter of this fascinating tale," Sir Charles said, reaching into his coat pocket for a newsletter. "The young barmaid, who died so tragically, was laid to rest in a simple ceremony near the village of her birth. A bulletin for the local happenings is published every fortnight and made mention of her funeral. I thought you might like to see it."

He gave the newsletter to Joanna and, with a tip of his derby, bid us good day and departed. We gathered around as Joanna read a neatly printed paragraph which had been underlined in red.

Martha Ann Miller was buried in a graveyard next to a small church outside Newcastle upon Tyne. Other than the vicar, the only person present was a handsome, young man of regal bearing with a decided limp.

Acknowledgments

Special thanks to Peter Wolverton, editor par excellence, and to Claire Cheek, his editorial assistant, who made such valuable suggestions. And a tip of the hat to Scott Mendel, my extraordinary agent, whose advice and guidance has always been spot-on.